A Long Road There

A Long Road There

Virginia Pickett

A Long Road There
Copyright © 2021 Virginia Pickett
All rights reserved. No portion of this book may be reproduced
in any form without permission from the publisher, except as
permitted by U.S. copyright law.
For permissions contact: sandpiperpublishing@outlook.com

This book is a work of fiction. Any references to historical
events, real people, or real places are used fictitiously. Other
names, characters, places, and events are products of the
author's imagination, and any resemblance to actual events or
places or persons, living or dead, is entirely coincidental.

Book design by Kevin Breen
The cover image, Toltec Gorge, Colorado by Thomas Moran,
was used thanks to the Cooper Hewitt Museum's participation
in the Creative Commons.

ISBN: 978-0-578-93009-1
Cataloging-in-Publication Data is available upon request

Manufactured in the United States of America

Published by
Sandpiper Publishing LLC, Spokane, Washington
Contact the author at sandpiperpublishing@outlook.com

DEDICATION

To my Great-Grandmother Magdalena Mok Altvater, whose courage and resiliency undoubtedly helped her travel her own *long road there.*

ACKNOWLEDGMENTS

My husband, Kerry, worked side-by-side with me throughout the entire process of writing and publishing this novel. His input and insights greatly enhanced the story, and his dedication and encouragement helped keep me moving forward. Ellie, our ridgeback of many years, came to work beside us every day without complaint. Now that she's passed on, she is sorely missed.

Many thanks to my readers, Linda Day and John Blake, Sharon Bowman and John Stockton, and Penny Hencz and Pam Miller. Their comments, criticisms, and suggestions proved invaluable and helped us create a better story. But mostly, I appreciate their love and friendship over many years.

Finally, I would like to thank Jon Gosch of Latah Books for taking a chance in agreeing to help us with the book. My thanks to Kevin Breen and the other Latah Books staff who worked on this project. Their time, effort, skill, expertise, and patience helped turn a rough manuscript into a finished, publishable novel.

FOREWORD

John Stockton

I met Virginia Pickett in 1973 when I was in the 6th grade. Gini and her husband, Kerry, were struggling law students at Gonzaga Law School in Spokane, Washington at the time. Both worked odd jobs at night to pay for school and their exceedingly sparse apartment carved out of the floor plan of an exceedingly humble house. They had few amenities or decorations that weren't handcrafted by Gini herself. They had a cat and an enormous, menacing dog that looked more like a lion, named "Mateus." The only creature in the world that scared me more than Mateus was her husband, Kerry L. Pickett, my new basketball coach at St. Aloysius Grade School that year.

Coach was a demanding sort, the kind that you don't like very much at the time but recognize later on as vital to your development as a player and a human being. We practiced three long hours every day, with a punitive running program afterward that would be considered abusive by today's standards. It was all rewarding in the end, but insufferable at the time.

What often went unnoticed were the other things that occurred that made our season memorable. We played older teams from schools all over town that weren't on a schedule. We had a Christmas tournament at our tiny, cracker-box gym with repurposed wooden steps as bleachers up on the stage, homemade popcorn concessions, and a PA announcer without any PA system at all. We had a father/ son game at the end of the season. We had both a Christmas party where we went caroling as a team and a post-season party replete with a robust game of charades and a cake that Mateus demolished before we got there. All of these special moments in time had Virginia's handprints all over them.

At first, we knew Gini only as Coach's wife. We never saw her at practice, but she drove half of us to each of our games. She kept the scorebook. She hustled and bustled about to get balls or air valves to fill them up. She administered to every detail that needed attention or that made our experience special. All of this she did behind the scenes—pleasant, competent, caring, and beautiful.

Despite the diminutive role she assumed in those days with our team, Gini possessed a quiet, internal confidence. Intelligence, a self-deprecating wit, a willingness to work, and a deep desire to help out wherever needed were talents woven into her very fabric. These qualities made her more than a match for Coach, Mateus, or any other formidable character, friend or foe.

In reading *A Long Road There*, I see many of these qualities in Magdalena, the main character and Gini's great-grandmother. As we enjoy Magdalena's journey through life, we come to know a young lady we would all be proud of. Independent and with a pioneer spirit, she remained steadfastly loyal to her family and the lessons they provided her. Her adventures wind us through historical events in war-torn Europe, transatlantic voyages, early immigrant days in America, and even the Oregon Trail—each providing insight and thoughtful reflection on what life must have been like in those wild days of yore that few of us could imagine, and even fewer of us could endure. She suffered countless heartaches and setbacks but learned from them and refused to be conquered by them. Magdalena was often scared and vulnerable but also courageous and strong. She didn't need to talk about it; she just was. Her upbringing told her so; no extraneous confirmation was necessary. Over and over again,

Magdalena succeeded by helping others succeed or simply enjoy life. I guess you could say she was the ultimate teammate.

Ultimately, Magdalena found happiness. She found it in places and with people she could not have imagined at the start. And yet, it was with the same type of people she left: hardworking, family-oriented, loving, hardy people. Her new family was like the one she left behind in body, but never in spirit. She found love, family, community, and purpose exactly like home, but had to make the journey to appreciate it.

I hope you enjoy getting to know Magdalena and all of the colorful characters she came across in *A Long Road There* as much as I did. Their personalities jumped off the page for me. I felt like I knew them personally. Maybe I did… right down to the pets. I could also picture, as if I was there, the Mok butcher shop, the train station, the SS See Falke, New York City and its taxis at the time. I endured, with them, the elements on the prairie schooners as they bounced across the plains and through snow drifts. Lastly, I could feel the complicated emotions attached to each place along the journey.

A Long Road There is a terrific story. I am grateful that Gini was willing to share a piece of her heritage with all of us. There is certainly a lot of Magdalena in Virginia. I am proud to call her my friend.

–John Stockton, NBA Hall of Famer

AUTHOR'S NOTE

Growing up, I visited my maternal grandparents regularly during the summertime in Colorado, just outside of Denver. I spent part of each visit admiring, through locked glass doors, cut glass and delicately painted porcelain dishes that had belonged to my great-grandmother. On one childhood visit, Grandma showed me an old wooden trunk, explaining her mother had brought it with her when she had traveled from Germany to Central City, Colorado by herself, crossing much of America in a wagon train. During my youth, cowboys, wagon trains, and westerns filled nightly television. Without realizing it, from then on, my great-grandmother was my heroine—having traveled by wagon train by herself. Unfortunately, I failed to question beyond that until well after Grandma had passed on.

Having traveled with my great-grandmother for over sixty years in my mind, I decided to write this story. Although *A Long Road There* was inspired by her journey, it is completely fictitious. Not knowing her actual circumstances, I went in search of the general conditions in Germany and then what a trip across American could have involved. In setting scenes and referencing actual locations or circumstances, I tried to be historically accurate.

EINGANG/ENTRANCE

Muddled Bearings
16 March 1871

This has to be a dream, Magdalena thinks. The deck railing is too cold to be real. Her papa seems to be disembarking with the other well-wishers who had accompanied the first class and intermediate passengers to their cabins. Scanning the dock for him, she takes note of the *zwischendeck* passengers slowly coming aboard. Papa hadn't let her travel with these people; passengers afforded the same level of comfort as steers.

Searching for her father's face in the crowd, she can't find him. Frightened, she's puzzled at the same time, watching the folding line of tattered souls gradually move inside the ship.

Suddenly, she spots Papa through the morning mist. He stands on the wharf and waves as though beckoning her to come back. With her expression, she tries to let him know that's impossible. Her eyes fill with tears. He shouldn't see her cry, so she tries to smile and wave. Her face seems frozen, and her arms are heavy. Acting confident and unafraid is more difficult than she imagined.

When all the people without cabins have disappeared, she can hear the gangplanks being drawn and see the docking ropes being pulled aboard. She's powerless to prevent the ship from gently easing away from its mooring. As the vessel glides into the harbor,

Papa gradually becomes harder to find in the crowd until only the ubiquitous aquatic horizon can be seen. She must be dreaming. Sometimes it's hard to tell.

OUVERTÜRE/OVERTURE

Village of Willenstat,
Kingdom of Württemberg
Circa 1850-1865

These were disruptive years in the Germanic states. A nationalist zeitgeist had been fermenting for some three decades. Times were hard. Food and work became scarce for many. People started leaving—mostly for America.

In the free village of Willenstat in the Kingdom of Württemberg, people valued their independence. The Mok family had farmed and butchered in the small village for generations. Like most of the kingdom's inhabitants, the Moks didn't view a unified Germany as an attractive prospect.

The Mok family had long valued education. Almost without exception, the men attended two years at the university at Stuttgart—just a ways down the road. Then, with equal predictability, the Mok men returned home.

Rudolph and Johannes Mok, like their father, Reinhold, followed this pattern. Rudolph, the oldest, studied agricultural science in preparation to take over the family farm. His father raised beef, pork, and poultry for the butcher shop. Younger brother Johannes returned to run that part of the Mok business. Oddly, he studied literature. Their sister, Ilsa, married a classmate of Rudolph's from a prosperous Stuttgart business family, making that city her new home.

The lettered meat cutter married the town tailor's daughter, Alexandria. The couple had four children: Kurt, Hans, Magdalena, and Elsa Emma, in that order. The butcher wasn't a man to bend with the wind. He and his wife expected their kids to do good and avoid evil and to figure out which was which early in their lives. Like most parents, they wanted their children to live long and happy lives, raise a family and become part of the Mok's stable legacy, all without wandering too far from home.

———————

Pretty much from the day she arrived on the 10th day of November in 1850, Magdalena tested the limits of her parents' patience and bent every one of their rules to the breaking point. They swore the stork had delivered her to the wrong family. Still, the child stole their hearts. Smart as a whip and better looking than most, she wasn't one to bend easily, either. In spite of her willfulness, the kid had a contemplative aspect to her. Under a twinkling night sky, the child could lie on her back and talk to the stars forever from the porch roof just below her bedroom window. She thrilled in speculation—big or small. What grand adventures might lie ahead? What might tomorrow hold in store? The stars didn't have to answer her. The little girl appreciated the heavens just listening.

In the light of day, Magdalena's life revolved around her two older brothers, Kurt and Hans. Brother Kurt was Magdalena's hero. Six years older, the boy was smart, athletic, and handsome. When he left for college, his little sister was certain he would join the pantheon of great German scholars. She stood a little straighter whenever she told her friends about anything he had accomplished—real or imaginary. Kurt was a first-rate student but hadn't yet reinvented mathematics or been appointed poet laureate as Magdalena often implied. Still, he was the oldest son and her oldest brother, which in her mind, elevated him a notch or two beyond his actual standing. He wore the Mok mantle after all.

Magdalena shadowed her other brother, Hans, as soon as she thought she could keep up with him and wanted to before that. By the age of eight, she considered herself an indispensable member of his gang, which was headed by their cousin Heinrich who, at thirteen, was three years older than Hans.

Being part of the bunch meant work on the Mok farm when the boys had finished school in the spring and fall and most every day, including all day in the summer months. This began for Johannes and Rudolph's boys when they reached the age of ten.

Magdalena seldom managed to stay out of the young workers' hair. But as crew boss, Heinrich required his laborers to tolerate his younger cousin. She played this trump card brilliantly until she had finally proven her mettle.

As you might suspect, these were Magdalena's favorite times. The boys fed, groomed, tended, slopped, and spread manure while she played, explored, and aggravated. Despite their Herculean efforts, they couldn't keep Magdalena from underfoot, especially when they had to hitch a team to a wagon. Horses exerted a magnetic attraction on the girl.

When the work was done, the gang would trek off into the woods for adventure. Magdalena was mesmerized by the forest. Her brother and cousin couldn't keep track of her, though she never thought of herself as lost.

Firing Uncle Rudolph's air gun could be dangerous business for young boys if they weren't careful, so that's what the fellows enjoyed most. The *Windbüchse* was no toy. Well past the turn of the century, it was regularly used in combat by the Austrian army. A strong believer in giving young men responsibility until they proved they couldn't handle it, Uncle Rudolph groomed the boys a target shooting course quite a ways into his woods. "Here's where you'll stay when you're shooting that gun," he told them, and they did—most of the time.

Late one afternoon, when there wasn't time to hike to the deserted shooting range before dark, the gang picked a spot a few steps into the woods out of Uncle Rudolph's line of sight—they hoped. Getting caught shooting off the range meant no more shooting, so Heinrich posted Magdalena to keep watch for his father—just in case. She was only there because she had snuck out of her second-story bedroom window onto the porch roof, into a flowerbed, and over a fence after being told she wasn't to go with her brother that day.

Sentry posted, the fellows hung a paper target on an odd-looking oak tree and started firing at it. As the sun dropped, it became harder to distinguish the bull's eye from the tree bark. That's about when they heard the cry, and everyone sprinted for the barn, except the lookout, who naturally ran for the scene of the crime when she heard the scream. When the fugitives got to the barn, Heinrich re-racked the *Windbüchse* as though it had never been disturbed, swore the fellas to secrecy, and ordered them to scatter.

Just short of the barn door, Hans stopped to look for his sister. She was nowhere in sight. Grudgingly, he turned on his heels and ran back into the woods. Near the spot where they had been shooting, he saw his little sister being interrogated by one of Uncle Rudolph's workers. The man's left arm was bleeding.

"What were you doing in the woods?" the farmhand demanded.

Even at nine, Magdalena knew if she told the worker the truth, her days in the gang were numbered. She had been warned more than once about snitching. In between a rock and a hard place, she cleared her throat and looked the farmhand in the eye. "Just walking."

"Then how did I get shot if you were just walking? Where's the gun?" he snapped, reaching out to grab her.

Hans jumped in between them, took his little sister by the arm, and ran for the barn.

7

Giving chase and dripping blood, the victim stumbled. Slow to get off the ground, he never caught up to the fugitives. When the outlaws got back to an empty barnyard, they realized their confederates had scattered, so they did the same.

No words were exchanged between brother and sister during the wagon trip home. The driver did squeeze his reins tighter than usual.

The fugitives weren't late enough for anyone to notice when Hans pulled the wagon into the barn. He quickly began pitchforking hay for the horses while Magdalena carefully retraced her furtive departure route—as she had done so many times before—to the safety of her bedroom. All's well that ends well, she thought.

For the next several days, Hans and Magdalena went about their usual duties. After some time had passed since the shooting incident, Papa found Magdalena working in the family garden.

"I want to talk with you about a serious matter. Your Uncle Rudolph and I have already spoken with Hans and your cousins. One of his farmhands was recently shot with an air gun. I want to hear what you know about that. It's important that you tell me the truth."

Magdalena's knees were shaking. She didn't want to lie to her papa, but she kept hearing in her mind Heinrich's repeated admonitions against ratting. She stared at the ground and, in a quivering voice, responded, "Nothing happened. We were just exploring in the woods."

She had rarely seen her papa truly angry. She grew petrified when he raised his voice and snapped, "I told you I knew what happened. Now, we'll try it again." Looking at the ground, she started to cry. "Stop your crying and tell me what happened. You put yourself in this position. Look at me. We're going to be here until you tell me the truth."

Realizing that she had made the wrong choice, Magdalena finally got her sobbing under control. Trying to look her father in the eyes, she truthfully described what had happened that day in the woods. She even implicated herself as one of the wrongdoers, even though that particular day she hadn't gotten to shoot.

Relieved and proud of his daughter, Papa nodded. "That's essentially what the others said." He understood that his daughter was only nine, but knew she was perceptive enough to understand the gravity of the situation. "I don't want you to come running to me every time someone steps south of a boundary line. But child, you must learn that some matters are more serious than others. It's crucial that you never lie to me. We must have a mutual trust. Do you understand that?"

"Yes."

"Your punishment will not be for what happened in the woods but for lying to me and disobeying your mother in the first place. Is that clear?"

"Yes."

Papa then listed what sounded to Magdalena like an endless list of penances.

The importance of having a mutual trust with her father wasn't something she'd ever thought about until now. She had been scared to tell her father a lie and then distraught that she had disappointed him so terribly. It wasn't long before she understood why her papa held trustworthiness in such high esteem. Still, even an absolutely truthful Magdalena was a handful, though not in her own mind. She saw herself as a determined Argonaut, braving the wilds of Willenstat. Growing up in the village seemed like heaven to the young explorer. As time passed, staying on the right side of the line didn't get any easier for the free-spirited little girl, though she honestly did try.

As the years passed and Hans became busier learning the art of butchering, the pioneer started spending less time with the old gang and more as Grandpa Mok's eager assistant. Since entering semi-retirement, the old butcher had started taking her with him on pickups and deliveries. He had a tolerance for her free spirit that others did not. Unsurprisingly, Magdalena badgered him about letting her drive from the first *giddy-up*. After many assisted sessions and a whole lot of pestering, Grandpa finally turned the reins over to his insistent twelve-year-old granddaughter.

Nearly every day, the intrepid twosome headed to Uncle Rudolph's to pick up product for the butcher shop. The route to his farm from town wasn't particularly hazardous, unless there was a young speed demon behind the reins. From her first day in the driver's seat, the kid pushed the limits of safety. One afternoon when she was buzzing faster than her grandpa would like, a covey of quail spooked the animals. Grandpa instinctively reached for the reins, but Magdalena pulled away and regained control on her own. Her hands paid the price. She finished out the trip where she had begun—in the driver's seat. She never said a word about her bloody hands.

When the injured driver and her grandfather Mok got back to town, she pulled the wagon directly in front of the tailor's shop. Her grandpa Brohmann had owned the place for the last forty-five years. Without so much as a *goodbye* to her delivery partner, she marched toward the shop's door. Before she was fully inside, she shouted over the cling-clang of the customer bell, "Can you make me a pair of leather gloves, Grandpa?"

Not surprised at his granddaughter's single-mindedness, the tailor calmly looked up from his ironing and asked, "Why?"

Displaying her wounds, Magdalena said, "I hurt my hands driving the wagon today." Her tone was matter of fact, as if she'd been at it for ten years.

Looking at the torn flesh on each of her palms, her grandpa suggested, "You need to have your mama take care of those hands, then we'll talk about gloves."

"I will, but I need to know first if you'll make the gloves for me."

A Long Road There

The tailor was amazed that his granddaughter seemed completely unconcerned with her nasty-looking palms. "Okay. I'll make the gloves," he said. Then, as Magdalena turned to leave, he asked, "How do you intend to pay for them?"

The girl was dumbfounded by his question. She had assumed her grandpa would make the gloves without charge. "I have no money, and I don't know how to get any."

"So, you expect me to pay for the leather needed for the gloves and for my time away from work? That's not how things work, young lady. You can't expect others, even though they may love you, to pay for things you desire."

His granddaughter hung her head and finally suggested, "Maybe I can get a job."

"Alright. I'll tell you what," her grandfather said. "You come work for me a few hours once a week. You can tidy up my shop and do whatever else I need. In exchange, I'll make this pair of leather gloves for you and new ones as you need them. Is that a fair deal?"

Delighted, Magdalena blurted, "Yes! Thank you so much. I'll come back in two days and work before I get my gloves."

"Only if you go straight home and have your mama fix you up right now. Do we have a deal?"

"Okay. That's a deal," she said, nearly skipping out of the shop door.

For several years after that, Grandpa Brohmann and Magdalena maintained their contract. To their great and mutual benefit, she received well-stitched leather gloves, and he employed her as the shop's young assistant. When Grandpa was finally gone, Magdalena missed their time together more than she could have imagined when they first struck their bargain.

Driving the wagon by herself greatly increased Magdalena's independence. She began pleading day after day that Papa get her a puppy to keep her company on her frequent butcher-shop

11

deliveries and her long sojourns into Uncle Rudolph's woods. Papa was aware of her solo explorations. He knew ordering his daughter to stay close to home would only fuel her forays further into the hinterlands.

Abe, the family shepherd mix, was twelve. He was mostly Papa's dog and had policed the butcher shop and guarded the family hearth for a long time. Papa knew he was ready to relinquish his duties, so he agreed to a new pup.

On a cold, winter Saturday in the same year that she began to drive the wagon by herself, Papa off-handedly suggested the two of them take a trek into the woods. Beside herself with excitement, Magdalena started heating rocks to serve as foot warmers. She quickly gathered blankets for the ride and began harnessing the horses to the sleigh, urging Papa to "hurry up." After all, he'd never taken her exploring in the woods before.

"Bring an extra blanket!" he yelled to his daughter. "It might get cold."

During the several-mile trip into the country, they talked about many things. After a while, the swishing of the sleigh over the snow and the soft clinking of the horses' harnesses were the only sounds in the forest. Magdalena became lost in the tranquility and beauty of the winter scene. It had snowed the night before; a break in the trees revealed glistening meadows and layered hills painted in white. "Look, Papa, there's a red fox!" she yelled, as a rufous-colored local resident emerged from the woods to check on the intruders.

"Yes, I see it."

"Where do you think it's going on such a snowy day?"

"Maybe back to its den after breakfast."

"I'm sure glad I don't have to traipse through the snow to find my meals!"

"I am, too," Papa replied as he put his arm around his daughter and pulled her close.

After they had gone a couple more miles, Papa let the cat out of the bag. "We're going to look at some puppies. If we find one we like, we'll take it home with us. What do you say to that?"

She couldn't speak, but she could hug. After a tight embrace, Magdalena found her voice. "What a perfect surprise!"

"Before you commit, you should know the pup will be your responsibility. You must train and care for him."

She offered her right hand and, with businesslike self-assurance, announced, "We shake on this bargain, Papa."

Stifling a laugh, the big-pawed butcher turned onto a lane toward a farmhouse visible in the distance. Veering onto a narrow drive, they quickly arrived at a large, snow-covered barn across from a well-kept farmhouse. Johannes' friend Herr Volkheimer came out to greet them. Papa shook his hand, then devilishly shot the breeze with his pal while his daughter squirmed in the sleigh. After an interminable minute, Papa mercifully offered, "Herr Volkheimer, this is my daughter Magdalena."

Brimming with excitement, she could only manage "Nice to meet you, Herr Volkheimer," before broaching the crucial issue. "Can we see the puppies now?"

Herr Volkheimer chuckled and led them to the barn. Inside one of the stalls was a large black female dog. She shielded a litter of ten rambunctious puppies, intent upon denying her any shred of peace. Mama was not nearly as taken with the uninvited intruders as were her offspring. Magdalena and Papa shopped like two little kids at Christmas, albeit gingerly, trying to avoid the pups' mother.

They watched the little rascals play, trying to make a choice. When they settled upon the most active and insistent—betting on a likely kinship with Magdalena—she scooped the pup into her arms and carried him off. While she and the pup settled into the sleigh, Papa paid Herr Volkheimer.

The little black ball was a beauty. The *Riesenschnauzer* breed had become a favorite of butchers and drovers. First cousin to the national favorite, the giant schnauzer was bred for strength, courage, and loyalty. They could also play with the best of them.

"Can we call him Max, Papa?"

"He's your dog, aren't you, Max?" Papa said. The pup, meanwhile, buried his head in Magdalena's mitten.

His daughter tried valiantly to discipline and teach her pup, though inevitably, the training sessions devolved into roughhousing and playtime. Fortunately, Papa had insisted that Max spend his days at the butcher shop while Magdalena was at school. Under the tutelage of the canine security chief and the head butcher, the pup quickly learned that following the rules was better than Magdalena's bending of them.

On their own, however, the pair quickly became devil-may-care adventurers. One or the other, often both, were always in hot water and forever repentant. Their two or four big brown eyes often pleaded for mercy, mostly from Papa, since he was the family magistrate.

This wayward path meant Magdalena missed many town socials, community picnics, and holiday open-market festivities due to punitive chores like cleaning Mama's heirloom china or shoveling barnyard manure. Occasionally, commutation, pardon, or parole was known to occur. Papa was a sucker for big brown eyes. Gradually, the pair moved toward changing their ways. Gradually.

TEIL EINS-PART ONE

KAPITEL 1

The Mok Butcher Shop
Spring 1866

The Mok family lot had gotten as rough as it could get. The previous autumn, Magdalena's oldest brother, Kurt, had been tragically stabbed to death in a Stuttgart campus riot presaging the Austro-Prussian War. Unimaginably, her father's brother Bernhardt had died as a student on campus in the same bloody way just eighteen years earlier. Such were the times in Germany the past quarter-century.

That fall, the butcher had received the tragic news that his son lay dying at his sister's house. He had rushed to Stuttgart, where Ilsa lived only a block from campus. Kurt's friends had managed to get him there, blood-soaked and clinging feebly to life's edge.

Johannes had arrived in time for the doctor to tell him that there was nothing to be done but pray. He had done that for the next several hours, to no avail, as he had watched his oldest son die.

Losing his brother had left Hans in pieces and feeling totally helpless. So, on a rainy April morning in 1866 at an ad hoc recruiting station located, ironically, across the town square from the family butcher shop, a confused eighteen-year-old became a soldier. Hans was desperately looking for some way to avenge his brother's death.

Papa had heard the enlistment news from a deliveryman that morning. His fury quickly turned to fright. His mind leapt to the night he'd been woken with the tragic news of Kurt. He would never forget that insistent knock at 3 a.m. The messenger from his sister had ridden three hours in pelting rain. His sister had suggested he come at once. Frantic and nearly out of her mind with fear, his wife, Alexandria, had demanded that he take Magdalena with him in the wagon and bring her son home to her so she could nurse him back to health. But his son had died before Alexandria had the chance.

Johannes was trembling again that morning at work. The memories of his boy's last breaths in his sister's dark bedroom haunted him. He could still see Magdalena beside him as they watched the life leave Kurt's body. He saw again the ride home, the corpse of his son's body in the wagon bed and his quivering daughter beside him. He pictured the day of the funeral when he had watched Magdalena stare at her brother's body.

So on that gloomy April morning when Hans pushed the butcher shop door open, Johannes exploded—as much from his horrid memories as from his son's indifference to putting him and the family in harm's way yet again.

"I've already lost one son. Isn't that enough? When did you make the decision to enlist in the army?" he demanded. Johannes wasn't in control of himself and he knew it. "Why? Why, I want to know, didn't you discuss it with me beforehand?"

Deep down, Hans knew he should have talked with his father before enlisting. As with most eighteen-year-olds, he had been feeling increasingly independent and knew that enlisting would be much easier if he didn't discuss it with Papa first. He hadn't expected, however, Kurt's ghost to be in the room with his father and him this morning.

Confused, the boy held his ground. "I'm eighteen. I'm a man now. I'm sorry that you heard it from someone else. I'm sorry Kurt is dead. But that's not my fault. This was my decision to make. I don't have to tell you everything I do. Someone in this family had to avenge my brother's death." As the boy spoke, he pointed his finger at the butcher. Hans was convinced that Prussian war agitators were responsible for pushing the knife blade into his brother's gut. There was never any solid evidence of that.

Papa moved nose-to-nose with his son. Hans was the taller of the two, and strong—especially for his age. Still, he was no match for his enraged father, and the boy knew it. Johannes picked his son up by the front of his shirt and slammed him against the wall, rattling the hanging knives and swaying the suspended meat products.

"You may be eighteen, but you're certainly not a man! As long as you live in my house and work in my shop, you must inform me of the choices you make. Got it?" After shouting at him, Johannes hugged his son more tightly than he ever had before.

Max and Abe were upset by what they witnessed. Papa leaned over and patted both of them. "It's okay." Max's tail accelerated.

For the moment, the horror of possibly losing a second son had let go of the butcher—until he thought of Alexandria. As his mind summoned visions of his wife's pain and anguish from losing her older son, he shuddered at what the loss of her younger son might do to her.

Papa picked up his knife and tried to cut meat. Then, spent of rage, he tried starting over with his son that was still alive.

"Things should have never come to this. Did you ever consider your mother? It hasn't even been six months since she lost her oldest son, and now you're going off to war. It would be hard enough for her if you'd been conscripted, but you didn't wait for that; you had to volunteer."

"I'm sorry. I didn't think about those things. I should have talked to you about it before I enlisted."

"You've got us in a hell of a mess. We're going to have to tell

Mama the news before she hears it from someone else. Make a sign and put it on the door to let people know we'll reopen in the morning."

When father and son entered the house together, Mama became alarmed. "What's wrong?" she asked, dreading their response. In over twenty years of marriage, she couldn't remember her husband leaving work early unless something was drastically wrong.

"Come sit down. Your boy wants to talk to you," Johannes told his wife.

Hans sat down next to his mother and tried to explain his impulsive act. "I enlisted in the Württemberg army this morning. Papa didn't know about it until this afternoon."

At first, Hans thought Mama was going to cry, but instead her face lost all expression. He tried to take her hand to comfort her, but she pulled it away.

He continued. "In ten days, I report to the training camp near Stuttgart for six weeks. After that, I don't know. I assume I'll find out while I'm there."

Mama sighed, then asked, "Is there anything that can be done to undo this?"

"No, I've already passed the physical and signed the papers."

Without saying another word, Mama rose as if supporting the weight of the world on her hunched shoulders. Hans watched as she willed herself up the stairs to her bedroom—nearly broken. He hadn't intended to do this to his mother.

When they were alone, Papa turned to his son. "Your sisters should be getting out of school soon and will be expecting us at work. Unhitch the team, then take Max and walk back to the shop. Tell the girls of your decision. Answer their questions. Don't lie. They need to hear the truth from you. Being a man, you'll find, means dealing with the consequences of your actions."

"Alright," the boy replied, stunned by yet another consequence he hadn't considered.

When the girls arrived after school to fetch Max, they saw the "closed" sign on the door. Just then, Hans and the pup walked up. Elsa Emma blurted, "Why is the shop closed? Where's Papa?" Ever since her brother's death, the girl was convinced that something unimaginably bad had happened whenever Papa wasn't where he was supposed to be.

Without answering, Hans led his sisters to the back of the shop. Making a place for the three of them to sit, he began trying to explain his enlistment. The girls were excited and had many questions. Where would he be going? What would he be doing? Hans did his best to answer. His sisters were in an imaginary world, concocting the exotic places their brother might be deployed, when Magdalena suddenly demanded, "Will you be killed?"

Remembering Papa's admonition against lying, he admitted, "I can't guarantee that I won't be. I'm going to do everything I possibly can to make sure I come back."

All excitement evaporated. There were no more mindless questions about travel to mysterious lands. His frankness had sobered them all. They walked home without conversation, which made Max uneasy for the second time that day.

The day Hans was to report to training camp, the family woke at sunrise. Papa hitched the team and loaded the wagon with his son's small duffle. The whole family climbed aboard. Not much was said on the short trip to the train station.

Hans held his mother close and shook his father's hand as the last boarding call for Stuttgart was made.

"Write your mother, boy," the butcher ordered.

"I will, sir," the young man replied, stepping aboard the train.

The station was crowded that day, mostly with other families sending off other brothers, sons, and husbands. The crowd seemed enthusiastic about the thrashing their boys would give the Prussians. Only after the train pulled away did some of those left behind begin to consider the more dire possibilities. The Moks knew all too well what those were. At fifteen, Magdalena was trying to make sense of everything. As Hans stepped aboard the train, she had a terrible feeling that he might not be coming home.

KAPITEL 2

War Battle Zones
Summer 1866

As the deafening barrage of artillery continued, Hans sat behind an earthwork with his rifle, wondering what he'd gotten himself into. His fury and zeal had completely vanished, leaving only his desire to stay alive.

This day in 1866 was turning out like all the others—retreat and regroup. After surviving the artillery storm, Hans and his unit marched with reinforcements that were also falling back. The June sun was beating down on everyone equally. Staying upright was the primary goal. He just needed to put one foot in front of the other—nothing more, but nothing less.

Hans heard someone groan from behind him. "Goddammit, I joined this army to shoot Prussians, not get kicked around by them." No one answered the soldier's gripe. Instead, the ranks moved forward, each soldier eating the dust of those ahead of them.

After a period of silence, someone did reply. "We're damn lucky we haven't had to fight the Prussians any more than we already have. I hope I don't have to remind anyone that we're getting our ass kicked." Hans shot a glance backward. He spotted the dour realist, dust-covered but still distinctive in his uniform from the Kingdom of Hesse-Darmstadt.

A Long Road There

Disgruntled curses, affirmations, grunts, and denials started to spread like a contagion through the ranks. It felt good to muster emotion of any kind.

"What the hell do you mean by that remark?" someone said. "Are you saying we can't fight as well as the Prussians?" The retort sounded like a direct challenge, though it couldn't have been since the accuser had no idea who the hell he was accusing.

Identifying himself, the Hessian quickly put up his hands, palms open in an apologetic manner, and offered, "I didn't mean anything about our fighting ability. We're as good as they are, but they have better rifles. That's all I was saying."

"What do you mean they have better rifles?" Hans demanded of the Hessian critic.

"Didn't you notice their guns, kid?" the Darmstadter asked, exasperated. "You missed one of the ABCs of a rifleman, son, if you didn't know what you're up against."

"No. I was too damn busy dodging the rounds that were whizzing by my head," Hans replied sarcastically to the dusty sage who couldn't have been more than three years his senior.

"Well, for your information, practically the whole damn Prussian army has those new von Dreyse breech-loading needle rifles. Our muzzle-loaders are useless antiques," the Hessian said, continuing his lecture on weaponry.

"How do you know so damn much about guns?" Hans asked, momentarily accepting his role as student.

"Not that it's any of your goddamn business, but my old man was a gunsmith in Darmstadt. I grew up handling, firing, and repairing more guns than you could count."

"A gunsmith, huh?" another soldier interjected. "That's convenient, but unlucky. Now, we know we can't win the goddamn war." A few chuckled at the wry comment.

"Hell no, we can't. You must be pretty thick-headed if you're just figurin' that out!" the Hessian said. Since complaining seemed to take his mind off their retreat, the gunsmith's son dug deeper. "Boy, are you guys stupid! The Württemberg army must've been desperate. Did you all sign up as cannon fodder?"

Hans gritted his teeth, thinking of those fast friends he had made and lost just as quickly. "You bastard! No one says that to us!"

"Is that so? Well, I just did!"

Quickly, a crowd began to circle, hoping for a fight. Hans and the Hessian quickly lost their packs and rifles, then went nose to nose, preparing for a showdown. When the MP stepped in between them, the Hessian feigned comradery. "He was just about to show me some self-defense moves, sir."

"That's right," Hans said. "We were just about to compare hand-to-hand combat techniques."

Luckily, the officer wasn't in any mood to make an arrest. "I suggest you save your goddamn energy to fight the Prussians. Now move out and keep up."

The betting circle immediately broke, and the two young gladiators picked up their gear and hustled on their way. As soon as the officer was out of sight, the Hessian turned to Hans, sticking out his hand, "How about a truce, ol' buddy? The name's Fritz Strasse from Darmstadt, Hesse."

Accepting the offered peace overture, the butcher's son introduced himself, "Hans Mok from Willenstat, Württemberg."

With their ceasefire in effect, the two began to direct their barbs at the army instead of each other. This was followed by a serious discourse on women, food, beer, and soft beds.

When the beleaguered troops neared their stopping point along the Taber River, a command passed through the ranks. All soldiers were to locate their respective units and report at once. With this, Hans and Fritz parted ways, wishing each other well. They pledged to continue their discussion over a tall stein at the first opportunity.

Since Hans had left, Mama had been exceptionally quiet and

A Long Road There

subdued—the way she was after Kurt died. She went about her normal chores but without any emotion. No smiles, no frowns, only habit. On one occasion, Magdalena found her sitting with needlework in her lap, staring blankly out the window, tears rolling down her cheeks.

Not knowing what to do, Magdalena went over and put her arm around her mother's shoulder. "What's wrong, Mama?" she asked.

"Oh, nothing. I was just thinking about your brother and missing him. I'm hoping he gets home soon in one piece."

"I do, too, Mama."

Suddenly, Mama got up as if Magdalena weren't there. "I better be getting to supper. Papa will be home shortly." She said this mostly to the air as she walked mechanically into her kitchen.

Magdalena's first instinct was to talk with Papa about her mother's despondence. But she quickly decided against doing that because he wasn't himself, either. She knew something needed to be done. *Grandpa Brohmann will know what to do,* she thought.

The next day, Magdalena was at the tailor shop, as she had been one day every week since their *gloves for work* bargain three years earlier. She decided to talk to Grandpa about his daughter.

After all the customers had left, and she and Grandpa were the only ones in the shop, she broached the subject. "Mama's sad almost all the time, and Papa's not himself either."

The tailor laid down the garment he was working on and slowly shook his head. Looking at his granddaughter, he said simply, "You just keep being a good girl and doing your chores. I'll talk with your grandmother. Maybe she'll have an idea that will help." Magdalena gave her grandfather a big hug, feeling better now that she'd said something to him.

A few days later, Magdalena and Max came home to pick up Papa's lunch. While there, Magdalena found Mama and Grandma Brohmann working together on an ornate embroidery piece. She

25

had a sneaking suspicion that her grandfather had motivated this new sewing partnership.

Over the next month, Grandma came over several times a week with sewing or needlework projects. Mother and daughter worked with increasing gaiety. Mama was gradually becoming herself again. The old tailor must have known the needle therapy would help his daughter and comfort his wife. It was also helping Papa—seeing his wife laugh again.

Hans came to in the tiny field where his company had been mercilessly shelled. He was certain he was in the middle of a nightmare or a small corner of hell. The big artillery guns had stopped, and the thick smoke was only a haze. There were torn, mangled bodies strewn across the pasture, most of them dead. When he tried to get up, he couldn't. His left boot was gone, revealing only part of a foot and his two biggest toes. Frantically, he splashed in a pool of his own blood, searching for the missing pieces. If he could find the parts, he could put them back where they belonged and wake up. When the stretcher-bearers finally came to retrieve him, he was in a hurry to leave. He didn't want to die in Hades.

The next time he woke, he was in an overcrowded hospital tent. His neck and head were bandaged fully, as well as what remained of his left foot. Doctors were screaming for assistance that didn't come. A pile of human appendages was being wheeled out the door. Hans vomited and passed out again.

The day after the July 27th truce, a long contingent of troops straggled down the road in front of a grassy knoll. The fellow Hans had almost tangled with on the long retreat a few days earlier was lying in the grass, finishing the last bites of his disagreeable supper.

"Well, if it isn't the damn gunsmith!" someone shouted.

Looking in the direction of the comment, Fritz recognized one of the soldiers who had been with Hans during the retreat. "Well,

A Long Road There

bless my soul. If it isn't one of the agitators from Württemberg? How the hell are you?"

"Fine, if I could just get out of here. How about you?"

"About the same. I don't see the other Württemberger. How the hell is he?"

"I'm afraid Hans got unlucky the day of the truce. He's over in the hellhole they call a hospital. I'm not sure he's all in one piece," the soldier answered before shuffling off with the rest of his company.

Fritz tossed his scraps to the birds and started for the hellhole.

The wounded were crammed together under a filthy, bloody canvas roof labeled "Hospital." Fritz didn't ask for help finding Hans. Both surgeons had their hands full. As he began the nauseating process of moving through the ward on his own, he saw Hans. His left foot was bandaged with blood-soaked pieces of cloth. The scrapper that had been ready to toe the line with him was gone. In his place lay a pale, gaunt boy. The bloody foot wound was so revolting Fritz nearly wretched.

"You sure picked a helluva time to get blown-up. Didn't you know the fightin' was over?"

Hans smiled weakly, managing, "I guess not."

Once the truce was officially signed, the non-professional soldiers like Fritz were free to return home. He didn't. There was something about this kid that he liked. Over the next ten days, the Hessian kept watch over his friend as Hans's wounds slowly began to heal. When the doctor at last said that it was time to go home, Fritz volunteered to make sure Hans got there.

KAPITEL 3

The Stuttgart Train Depot
Summer 1866

The boxcar carrying the wounded and their caretakers south from Würzburg was packed. Compared to Hans, most of the fellas had lost bigger pieces of themselves. With the connecting troop transport delayed overnight in Stuttgart, Fritz and Hans spent the dark hours on the crowded station floor. Trying to pass the time, Hans went on and on about his family. Fritz only listened; his family stories weren't ones he enjoyed telling. After his father's death just a month short of Fritz's sixteenth birthday, things had deteriorated at home. His older brothers fought over the small estate, and his sisters went their own ways—many quickly to the altar as a matter of survival. No, going home wasn't in the cards for the young Hessian.

With first light, Fritz sent a telegram for Hans to his Papa, letting him know they'd be home on that day's train.

———

"You got a telegram, Papa!" Magdalena said as he returned from his long delivery. He accepted the envelope and ripped it open, shouting, "It's from Hans! He's coming on today's train." Magdalena immediately gave Papa a powerful bear hug.

A Long Road There

"Did you and Max have any problems while I was gone?" the butcher asked.

"Nope! We didn't, did we boy?" Magdalena asked her canine helper. Max promptly shook his head *no*. "I taught him that while you were gone," Magdalena said proudly.

Papa smiled and shook his head, marveling at the productivity of his staff.

"You and Max take the wagon and give your mama and the rest of the family the good news. Tell everyone Mama's preparing a welcome-home dinner. Come straight back so I can get to the station. You two will watch the store again while I get Hans."

Bursting at the seams with happiness, the courier and her assistant scurried out to the wagon to begin her joyful errand.

As Magdalena delivered the good news to their other relatives, Mama sat at home looking out the window like a kid waiting in a snowstorm for *Sankt Nikolaus* to arrive. Dinner was going to have to wait until her boy got home. She kept thanking the good Lord over and over again. God understood.

———

Papa finally heard a distant whistle. He strained to find a cloud of black smoke. Suddenly, the iron dynamo was in sight.

When the belching giant finally chugged to a stop, tears filled his eyes. His boy was almost home. At the end of a long de-boarding process, a crooked, wooden crutch, followed by a bandaged foot, emerged from the train.

"Papa!" Hans shouted. He nearly toppled while trying to negotiate the two steps to the ground. But before he fell, a dark-haired young soldier in an odd-looking, crumpled uniform caught him. The butcher's knees buckled when he saw his son struggling to get to the ground.

"You've come home," was all Papa could muster, hugging his boy. Though a piece of his son was missing, Papa was overjoyed to embrace what had returned.

"I'm okay, Papa. Where are Mama and the girls?"

"Magdalena's at the shop. Mama and Elsa Emma are home. I didn't know if we'd have enough room in the wagon."

As they rode along, Fritz took the first quiet moment to introduce himself. "I'm Fritz Strasse," he said, extending his hand to Papa.

Gripping it, the old butcher squeezed hard and long in gratitude. "Thanks for bringing our son back to us."

Max heard the wagon wheels first and bolted for the shop entrance with the morning boss and a limping 15-year-old senior sentry in hot pursuit. Hans was immediately buried in the wagon bed below a wild threesome smothering him with licks and kisses. "Take it easy," Papa cautioned. He didn't have to. The dogs had already begun smelling and licking at Hans's bloody bandages. Magdalena had pulled back in horror.

"I'm alright, sis. I left three toes and a little piece of my foot in a farmer's field is all."

Magdalena was now staring at the jagged scar on his neck. It wasn't disfiguring, but it caught the girl by surprise. Her brother saved her from any embarrassment. "Looks a little like a lightning bolt, don't you think?" Without answering, Magdalena buried her head in her brother's chest and began to cry.

As soon as Mama saw the wagon some ways up the drive, she rushed outside. She had her son in her arms before the horses had come to a stop. She didn't notice his foot or his scar as she smothered him in hugs and kisses. Hans made it easy for her when she paused for an assessment. "You've got yourself a seven-toed son now, with a bolt of lightning on his neck. You'll get used to me. I already have." With that, Hans hopped down on his good foot and quickly balanced on his crooked crutch.

"You're beautiful," was all Mama could say.

Fritz introduced himself first to Alexandria and then Elsa Emma, both of whom had come outside by now. Damn, Fritz thought, the kid really does have quite a family.

Max, though trained to be leery of strangers, didn't think Fritz fit the category. Instead, the sentry introduced himself with a friendly nudge and wagging tail. Fritz dropped to one knee, and the two wrestled playfully until they were both sure each had made a friend.

Papa let everyone know that Hans's caretaker would be staying for a while. That was about the only thing he had established with the young soldier on the short ride home from the train.

Mama's dinner that evening was scrumptious. Tears and laughter filled the room after everyone had gotten over the shock of Hans's wounds. Grandmas and grandpas, cousins, aunts and uncles, all welcomed their warrior home. Magdalena watched as her brother and Fritz shoveled food into their mouths, washing it down with plenty of beer. It made her feel calm, sitting around the dining room table and watching them eat. Hans already seemed whole to her. Plus, the nifty scar on his neck made him seem mysterious.

After supper, her brother made himself comfortable on his favorite sofa and told Papa that Fritz had saved his life. As the men talked in the front room, the ladies finished the dishes, gabbing among themselves.

Eventually, everyone gathered around Hans to tell stories and toast his return. The family's underlying fear of losing him was finally gone. The evening was a new beginning. Hans's missing toes and his small permanent limp became the subject of jest and stories from that evening forward.

Magdalena was glad the war was over. She was happy her brother was home. Everyone shared those feelings, including the furry twosome curled in the corner together. Hans was lucky to have a friend like Fritz, she thought.

KAPITEL 4

The Mok World in Willenstat
August 1866

The next morning, Mama and Papa got up together long before everyone else. They sat at the kitchen table holding hands and drinking coffee, quietly soaking in the fact that Hans had come home to them.

Fritz and Magdalena got Hans to the doctor that morning for a thorough going-over. While Hans was being inspected, Fritz fell asleep in the sun-drenched wagon bed. This gave Magdalena the perfect opportunity to conduct her own silent appraisal of her brother's friend. Standing by the wagon bed as he napped, she watched as his chest rose and fell in a comforting rhythm, occasionally interrupted by a jerk or mumble as though he were having a bad dream.

Although she wouldn't admit it to anyone but herself, she liked her brother's handsome friend. His brown, slightly curly hair was long and a bit askew. She wanted to reach over and gently comb it back into place with her fingers, but she didn't dare. She studied his face, the wide jawbone and the small, jagged scar below his lip on the left side. His nose was just a little crooked. It started out straight but veered slightly to the left toward the tip. She wondered why. Even with his wide shoulders, his slim body didn't fill out her brother's clothes that Mama had given him. He looked kind of funny in the oversized garments but handsome with his tanned skin.

At Papa's urging and being in no particular hurry to be on his way, Fritz agreed to stay and cut firewood for the winter. The biggest downside to this arrangement was that Hans became an insufferable supervisor. Magdalena's curiosity about her brother's handsome friend grew. She even consulted the wise old family owl.

Almost late for work as usual, Magdalena and Max were sprinting for the tailor shop when Grandpa saw his young apprentice. Welcoming her with open arms, he exclaimed, "Ah, you love the sewing so much, you race to the thread!"

Gasping for air, she managed only, "I didn't want to be late."

"What a loyal worker. *Wunderbar*! Go get a drink of water, then come see me," the tailor said. "Max, you stay here and guard the front porch." He threw the dog a bone just as he did every day when Magdalena came to work.

When his granddaughter returned from her drink, Grandpa handed her a pair of men's trousers. They were turned inside out and made of sturdy material. Giving them to her, along with a needle, thread, and a thimble, he explained, "These are for a young man who does hard physical work. He needs a strong pair of trousers. I've sewn them once, but I want the seams reinforced with short, sturdy stitching. I'm hoping you can finish before you leave today."

Magdalena took the trousers and started sewing. Although she'd helped her grandpa for more than three years, he rarely gave her stitching work. Grandfather was the master craftsman. She was a backup—until now. Seeing that both the material and thread were dark blue, she figured she couldn't mess up too badly.

Grandpa began to work on what looked like a man's work

33

blouse. Both the tailor and his assistant stuck to their stitching with only an occasional comment passing between them.

"How old were you and Grandma when you got married?" Magdalena inquired out of the blue.

"Where did that come from? Are you thinking about tying the knot?"

"Heaven sakes, no! I was just wondering," the blushing fifteen-year-old assistant replied.

"That's good to hear. To answer your question, I was twenty-five, and your grandma was seventeen."

"Grandma was so young," Magdalena said. "I won't be ready for such responsibility by then. She must have been a very mature girl."

"It happened more back then. Girls are waiting longer nowadays Like I said, it was common. The men were older, mostly because they needed to have a job to support their families. I was working by then, and we loved each other, so we got married. I've been glad we did ever since." After a pause, the tailor surprised his assistant. "You're not thinking about Hans's good-looking soldier friend, are you?"

"Grandpa!" Magdalena demurred. "I'm way too young!"

"I agree, but there's no harm in looking so long as that's all you do."

"He doesn't even know I exist, Grandpa."

"Does he talk to you?"

"Sometimes, but mostly he just teases and makes fun of me."

"A pretty gal like you? You bet he knows you exist."

Grandpa enjoyed talking with his granddaughter. He was happy she trusted him enough to discuss just about anything that seemed to be puzzling her.

He finished his project before his assistant completed her seaming, but it wasn't a minute or two before she proudly announced that the pants were done. From behind his spectacles, the tailor scrutinized the assistant's work. "A complete success!" he declared. "You did a nice job, sweetheart. Now press the blouse and trousers. When you're done, it'll be about time for you to leave."

Magdalena ironed with the confidence of experience. Over the years, Grandpa had her put the same finishing touch on many projects. When she finished ironing, Grandpa carefully wrapped the garments and included a card on top of the package. "Give this to Fritz," he said. "Now, you better get home. Thanks for your work today. I enjoyed our visit. I'll see you next week."

Magdalena gave her grandfather a kiss on the cheek and hurried out the door. She skipped most of the way home, feeling like a young woman.

That evening when Fritz got his package and Grandpa's clothes, he was overwhelmed. People didn't do that sort of thing in his family.

After he finished putting up the winter's wood supply, the soldier extended his stay for another twelve long days of harvest in Uncle Rudolph's fields. That year, Hans could only help by driving a wagon. For Fritz, Grandpa's clothes were a Godsend both when he was logging and behind the scythe. When the last strands of hay were finally baled, it was time for Uncle Rudolph's harvest celebration.

Unfortunately, life cruelly intervened just as harvest was winding down. Papa rose for work as usual and went to wake Abe. "Get up you old slacker. We've got meat to cut." Lying in his usual sleeping place at the foot of the bed, his dog didn't move. He had passed peacefully in the night.

At first, Papa didn't want to accept what he saw. He sat down on a chair and wept. Together, Abe and Papa had shepherded the shop for a long, long time and, with Mama, had raised the Mok children.

Papa took Abe to the woods on the farm and buried him. He

35

sat and reminisced with his old friend, gradually coming to terms with his loss. The butcher went to work that day without his dog. But no day passed after that he didn't feel the old sentry in his corner watching over things.

When Magdalena learned Abe had died, she quivered, thinking that someday she would lose Max. She was all too aware that tragedy could barge in uninvited during the best of times.

KAPITEL 5

The Mok Farm Curtilage
Late Summer 1866

The morning after the haying was done, the girls were too excited to be tired. They helped Mama prepare for the feast—sort of. Neither one of them could concentrate on their work. At last, Mama told them to skedaddle and get themselves ready for the party. The thirteen-year-old Elsa Emma became lost for hours in the monumental problem of which dress to don and what hairstyle to wear. Magdalena, on the other hand, knew what she was going to wear, so she and Max spent most of the time chauffeuring relatives from the train station and running errands for Papa.

For Magdalena, Uncle Rudolph's celebration was always the event of the year. The guest list was especially large this fall, adding to its mystique. It included the entire extended Mok family, as well as all the Brohmann clan, and customers and friends from hither and yon. Everyone contributed to the bacchanal, which was preceded by an assortment of competitions. Dancing followed until the early morning hours. This year Magdalena was focused on becoming a member of the horse-race relay team.

The annual event was an all-male contest, not by rule, but by unassailable custom. This year, Magdalena was determined to take Hans's spot, despite the event's long chauvinist tradition.

When she told Hans and Heinrich of her plan, the three had a heated exchange before the boys capitulated. They knew she could out-ride most of the men in town. Word quickly spread of the unthinkable—Magdalena would be joining the Mok team. The old-timers were already upset that Fritz, a presumed ringer, was taking Johannes' place in the saddle. In the end, the elders agreed to the blasphemous arrangement, believing that Magdalena would be a hopeless drag on the team and that her poor performance would shatter any future of girls in the saddle.

It was now official: the Mok racehorse relay team would consist of Heinrich, Fritz, and Magdalena. The opposing field was comprised of the archrival all-Brohmann riders and the heavily favored "Area" team.

When word spread that Hans and Heinrich had given the okay for her to ride, Magdalena knew it galled Heidi, Heinrich's latest long and lean fraülein. Hans's good-looking *nurses*—and there were a lot of them—just shook their heads at his tomboy sister. It's fair to say that the new female jockey felt she had plenty to prove to all the skeptics, but most particularly to her genteel detractors.

Of course, she didn't want to let her team down. If she did, who knew, Fritz might fall for one of the empty-headed, slim-waisted admirers always hanging around her brother and cousin. So, when the gun went up, there was going to be a whole lot at stake for Magdalena.

The race consisted of three laps around Uncle Rudolph's hayfield. An oval had been carefully cut some years prior and was refurbished annually for the event. As the bugler called the teams to the starting line, the riders stood by and steadied their mounts.

As always, Grandpas Brohmann and Mok were the race stewards. This ensured no advantage to either surname. All the riding trios were instructed on the rules before the gun sounded. Magdalena had somehow convinced her teammates she should ride anchor, being the lightest by far. Heinrich agreed to begin, leaving Fritz to ride second. As the gun was raised into the air, Fritz winked at Magdalena, saying, "We've got this, kid."

The pistol fired, and the steeds broke cleanly. The entire picnic became a frenzied gallery of rooting maniacs cheering for one troika of riders or another. Well into the first trip around, the Area jockey surged a length beyond Heinrich and his Brohmann cousin, who were nose-to-nose.

The exchange zone was marked with bold red chalk. It started about fifty meters from a full lap. Dust flew when Fritz broke legally, still a length off the pace. The Hessian remained tied for second, with young Tomas Brohmann full around the stubbled oval.

Magdalena began the bell lap eating dirt, still about a length off the pace. And yet, to this day, no one in Willenstat can remember a more exquisite homestretch than the one she rode. Magdalena crossed the finish line a nose ahead of the deadlocked second-place finishers.

Fritz was the first to the winner's circle, grabbing Magdalena out of the saddle and tossing her high in the air. As soon as she touched the ground, Cousin Heinrich launched her skyward again. Before she came back to earth, the three jockeys were swallowed by the crowd. Magdalena rode to the trophy stand on a hundred raised hands. Grandma Brohmann proudly presented the first-place trophy to her granddaughter. Magdalena didn't part with that cup for the next few hours as the remaining events unfolded. The Mok team was dethroned at the horseshoe pit but staged an epic comeback in the three-legged beer chugging race.

When Uncle Rudolph rang his dinner bell, the crowd rushed for the heavily laden tables. The *legend of the lady rider* was born that evening—with a little different version spun at every table.

After dinner, the men made short work of the cleanup while the gals freshened up for dancing. Magdalena donned the new dirndl her mother had made for her. Then, her cousin Elsie helped fix her thick, black hair, pulling it back and tying it loosely —a far cry from her usual single braid. She looked like a woman—beautiful and delicate—which made the jockey uncomfortable and the fellas pleasingly mystified.

When the ladies returned, the men took off their aprons, stood up straight, and started clapping, as their wives and sweethearts promenaded around the dance floor. The applause ran deeper than a simple *thank you* for the picnic. The moment was intended to recognize the indispensable and underappreciated day-to-day contributions of the women of the Willenstat households. When things quieted down, the husbands found their wives for the traditional first polka. Brothers, cousins, and friends stepped in to dance with the unattached. Heinrich surprised Magdalena by taking her hand. To her delight, Fritz found Elsa Emma.

As the day gave way, lanterns flickered around Uncle Rudolph's humble dance floor. Music broke the stillness of the late summer night for the next several hours. Magdalena didn't miss a dance. Everyone wanted a turn with the champion, not because of her winning ride, but because tonight she was the belle of the ball. Happily dizzied, she returned to her chair for the first time in an hour as the traditional harvest waltz began. No sooner had she sat down than Fritz tapped her on the shoulder from behind, "May I have this dance?" he asked.

They moved effortlessly around the makeshift floor from their first step. Watching, Grandpa Brohmann smiled from his chair as he remembered his conversation with his granddaughter on love and marriage. He was now certain the young Hessian was acutely aware of her existence and that she was equally enchanted with the young soldier.

As the last notes of the waltz lingered, the pair stood motionless in a lovely place of their own, until Fritz reluctantly returned his

A Long Road There

partner to her chair. "I'll never forget your ride, kid. And thanks for the dance."

The party extended, as always, closer to morning than dusk. It was certainly an evening to remember. Only the old tailor had a notion of what was in store.

———

The next day Fritz began packing. He had decided it was time to leave. Papa tried to talk him into staying permanently, with no luck. He did manage to get a commitment for the spring planting and the fall harvest again.

After breakfast, Fritz made all his sad goodbyes. He even walked over to the Brohmanns and hugged them both. When he found Magdalena in the barn with Max, she was crying.

"Hey, kiddo, are you that happy that I'm leaving?"

"No. I'm not happy at all. Max and I want you to stay," she said with no attempt at hiding her emotions.

"I'll be back. I promise." He gave her a hug— not a casual one, but a long embrace with meaning.

She smiled up at him, saying, "Please hurry back. Max and I will miss you terribly."

"Stop crying. I'll be back sooner than you might like," Fritz said, turning away so the kid couldn't see his own tears. Hans had been right to brag about this family of his, he thought. They were certainly more than he had expected, especially his friend's oldest sister.

KAPITEL 6

The Village
Fall 1866 – Fall 1867

With harvest finished, Magdalena and her classmates returned to school. She was finding her subjects more interesting. She couldn't figure out why. Even Mama, the family skeptic, made a passing comment about her improved study habits. The boys caught her attention more, too. They were all a little taller and pleasingly bronzed. Bigger muscles attested to their many hours in the fields. Her scrawny pals were gone forever.

Magdalena was different, as well, and the boys were also taking note. She had discarded the two braids and now softly pulled her hair back in one long plait that swung slightly when she walked. Her body, too, was beginning to show changes. The skinny tomboy was transforming into a young woman. Instead of always challenging the boys, she enjoyed having their undivided attention. As the fall deepened and the leaves colored, Magdalena was transforming alongside them.

In January, Hans left for the university in Stuttgart. He wasn't excited to go. Times were lean since the war. Staying at home to

A Long Road There

help Papa made more sense to him than going off to college. Kurt's death still left a sour taste in his mouth for the university. Still, his papa wanted him to give school a try, so off he went.

Hans was Magdalena's best friend. She loved having her brother back from the war, limp and all—even if he wasn't quite the same as before he'd gone. She still couldn't erase from her mind the exchange they'd had in the first few days after he came home. She had been changing the bandage on his foot while no one else was around. Perhaps foolishly, she had decided to ask him what it was like to be in battle. The tortured expression that came over his face would never leave her mind. He continued to look directly at her, but he wasn't seeing her. His eyes were glazed and distant. When she had touched his trembling hand, he came back.

"Horrible. Indescribably horrible. Promise me, if it's within your power, you'll never let anyone you love go to war. Promise me, dammit!" he had demanded.

"I promise," she'd blurted. Hans had never spoken to her in that way. The exchange would linger for a long time.

The memory of Kurt's death had never let go of her either, and now Hans was going back to that place where her oldest brother had been killed. That conjured only the darkest of possibilities for the young girl. So, when the time came to put her brother on the train, she hugged him tightly, unable to hold back her tears. "I'm going to miss you terribly. You come back home safely. Do you hear me?" she said, confronting her brother directly. She hugged him a second time, harder still.

"I will. I promise," Hans said, trying in vain to comfort her.

After her brother left on the train, she and Max went for a long walk in the woods, where she sobbed. Max snuggled her for as long as the tears flowed. When they came back home, she felt better, although she couldn't completely shake the dread.

Magdalena got her first kiss that year. Erik, the tall, shaggy-haired blond that sat in the desk behind her, had asked her to go ice skating. After zipping across the ice all afternoon, with their skates now hung around their necks, they walked home in the twilight. Then, Erik took the big step. Their blades clanged, and their noses bumped.

That night as she tried to sleep, Magdalena kept replaying every detail of the walk home. She wondered if kisses were always that awkward. It certainly wasn't what she'd imagined. It didn't seem as nice as the short pecks Papa gave Mama as he was leaving for work in the morning. No matter, she thought. A first kiss nonetheless. She wondered if a kiss from Fritz would be any different, then quickly dismissed the thought, scolding herself for such silliness. Such a kiss is never going to happen anyway, she concluded, with enough uncertainty to leave the door slightly ajar for the possibility that it just might.

As promised, Fritz returned the next spring and fall to help Uncle Rudolph. During Fritz's autumn stay, he built up the Mok and Brohmann woodpiles again before helping Uncle Rudolph with his harvest. He stayed a little closer to Magdalena this visit, just as Grandpa Brohmann had suspected he might. When the harvest ball came around, he and Magdalena were hard to separate. The last waltz found the two snugly in each other's arms.

Magdalena took Fritz to the train as she had done ever since his first visit. The ride this time was especially quiet. Both knew what was happening. "I'll be back," he said, kissing her softly on the cheek before stepping aboard.

As the track continued to disappear behind him, Fritz kept telling himself how much he enjoyed being with the entire Mok family. That was true, of course. But Magdalena was the one that kept creeping into his thoughts.

KAPITEL 7

Der Weihnachsmärkte
Winter 1867

While Magdalena was making her way toward seventeen, the fall of 1867 brought continued change. Many classmates had stopped their schooling and begun working. In the wake of hard economic times, several had immigrated to America, mostly with their families but occasionally by themselves. More than a few of the girls had gotten married.

Magdalena now found school generally uninspiring, though she did enjoy the tutoring assignments her teachers had been giving her. She had decided not to return for classes next year. Tying the knot with an established older man of the community certainly wasn't in the cards, either. She vowed to greet the future and whatever it held in store with all the wisdom of her seventeen years.

In early December, Fritz arrived unannounced by train for a holiday visit and a talk with Papa. He came bearing gifts—Moroccan oranges from a wagonload he had delivered just north of Willenstat the night before. The ex-soldier had been working steadily as a long-haul teamster. The long, lonely miles gave him plenty of time to think about where he was headed. Those deliberations led him to two conclusions. One, he was going to Colorado to get rich alongside his uncle. Whatever had to be done to make that happen, he was going to do. Two, Magdalena would be beside him. He hadn't yet worked out the details, but he was certain of what he was going to make happen.

Entering the village square at the end of his ten-kilometer walk, the sounds of the season filled the air as he made his way to the butcher shop. Carolers and musicians were serenading browsing shoppers amid gently falling snowflakes. Fritz hummed as he walked through the magical scene. The *Weihnachsmärkte* had begun a few days earlier and was in full swing in the village square. The street bazaar was the winter event of the year. The village merchants and artisans hawked their wares from inside the small booths each had put together. Customers and browsers alike were lured by the aroma of bratwurst and sausages. They chased that down with warm glasses of *glühwein*, the favorite spiced wine of the hoi polloi. Gingerbread delicacies like *lebkuchen* and other sinfully delicious pastries tempted Fritz and guaranteed that even the most frugal visitors would open their wallets for a Christmas purchase.

Fritz could hear Papa rendering "O' Tannenbaum" through the shop door, but didn't expect an accompanying voice. Hans had tried the university for a semester before joining Papa behind the counter. Fritz dropped the gift of oranges he'd brought on the floor and embraced Hans with tears in his eyes. Seeing both men behind their dirty aprons again tugged at his heartstrings. He'd fallen for this family.

The shop was crowded with customers, so Fritz grabbed an apron and stepped in to wrap and bag. After an hour or so, the first lull in traffic permitted the bagger to call Papa aside. "Herr Mok, I think Magdalena's wonderful, and I think she likes me, too. I want your permission to court her."

"You've got it, my boy. I think you know what you're getting yourself into," Papa continued, only half-joking.

"He better!" a snooping Hans added from behind the counter.

"You just stick to meat cutting, Hans." With that advice, Fritz took off his apron and scooted out the door, hollering back, "Thanks, Herr Mok. I'll see you two at closing."

Max sprinted to greet the welcome visitor from quite a ways up the Mok drive, landing two paws full onto his chest.

"Where's Magdalena, boy?" Fritz asked, regaining his balance.

Max turned and raced for the chicken coop. When Magdalena saw the four-legged freight train bearing down on her, she dropped the squawking hen back on her eggs and prepared to meet the engine head-on. That's when she saw Fritz. He caught her mid-air, lifted her eye-to-eye, and gave her that kiss she'd left the door cracked for.

"Fritz," she managed, kissing him rapid-fire all over his happy face.

"I promised I'd be back, didn't I? I'm just sooner than you figured," he teased.

He kissed her again, more tenderly this time. She relaxed in his arms, thinking the soldier's kisses were better than the ones in her dreams.

Fritz stayed for a couple more days, helping the family where he could. He put on an apron again at Papa's shop. Staying clear of cleavers and knives, he stuck mostly to wrapping and bagging. The handsome young soldier also tactfully assured clamoring holiday customers that Papa would be specially attending to their orders next.

At the family's *Weihnachsmärkte* booth, he used his natural charm. With the skillful use of his irresistible smile, he persuaded the ladies to open their pocketbooks in record numbers.

Fritz and Magdalena did manage some time alone. During one of their purloined hours, the couple found themselves talking seriously about the future. "I have to leave by Saturday, and I don't know when I'll be back again. As soon as I can, that's for sure. How about you and me starting to write each other? You're always in my thoughts. If we're writing back and forth, that'll make the long miles less lonely for me."

Having thought many times what she might say in the quiet of a letter, she answered quickly, "I'd love to write."

For the next year and a half, Fritz worked close to full-time as a teamster running out of Darmstadt, though he did arrange time off with his employer each spring and fall to work on Uncle Rudolph's farm. Whenever he didn't have the prospect of a load for several days, he'd jump on the train to see his sweetheart.

In between visits, he and Magdalena wrote to each other faithfully. The letters quickly became romantic. They'd fallen hopelessly in love. It wasn't long, either, before Magdalena shared Fritz' dream of traveling to America. She presumed once they had their adventure, they'd return to the loving arms of family and friends as if they had never left.

KAPITEL 8

Willenstat Train Stop
Winter 1869

It was nearly 1870, and Magdalena was on the cusp of nineteen. Throughout Fritz' many visits, Magdalena remained a virgin, but that was not of her choosing. She had all but demanded that the two explore the splendor of complete intimacy. Fritz balked. He was determined to do right by Papa, though as time went on, even his resolve was waning.

The sadness of life again intervened that late November when Grandpa Brohmann died in his sleep. Magdalena lost her North Star. She waited until after the funeral to write Fritz, knowing he was in the middle of a round-trip to France, hauling hardwood over and returning with French champagne for the holiday revelers at home. France wasn't his favorite route, but the money was good.

The sad news awaited him at the post office when he returned to Hesse. It brought tears to his eyes. Grandpa Brohmann had held a special place in his heart. There was no doubt in his mind that he needed to pay his respects to the family at once. He left that afternoon.

The snow was falling hard when he stepped from the train. The ten-kilometer walk ahead of him wasn't a pleasant prospect. Like a good soldier, he put his head down and leaned into the wind, high-stepping through the deep snow. But before he made it far, he heard a familiar voice.

"Get in here, Fritz," the captain of their winning relay team demanded. "The snow's too deep for walking. These horses aren't real happy to be out in it themselves." Heinrich smiled and peeked out from beneath his blanket.

"That's 'cause the horses got good sense," Fritz said, climbing up next to the driver. While brushing off a little snow, he added, "I'm sorry about Grandpa Brohmann. He was a good man. When I got Magdalena's letter, I wanted to come and pay my respects."

"He was a good man, Fritz. It'll mean a lot to Magdalena that you've come."

Heinrich dropped Fritz at the butcher shop and left. He needed to get the wagon parts he'd picked up back to his father.

"What a surprise!" Papa said, looking up at the snowy man shaking himself off just inside the shop's door.

"Don't you know enough to stay out of a blizzard?" Hans asked, happy to see his friend.

"I guess not," Fritz said before turning serious. "I'm sorry I missed Grandpa's funeral. I just got Magdalena's letter."

"You came when you could, my boy," Papa told him. "We're happy to see you. Magdalena will be back from her delivery shortly. Sit down and warm yourself. She'll be even happier to see you if you're thawed out. The kid has been busy between the shop and the *Weihnachsmärkte*. I think she's frantic about what Father Christmas should gift her boyfriend." The butcher said this with a back slap and a big laugh.

"I'll see you two later," Fritz said. "I'm going over to Grandma Brohmann's."

A Long Road There

Fritz stood outside thinking. The *Weihnachsmärkte's* two blocks in the opposite direction, he said to himself. If I'm going to get a bouquet, I'll have to do it in the blizzard. But Grandma Brohmann is worth every step, he decided, pulling his hat down over his ears.

"Fritz, I'm so happy to see you," Grandma said as he handed her the snow-covered flowers.

"Just picked 'em," he said with a straight face. The two sat drinking hot tea and talking for the better part of an hour. "I need to go find Magdalena, Grandma. Is there anything you need, anything at all?"

She stood up and fastened his overcoat's top button, then tugged his scarf tight. "That's very kind of you, but your visit is the best help you could have given me. Magdalena will be excited to see you. Get along now and give that granddaughter of mine a big snowy kiss when you see her."

"These are for you," Fritz said, handing the imported violets to Alexandria as she opened the door. Violets were her favorite flowers.

"What a surprise," she said, braving the weather to give her daughter's sweetheart a huge hug and a big kiss on the cheek.

"Come in, come in. I'll get some hot chocolate. Sit by the fire," she told him, wiping the cold snow from her apron.

"Have you seen Magdalena?" she asked, handing Fritz his hot chocolate.

"Not yet. She was on a delivery when I stopped at the shop. I went directly to Grandma Brohmann's from there. I'm so sorry I missed your father's funeral."

"You didn't know he'd died. Seeing you now is a wonderful gift. Put your gear upstairs in your room. Magdalena will be wondering if you came to see her or her mama and grandma."

"All three!" he said, bounding up the stairs.

When Fritz got back to the butcher shop, Max knew he was there before anyone else. He immediately started barking. Magdalena flew out the door and into Fritz's arms, where they kissed as passionately as they could, knowing Papa and Hans would be snooping.

When their lips parted, Papa laughed, Magdalena blushed, and Max barked as the pair quickly left the shop.

"Take the sleigh—the snow's deep. Pick us up for supper," Papa hollered after them.

"Thanks," his daughter yelled, before telling the horses to "giddy-up."

Fritz wanted to visit Grandpa's grave, so the excitement of being together collided with that somber task. As Magdalena steered the team toward the cemetery, there wasn't much talk.

At the grave, Fritz dropped to one knee in the deep snow and bowed his head at the old tailor's resting place. For several minutes, Fritz spoke privately with the tailor. When Fritz got to his feet and came back to Magdalena, tracks of tears lined his cheeks. Feeling grateful that Magdalena had given him time alone with Grandpa, he said simply, "Thanks."

Before they were out of the graveyard, Fritz turned and said, "I'm afraid that we're both going to miss that man terribly."

The ride back into town was subdued most of the way. After a while, they shared a few stories of their time together with Grandpa. By the time they got back to the shop, the young couple was laughing—as the old tailor would have wanted them to do.

KAPITEL 9

Mok Family Kitchen
December 1869

After dinner that night, Fritz asked Papa to speak to him alone in the living room. "It's my intention to ask Magdalena to marry me—if you have no objections."

"Congratulations!" Papa said, slapping him on the back before putting the young man's hand in the vice and squeezing it with approval. "Alexandria and I couldn't be happier. I suggest you get on with it. That daughter of mine is chomping at the bit."

The next morning after helping the women set up their booth at the open market, the couple left to play in the snow. Actually, they were a trio. Max was better at every little game they played, except snowball fighting, though even there he was faster than their snowballs. The dog considered piling on top for the downhill sled ride but chose instead to race the tandem riders, barking at his playmates the whole way. Later, in front of the fire, Max tried to horn in on the cuddling and hot chocolate, but that's where Fritz drew the line, commanding "lie down."

Magdalena was making dinner for the family that night. She was nervous as all get-out. In fact, she was so frazzled that she never went back to the booth that afternoon as promised. Mama and Grandma only giggled, remembering back to the first meals they'd cooked for Papa and Grandpa.

When she stopped at the market for groceries before heading home, she bought twice as much as she needed, certain she wouldn't have enough. After all, she'd never made a fancy schnitzel before. But that was Fritz' favorite, so schnitzel it had to be.

She started to second guess herself as she struggled to open the kitchen door with two bags of groceries. As she struggled with the bags, the door, and the snow, two familiar arms came to the rescue. They snatched her load, pulled her inside, and closed the door. Then, she got a very big kiss from the man attached to those arms.

"Fritz, I didn't know you were home."

"I know. I wanted to surprise you. Did I?"

"You know darn well you did, but I'm glad you're here."

"Good 'cause I wanna talk to you for a minute."

"It can only be for a minute. I have work to do. I've gotta get your fancy schnitzel ready. Papa doesn't like to wait to eat when he gets home from work. I don't have time for nonsense right now." Though she tried being as serious as possible, Magdalena wasn't up to the task. Her matronly persona dissolved into a smile and became a full-fledged laugh before she could finish shooing Fritz away.

Taking her hand and falling to one knee, Fritz tried to stay solemn in the face of Magdalena's giggles. He cleared his throat. "I love you. I want to spend my life with you. Will you marry me?"

Assuming it was a dramatic prank, Magdalena feigned great anxiety and ambivalence.

Her performance was so good, Fritz panicked. "Will you marry me or not?" he demanded.

This time, the suitor's actual desire to marry her hit home. Gushing with glee, she flung her arms around his neck, "Oh, yes. Yes. Yes! When?"

Fritz smiled from ear to ear and parried her direct question, "We'll talk about that later—when we've got more time. I think my minute's up. Even though I want one more."

They kissed softly. As he left, Fritz insisted truthfully, "I don't wanna mess with the cook."

When he was called for supper, Fritz went directly to the chef and whispered in her ear. She smiled and nodded. After an especially delicious schnitzel, Fritz invited the entire family into the front room, including Grandma Brohmann, who had come for dinner.

"I know it's not quite Christmas Eve, but since I won't be here, I brought your gifts tonight," he said, beginning to hand out presents. "Ooohs" and "ahhs" filled the room as Grandma, Mama, and Elsa Emma found delicate, lace handkerchiefs inside their beautifully wrapped boxes. Papa and Hans had already torn open their less carefully wrapped beer steins.

"*Wunderbar!*" Papa announced, holding his stein above his head. The ladies, meanwhile, fawned over their lace gifts.

Hans, who had made a beeline for the kitchen the second he'd laid eyes on his gift, returned with a cold bucket of suds and immediately began pouring.

"I have one more gift," Fritz announced, "before I propose a toast." Pulling a small package from his pocket, he handed it to his sweetheart. "This is for you, Magdalena. It's a symbol of my love," he told her, before informing the family, "Magdalena has agreed to marry me."

The beguiled bride-to-be quickly unwrapped her gift and found a small oval-shaped ivory broach. Her eyes glistened with happiness as her fingers ran gently over the delicately sculpted perimeter that surrounded a turquoise-colored inset. When one finger came to rest on top of the raised center and began exploring the tiny ivory flowers, she tried speaking but couldn't. With tears streaming and eyes sparkling, she ran to Fritz and wrapped her arms around him.

She could only manage, "thank you." Her actions spoke louder than anything she could have said at that moment.

Now, it was time for a toast and several others that followed. As the broach was passed around, Fritz proudly let everyone know, "I found it in Italy. When I saw it, I thought it was almost pretty enough for my girl."

"I think it's time we refill the steins before everybody starts crying," Papa said.

Having figured a celebration might be in order, Fritz quickly dashed outside and returned with a snowy magnum of French champagne. Handing the bubbly to Papa, he announced, "All the way from Paris, ladies."

Mama found her crystal in time for each lady to catch a little of the white foam from the ceremonial geyser Papa had uncorked. The rest of that night, the room overflowed with happiness as well.

The next few days went by quickly. Magdalena and Fritz tried to steal quiet moments alone, without much success. When they did manage, the conversations immediately went to the wedding date. Magdalena wanted to marry soon. Fritz tried to explain to her that they needed money. He told her of the flyers he'd seen recruiting arms specialists to enlist in the Prussian army. The advertisements featured the carrot of a cash bonus in exchange for a one-year enlistment. Even if war broke out, he noted, he would be enlisted as an instructor only. The bonus, together with the money he'd saved already, would be sufficient to take them to America. Magdalena balked, saying they should get married at once. Fritz asked her where and how they would live. She hadn't considered that.

"We could live with Mama and Papa for a while," she said.

"No!"

The back and forth continued for the next day and a half. Magdalena insisted he not enlist in the army. The spat put a chill over the rest of the visit.

A Long Road There

The night before Fritz left, Mama was clearing the table after supper when Papa stopped her. "Leave the dishes, Alexandria. Fritz and Magdalena will take care of them after I'm done talking with them." He, Fritz, and Magdalena stayed seated at the table with no one speaking. Then after a few moments, Papa broke the silence. "While you clean up, I suggest you attend to the anger between you. If you don't, I fear it'll only act as poison to both of you. In the future, don't bring your squabbles into my house and to my dinner table."

Papa left the kitchen. The two young lovers set to the task of cleaning and mending fences. Slowly, the ice melted. They didn't resolve all their differences, but they stopped pouting and agreed to work things out.

When Magdalena took Fritz to his train, their parting was sad and filled with kisses as usual. But neither had retreated. Magdalena had made a promise to Hans, and Fritz wanted to make enough money to go to Colorado.

After returning from the train station, Magdalena sat down at the kitchen table, missing Fritz already. Being caught up in the issue of enlistment, she'd forgotten how happy she was that he had asked her to marry him. When Mama came and sat, Magdalena—without a *hello* or a *good morning*— asked, "How do I thank God properly for all of my good fortune?"

The question was strange coming from her oldest daughter, so Alexandria paused before answering. She knew Magdalena wasn't given to wearing her religion on her shirtsleeve. Finally, she answered, "I don't expect there's any proper way, sweetheart. I just know it must come from your heart."

"Thank you, Mama," she said, popping up from the table like a jack-in-the-box. "Life is *wunderbar*, simply *wunderbar!*" she shouted. Mama smiled and shook her head as her daughter shot out of the kitchen door.

Magdalena quickly found Max and re-hooked the team to the

57

sleigh. The two were headed for Uncle Rudolph's woods. There was a beautiful blue sky above a glistening white blanket of snow. Some ways into their ride, Magdalena saw a red fox and thought of the one she and Papa had seen the morning they'd gotten Max.

She stopped the sleigh in one of Uncle Rudolph's fields, just before her beloved woods. Neither she nor Max needed any encouragement to begin romping in the chilly white powder. In seconds, both were indistinguishable from the snow. Out of the blue, Magdalena stopped roughhousing. Looking to the heavens, she bellowed, "Thank you, God. Thank you," before tackling her partner in the snow again.

KAPITEL 10

Bureaucracies to Brookside
Spring 1870

In February, after his holiday proposal, Fritz enlisted for the advertised one-year position as an arms instructor. Certain it was best for their future, he made the choice without further discussion with Magdalena. By the spring of 1870, war between France and Prussia seemed all but inevitable, but Fritz didn't give it a second thought. He knew he'd enlisted as an arms instructor only.

When she received the letter with the news of Fritz's enlistment, the bride-to-be was furious. After stewing for a few days, she talked with Mama and Papa. Gradually, she saw the merits of the financial security the enlistment offered. "In one year, I'll be Mrs. Fritz Strasse," she told herself, pushing aside her pledge to Hans.

After three months of training in both small arms and light artillery, Fritz was certified to instruct in both. When he received his bonus and a ten-day furlough in mid-May, he headed straight for Willenstat. Feeling unshackled as he stepped down from the train, he shouldered his duffle bag. He headed directly for the butcher shop; Fritz wanted to surprise Magdalena.

59

Popping in the front door, he braced himself for an attack by a pretty girl and her four-legged sidekick. Unfortunately, all he got was a "hey, Fritz" from two butchers wearing bloodstained aprons. In fact, they barely glanced up at him. This wasn't the cold shoulder treatment—far from it. In a way, it was the ultimate compliment that they were treating Fritz no better or worse than any other member of their family who might have dropped by the shop on a busy day.

In between bacon slices, Papa managed, "Fritz, it's good to see you. Magdalena's making deliveries. I think she's stopping by the house afterward." Busy as he was, Papa wasn't blind. Fritz was clearly disappointed his sweetheart wasn't there to greet him. "I'm giving your fiancé the day off tomorrow. Love birds need time alone," he said, trying to repair the young man's deflated enthusiasm.

"You bet we do, and we don't get much," Fritz replied, perking up. "I'm headed to visit the better-looking members of your family before I get used to the two of you."

"Get out of here," Hans said, launching a piece of gristle at Fritz as he stepped out the door.

The fellow in search of a big reception got one in the Mok driveway. Max greeted the surprise visitor with two front paws to his chest. They both went down, and Magdalena piled on. Fritz's absence had made at least two hearts grow fonder of him. Immediately, he offered an olive branch for enlisting without notice. That wasn't a military code violation, but he knew his small indiscretion could get him guillotined by the civilian authority on top of him.

"I'm sorry I signed up without letting you know," he managed from beneath the shower of kisses. "I just thought it was the best thing for. . . ." He didn't get to finish because he got another big kiss first.

"I know that," Magdalena told him. "It just took me a few days to settle down after I got your letter."

"Then, how's about we take care of some wedding plans? We can begin tomorrow," Fritz said, hoping to cement his pardon.

Now that he was back in his fiancé's good graces, the soldier figured this would be a good time to show his girl the travel brochures hawking America he'd brought with him. He was right, because Magdalena was immediately hypnotized.

The next morning, Fritz had a degree of buyer's remorse as the couple entered the marriage bureaucracy. But Magdalena was not about to let him out of his bargain.

They began by waiting in a long line to apply for a marriage license. After an hour, they finally stepped up to the counter. Examining their application, the near-sighted clerk announced without a smidgen of remorse, "I'm sorry. No marriage license applications more than six months prior to the anticipated ceremony."

"No worries," Magdalena told her steaming beau. "We can still meet with Pastor Rheinhart," she said. What salvation, Fritz thought.

When the reverend arrived in his anteroom, it was clear that his white collar was too tight, because his face was apple red. "I'm sorry, my children. You're too early to get the Lord's blessing. He doesn't give it more than six months before the blessed day," the conservative old proxy assured them on the Lord's behalf.

That was enough, even for Magdalena. They both raised the white flag.

Hustling by the house, they picked up a picnic lunch along with Papa's fishing gear. Riding double toward Uncle Rudolph's farm on top of Papa's old mare, Red, the pair made an odd picture–carrying their fishing gear and a picnic basket while being chased by a large black dog. The riders didn't give it a second thought.

It wasn't long before Red was ambling down a narrow pathway between knee-high hayfields. The family fishing hole wasn't far down the quiet creek that flowed gently along the edge of Magdalena's cherished woods. The sun was shining, with only an occasional wispy cloud drifting by as the couple spread their picnic blanket on the grass. Red grazed, while Max took off to inspect the woods he knew every inch of by heart.

For once, no one else was around. Springtime was at the wheel, and nature took its course. When things began to overheat, Fritz suggested they cool down. Magdalena pulled him back down on the blanket. They kissed harder, then started untying, unbuttoning, and undoing more fasteners than either thought they had. Their yearnings drove them all the way to the mountaintop. When passion subsided, they snuggled. Both were at ease even after the splendor turned to contentment.

That evening at supper, the young couple was walking on eggshells as they shared their plans to go to America after they were married. They figured Mama and Papa would explode. But the fuses they thought they were lighting promptly fizzled. The lettered butcher and his wife became philosophical, waxing about youthful dreams and ambitions. They knew all too well that the best-laid plans could go astray. Happy to hear the couple had tried to make wedding arrangements, they just smiled and listened to the children's musings on Colorado, content to wait and see what happened.

The lovers climbed the same mountain of desire they'd scaled on their picnic several more times during Fritz's visit. They discussed the possibility of pregnancy, and both agreed they would welcome a child by simply moving the wedding date forward.

When Magdalena took her fiancé to the train station, she was sad to see him leave, but this time she was pleased with what the future had in store. She could wait for it.

KAPITEL 11

A Battlefield: Wörth, Alsace, France
6 August 1870

Upon his return to base, Fritz began instructing recruits. He seemed to have a knack for teaching and was enjoying his duty. Having grown up the son of a gunsmith, he was comfortable with firearms and knew what made them tick. He missed Magdalena and was hoping to have another leave in the next two or three months. Even though he had originally said they should wait to marry until his one-year hitch was up, after their last time together, he was starting to think the sooner the better.

On July 16, 1870, the French parliament voted to declare war on Prussia. They invaded German territory on July 19. On July 20, Fritz received notice of his transfer to a field artillery unit as a second lieutenant. He was fit to be tied and marched directly to his commanding officer.

"I just received these orders for a field assignment. There must be some mistake. I have an agreement here. . . ."

Interrupting, his commander had little consolation for him, "Son, you're the seventh soldier today that's come in here with a similar gripe. This is war. That agreement isn't worth the paper it's written on." Walking out of his commander's office, Fritz didn't see that he had any choice but to follow orders.

On August 6, at the Battle of Wörth, the French suffered 20,000 casualties. The combined German armies counted just over 10,000 soldiers killed, wounded, or missing. Second lieutenant Fritz Strasse's name was on the list of those killed.

On September 6, a letter arrived at the Willenstat post office. Fritz had listed Magdalena on the army's paperwork as his next of kin and beneficiary in case of his death. It took the Prussian army some time to send her the notice that Fritz had been killed. When Mama picked up the mail, she saw the letter from the Prussian army addressed to her daughter. She grabbed it and hurried to the butcher shop.

Magdalena and Max were out on an errand when Mama arrived. She handed the letter to her husband immediately. His face became ashen. Even though it was addressed to his daughter, he opened it, fearing the worst.

Pulling his wife close, he whispered, "Fritz has been killed." Mama started to sob. Hans didn't have to ask what had happened. He locked the front door and drew the shades. As the three of them sat in the shadows waiting to deliver the unthinkable news to Magdalena, they were silent. There was nothing to say.

When they heard Max at the shop door, time seemed to stop. Papa was still searching for some way to tell his daughter. When Magdalena saw the "closed" sign, she feared something bad had happened.

As she came in, Papa couldn't find any words. He was trembling. Hans took the letter and handed it to his sister, "I'm sorry, so sorry. Fritz is gone."

Magdalena walked to a corner and sat motionlessly. Her head fell of its own accord. Mama, Papa, Hans, and Max tried squeezing her tightly in a protective ring. The pain, like a virus, breached the perimeter.

A Long Road There

On the way home, Magdalena lost all sense of time and place. Only one utterance trickled from her lips over and over, "This can't be true."

Mama cradled her. Max seemed to know comfort wasn't in his power. He lay at her feet, helpless like everyone else. Magdalena felt as though the grim reaper was dealing from the bottom of the deck.

When they got home, Magdalena and Max went directly upstairs to her room. Mama and Papa decided they needed to carry the heavy burden of unimaginable tidings to their extended family. Everyone was deeply saddened when they learned of Fritz's death. Most had carved out their own special relationship with the charismatic soldier. Grandma Brohmann took the news particularly hard, having been especially fond of the boy. She feared now that Magdalena would be irreparably broken. Magdalena, as her grandma had suspected, felt as though she'd been shattered into a thousand pieces.

Foundering, she remained in her room for most of the next three days, refusing food and consolation. She went through the motions of walking Max as if she were dead herself.

By the third morning when his oldest daughter didn't appear at breakfast, Papa knew he had to do something. He headed up the stairs, knocked on her door, and entered without waiting for an invitation. Magdalena turned over in bed and began to cry. Papa spoke with absolute authority, the kind that precluded choice on his daughter's part. "Get up now and get dressed. You and I have things to do. You have ten minutes to be downstairs, dressed, and ready to go."

Instinctively, Magdalena responded. She rose, washed her face, combed her hair, and dressed—all mechanically. She walked without conviction. Max was almost pushing her by the time she reached the kitchen table where Papa waited.

"Mama left you a little something to eat," he said, pointing to the food in front of her.

65

"I'm not hungry, Papa."

"You must eat."

Morsel by morsel, she moved her food from plate to mouth. Papa started talking about death, loved ones, grief, and grieving. Magdalena tried to listen, but mustering the will to do so was proving nearly impossible.

He continued to talk mostly about different people's reactions to death. He reminded her of how Mama had seemed to lose her purpose, going only through the motions of life after Kurt's death.

"However you take the blow, daughter, you must get up and move on. Despair is not an option."

She knew he was right. He reminded her of how worried she had been seeing Mama stare vacantly out the window for days after Kurt's death. Sitting at the kitchen table in that moment, she felt some empathy for her mother. It was a tiny step forward. Papa sensed the spark and hoped for a rekindled fire down the road.

Her favorite jam was sitting next to a couple of slices of Mama's bread. She submitted to the pleasure. Finishing, she pondered out loud, "I hurt so bad. I don't know how I'll keep going, Papa."

"You just do. You'll find a way," her papa assured, wrapping her in his arms.

Papa went on to explain that after Kurt's death, his responsibility to loved ones had helped to motivate him in the darkest hours. He added that keeping busy—doing things for others, when possible— had started him toward recovery. Then, he gave his daughter a simple directive, "Magdalena, you will get up and make breakfast every morning. You will also split wood each day from the smaller sections Hans gives to you. The winter wood supply for us and Grandma Brohmann will be your responsibility."

She nodded silently.

"You and I are going to work now. We'll walk together," he told her. Max made it a threesome, with his tail wagging for the first time in a while.

From that day forward, Magdalena rose early each morning to fix breakfast for the family. She worked each day at the butcher shop and helped Grandma and Mama with their gardens. Each evening, she split wood. It was Papa, not Hans, doing the quartering for her. She wondered if he was trying to stay a step ahead of his own hurt; after all, he had lost Fritz too.

She did all this and anything else her parents asked. But soon, Magdalena found that staying busy could only chase the blues so far. Hard work wasn't enough to get her through the long nights. She came to fear the dark hours. Her smiles remained few and far between.

A terrible vicissitude of life had visited the happiest girl in Germany and knocked her down hard. She did not yet know how to get back up.

About three weeks after the news of Fritz's death, Magdalena received a small package in the mail from the Prussian army. It was filled with his personal effects—all that the army said remained of Second Lieutenant Strasse. Since most of the fallen rested with their comrades in battlefield graves, the package was limited to Fritz's possessions left behind at camp. The largest thing in Fritz's parcel was his pistol. Not the weapon the army had issued him, but the one he had taught Magdalena to shoot with. A watch, a few pieces of clothing, odds and ends like a razor, a small shaving mirror, and a batch of letters—mostly hers—were also included. Near the bottom of the menagerie of relics was a small, blue savings deposit book for the Willenstat bank. Fritz had often said he was saving for their future, but she'd never given it another thought. She slowly turned the bankbook over and over, not certain she was the person to open it. The money rightfully belonged to Fritz's family.

He'd been so proud of scrimping for their trip to America, announcing in every letter that more coins for America had been placed in the bank. Opening it, mostly because she knew he would have wanted her to see the fruits of his labor, she was puzzled to read, "Fritz Strasse, Magdalena Mok, Account No. 127." On the back inside cover was the standard legalese: "In the Event of Death." She started to cry. The reluctant soldier had made her a cotenant on the account. He had deposited enough for two ship tickets to America and a good start toward paying for the rest of their trip.

Staring at the items strewn on her bed, she heard Papa knock on her door and ask to come in. "There's no good time for me to give this to you, I suppose," he said, handing her the letter Fritz had asked that he deliver only if he were killed.

"Unless you want me to stay, I'll leave you alone," Papa said, patting her on the shoulder.

"I'd like to be by myself, Papa. Thank you."

As her father left the room, she opened the letter and read,

> *My dear beloved Magdalena,*
> *If you are reading this without me by your side, it means I am no longer on this earth. It makes me very sad to even think of such a possibility.*
> *I want you to know that I love you more than I ever imagined. The times we shared together were beyond wonderful. If it can be done from this side, I will always love you and protect you. But I am gone, so you must forge on. Please don't be sad. Be as happy as when we were together. You'll find another true love. Don't settle for less. You can do anything you decide to do. You're amazing. Now, go show the world that I'm right.*
> *With all my love forever,*
> *Fritz*

With tears streaming down her cheeks, she held the letter close to her breast for a moment before putting it away with the others. The one on top of the pile was from Fritz' uncle in America.

Glancing back at the revolver lying next to the correspondence, she paused to reminisce. Smiling through her tears, she saw Fritz once again covering every detail of handling and cleaning the weapon. He always fussed whenever her attention waned. Tired but rekindled by Fritz's visit, she laid down next to the pistol. For the first time since her sweetheart's death, Magdalena fell asleep peacefully.

KAPITEL 12

The Mok Front Porch Swing
Fall 1870

For the next several weeks Magdalena's demeanor didn't change, but she kept putting one foot in front of the other. The spark Papa had seen never went out completely, but its glow remained faint. No one knew how to help her. Magdalena was spinning her wheels. Out of ideas, most of the family petitioned the Lord, each in their own way.

As time passed without much change, Papa gave his blessing to his friend Otto Diller to begin calling on his daughter from a heart desperately seeking any solution.

The butcher had given the matter much thought. A cabinetmaker and widower, Diller was around fifteen years older than Magdalena and had four children ranging in age from three to twelve. Their mother had tragically died of influenza the previous winter, so he had hired an older woman to keep house and tend the children. He wasn't a rich man, but he was secure. He was looking for a wife to care for his family and to offer him comfort at night. A short man that had never been handsome, he was solid. Papa thought he might just be the anchor his daughter needed. He was searching for anything. A stably employed man and a fixture in Willenstat, Otto was worth a try.

Later that month, the cabinetmaker called at the house. Magdalena was shocked when he announced that he had come to see her. Papa had casually mentioned his friend's situation, but she hadn't connected it with herself.

After an uncomfortable half-hour visiting in the front room with Mama and Papa, the butcher suggested Magdalena show his friend the new porch swing. It was all downhill from there. When the widower told her in no uncertain terms he was shopping for a wife, Magdalena told him in equally clear language that he was in the wrong store. Wheeling, she headed directly upstairs to her room.

The courtship never went any further—not for want of effort by Herr Diller. It was simply dead on arrival that first night. Still, Mama and Papa would persist in playing cupid. There was Herr Bittmann, the bank clerk; Herr Willmann, the farrier's apprentice, and other gentlemen of Papa's choosing. Over time, her parents' quest weighed heavily on her. Their match-making efforts only led to inevitable comparisons with Fritz. No one withstood the scrutiny.

As the first November snowfall covered the remaining vestiges of fall color, Magdalena felt as though the cold, white blanket had extinguished the spark Papa had seen. If she had been able to look beyond herself, she could have seen the misery around her.

The Franco-Prussian War raged on, amplifying burdens of all kinds for almost everyone. Since the end of the Austro-Prussian war four years earlier, the kingdom and most of its people had fallen on hard times. Württemberg had paid a heavy price for tossing her support behind Austria. War reparations were suffocating the economy. Fortunately, since Willenstat was a free village—not owned by a noble—its inhabitants had only to pay taxes to the kingdom. Even these were a heavy load. Opportunities of every kind were becoming scarce. People were leaving the kingdom—often for America. The butcher shop didn't fail, but growth had slowed for the better part of five years. Fellow feeling eluded Magdalena, though it wasn't in great supply anywhere, as people struggled to take care of their own.

Only the forest seemed to offer Magdalena any refuge. It summoned something that made her feel alive again. Max became irrepressibly buoyant in the woods, and that was contagious. So, as the pair came onto their favorite spot in the giant oak grove, Max's windmilling tail lifted Magdalena's spirits—until a crazed cat leaped from a tree, knocking her into the wagon bed. Somehow before the lynx got to her again, Max got to him. Magdalena could only watch as predator and protector tore at each other's flesh.

Ripped and broken, the feline finally surrendered, limping off. Max stood defiantly, readying for a second charge that didn't come. After a moment of silence, the canine paladin fell to the ground. His belly was ripped wide open. Magdalena dropped to her knees in the bloody snow beside him. She repeated his name over and over as if it might get him up from the ground. Her old friend managed to paw the dirt beneath the snow and pull himself close enough to nuzzle her leg, before wagging his tail one last time.

Nearly an hour passed before Magdalena moved. She didn't have the will or desire to get up.

In all the places to find purpose again, this desperate scene didn't seem like a likely candidate. But as Magdalena kept picturing that last tail wag, she began to find some will. Max had gone down trying to help her. It wouldn't be in vain, she decided.

Right then and there she made up her mind to stop being life's punching bag. She would go to America to fulfill the dream she had shared with Fritz. Why not America, she thought. Papa's matchmaking efforts had convinced her she didn't have a future in Willenstat. After that, happiness became embodied in a place, in a journey. Whatever lies ahead, she figured, had to be better than where she was now.

As she lifted Max into the wagon and headed home, his blood stained her hands and clothes. Carrying his body into the barn toward Papa with her head bowed, she didn't look up until she laid Max down in his old stall. Johannes watched in silence. "We were ambushed by a wild lynx," she sobbed. "Max was killed saving me." Finally, after a somber silence, Magdalena whispered, "Let's go bury him next to Abe."

The two guardians now rested together. Watching his daughter cry as she drove the wagon home, Papa was looking for answers. Life sure seems merciless sometimes, he thought.

Magdalena called out for Mama as she walked in the front door, then headed for her voice in the kitchen. "Something horrible has happened, Mama," she began, crying. When her mother came to hug her, she asked to finish, doing everything in her power not to break down again. "Max and I were attacked by a wild lynx. He was killed saving me. Papa and I buried him next to Abe. I'm all right, I promise. I'd like to go to my room to think for a while, though."

"You go right ahead, sweetheart," her mother said, wanting to embrace her daughter tightly right then. Alexandria was hurting deeply inside for her child. "Hasn't the girl had enough? Please, Lord," she muttered, watching her daughter go up the stairs without Max. That seemed so cruel to her.

Magdalena sat on her bed and reflected for a bit before looking for the packet of letters from the army. She wanted to find one from Fritz's uncle. When she did, she took particular note of the ending, "*I think you would thrive in America, nephew. Come and give it a try. Uncle Hermann.*"

Putting the letter aside, she dipped her pen in the inkwell in front of her and began to write,

Dear Mr. Strasse,

My name is Magdalena Mok. I write to you with the saddest of tidings. Your nephew Fritz was killed in action fighting as a second lieutenant in the Prussian army at the Battle of Wörth. This happened in August, and I'm not sure whether or not you were notified.

Fritz and I were to be married. It was his dream that we come to America to see you after he was discharged. This was not an idle musing. We made plans and saved our money.

Now, I find myself lost without him. I am considering chasing our dream alone and coming to Colorado. I want to ask you what you think of that idea.

I hope to hear from you soon.
Most sincerely,
Magdalena Mok

After re-reading the letter, she sealed it. Grabbing her cloak and running down the stairs, she hollered to Mama, "I'm going to help Papa and Hans close up. I'll see you at dinner." On the way to the butcher shop, she posted her letter.

No, Magdalena hadn't seen or felt the hard times up close like so many people had experienced during the war-torn years of the past decade. Papa had made sure of that—to the extent it was within his power. So, now, at nineteen, getting back up after life had knocked her down would test her further. Mama had never fully recovered from Kurt's death, and in some ways, Papa hadn't either. When Max left her kneeling in the bloody snow, with his last spirit-raising tail wag, it was the smallest of beginnings. Young or old, the search for solace can be a long road for the grief-stricken. Time can heal all wounds, they say, but not always quickly.

Waiting weeks for a reply from Fritz's uncle was hard. Her

A Long Road There

resolve to leave for America was strengthening with each passing day. She was committed to fulfilling the dream she and her dead fiancé had shared, finding purpose in that quest without really knowing why. Maybe it was because she felt she needed to achieve something that seemed unimaginable to everyone around her. So, even before she heard back from Fritz's uncle, she began pursuing the dream she had shared with Fritz. Learning the English language became her late-night pursuit by the light of the candle next to her bed. Although she didn't expect to leave until sometime in the spring, she felt she needed to begin preparing now. She began researching ship fares and sailing dates, together with the varying means of travel from New York City across the vastness of America to Colorado. Figuring out how to get from the port of New York to Central City, Colorado was proving complicated. The alternatives abounded—trains, steamboats, stagecoaches, and wagon trains. Some went all the way, and some didn't. Money was certainly an issue, so it was going to take time, research, and figuring to decide what was the best and least expensive way to go. Preference, of course, played a role from the beginning as she lost herself in preparation for the pilgrimage.

Like her brother Hans when he enlisted, she did all these things without sharing her intentions with anyone. Magdalena grew more certain that she would go to America, so trying to explain it to her family would only make it harder to push forward with her plan.

Over time, though, keeping her secret became all but impossible. Telling Mama and Papa couldn't be put off any longer. She'd come this far and had no intention of changing course, no matter how they took the news. One evening after supper, she asked them to come and sit in the main room. She began speaking without preface.

"I'm going to America. I've written to Fritz's uncle in Colorado, the one he'd spoken of so often. I'm not doing this because I'm sad or desperate. I feel very comfortable with my decision," she said, stretching the truth. "If I don't like it, I'll return home. If I do, I'll

come back and visit often. Please understand I need your support."
Watching her parents as she finished her shocking pronouncement,
she sensed she had hurt them both. The scope and extent of the
consequences of her decision were beyond her, just as the possible
damage from Hans's enlistment four years earlier had completely
escaped him. The dread on Mama and Papa's faces now was an
undeniable sign she didn't have a clue what she was getting herself
into.

She hadn't asked them; she had told them. Her tone had
foreclosed the possibility of reconsideration. She had expected an
argument and was prepared to stand her ground whatever it took.
Instead, Mama and Papa surrendered. Mama sobbed, and Papa
slumped into his chair. Both had presumed that when Fritz was
killed, this going to America business would be the last thing their
daughter would consider.

"We love you, Magdalena. Why would you want to leave?" Papa
asked, hoping for a reason he could understand. He got, instead, an
inalterable pledge to fulfill a dream, as if it were a matter of honor
to his daughter.

Would he have understood if she had told him that his
matchmaking had played an outsized part in her decision? Maybe,
but that wouldn't have been the whole truth, either, because not
even Magdalena knew what truly motivated her decision.

When things settled a bit, she asked her parents to let her tell
each family member in her own way and time. She also wanted to
have a family gathering to say goodbye when the time grew nearer.

"I love you all so much. It'll be hard to say goodbye, even if it's
for a short time."

Then why are you leaving, Mama and Papa thought to
themselves. At nineteen, their daughter was a grown woman. Yet,
both knew life hadn't yet wrung the kid out of her—not by a long
shot. Papa couldn't force his daughter to stay, but he knew she
shouldn't be leaving. He was hurt, angry, and afraid for her all at

the same time. Mama was mostly gripped with fear. The thought of losing another child was more than she could take. Picturing Magdalena traveling all alone in a strange land with no place to call home made her tremble. Still more terrifying to her was the notion that her daughter might never return.

Within a few days, Magdalena had told everyone in the family of her decision to leave for America. It didn't sit well with anyone. The reactions were mostly predictable, though one caught her by surprise.

She had never heard or seen her Grandmother Brohmann really angry. The woman had always found a way to see whatever it was Magdalena had done wrong or decided foolishly to do as understandable, or at least less severe than Mama and Papa saw it. Today for the first time in her life, Magdalena had stepped over her grandmother's line.

"This is heartbreaking news, Magdalena," she had said when her grandchild told her she was going to America. "I've never seen you as a foolish person—impetuous, yes, but not foolish. You've had time to see that the path you're suggesting is the wrong one. There's no reason to do this. None whatsoever. Fritz is dead. He was a fine man. Yes, I wish he were alive and you two were married, but that didn't happen. Going to America will never change that. I can't say exactly where your mixed-up mind is, but you must change course. If you keep on your current path, it will only bring you and your loved ones loneliness and grief."

When Grandma finished, she hugged her granddaughter, saying, "I love you and I always will, whether you do this or not. But I'm against it, and you should know that." When she finished, she left Magdalena standing alone in the kitchen while she walked up the stairs to her bedroom.

The blow from her long-time champion was unexpected. Walking home, Magdalena convinced herself that Grandma was getting old and didn't understand. Magdalena either couldn't see

Virginia Pickett

or was unwilling to concede that the trip to American was not her only way forward. Her resolve to go only strengthened.

KAPITEL 13

Willenstat
Fall 1870 to Early Spring 1871

It would be wrong to say that things returned to normal after that talk in Grandma's kitchen. Hans, the same fellow who had enlisted in a rage to kill Prussians, told his sister straight out he thought the whole business was half-witted.

"You need to stay right here with your family," he'd said, pounding the kitchen table. Magdalena had been his best buddy for a long time—even if she had sometimes been an unwanted responsibility. He couldn't imagine his everyday life without her. If she left and didn't return, it would crush him, although he would never admit that. He would have gone with her in a minute and taken care of her had he not known that losing two children would break Mama and likely bring Papa to his knees.

But after their initial protests, neither Papa nor Hans ever really tried to persuade her to stay. Both were deeply hurt, taking her decision to leave personally—almost like she was betraying them. Her trip remained the elephant in the room until the day she left. Not talking about it was like walking on eggshells for everyone. Only an occasional cleaver buried deep into a cutting board at work ever alluded to the Mok men's dread of Magdalena leaving.

No one's perspective changed over the next few months. It was a strange mixture of anger and angst for everyone but Magdalena. She became nearly obsessed with her preparations for departure, oblivious to any wisdom in her loved ones' warnings.

Toward the year's end, in contrast to September and October, the days flew by for Magdalena. The Christmas season and the winter open market had come and gone before she knew it. In spite of that, her loneliness did spike with the holidays. After all, it was the first time in several years that Fritz wasn't here. She was determined not to return to those horrible months that had followed his death. In her mind, feelings and memories were the enemy, so she simply re-doubled her preparations, refusing to let grief intervene in her plans. Sadness, however, proved to be a stubborn foe. Sweeping it under the rug was easier than showing it to the door.

Halfway through January, Magdalena figured, was the earliest she could possibly hear back from Fritz's uncle. On an especially cold evening upon returning from work with Papa, Mama told her she had a letter from Colorado. She flew across the room and grabbed it. She wanted to read it alone, so she raced upstairs.

"Dinner's nearly ready, Magdalena!" Mama hollered after her. "Five minutes. Please don't be late and upset your papa."

Dear Magdalena,

Thank you for sending me the news of Fritz' death. I had not heard. I was sad to get such news. He had written often that you two were planning on coming to Colorado. I'd been looking forward to having family here.

You asked what I think of you coming to America by yourself. The country offers great opportunity, especially for those determined and willing to work. It's not for the faint of heart. If you're looking to marry, the west is begging for young women. Eligible men far outnumber them here. Fritz wrote of your independent spirit, as well as your butchering and teamstering skills. So, married or single, if you're possessed by pluck, my hunch is that you'll do well here.

If you do decide to come, I've heard good things about a wagon master in Independence, Missouri. His name is Robert Douglas. People seem to have the best success traveling by train from New York to Independence. It is from there the wagon trains leave, usually no later than May 1st. Travel as light as you can.

If you're still of a mind to come, let me know your schedule. I should be in Central City late summer or early fall. If I'm not there, the postmaster will know where to find me.

Best wishes and good luck.

Hermann Strasse

"*Wunderbar,*" she whispered softly to herself as she put the letter safely below the clothing in the top dresser drawer. She shared the heirloom with her sister. Elsa Emma knew the wrath of God would come down upon her if she were to ever open that drawer. Satisfied with the invitation's safety, Magdalena sprinted back down the stairs directly to her chair at the kitchen table, not five seconds before Papa came into the room and sat down to begin the blessing.

That night she lay awake for a long time, thinking about the letter and how she would get to Colorado. The travel brochures mentioned working across America for a wagon master. Running figures in her head, she considered how she'd get to Central City. There was no question she'd take the train from New York to Independence, Missouri; it was fast and affordable. From there, it had to be a wagon train rolling west over the new land. With that thought, she fell asleep dreaming of Fritz and her around warm campfires crossing America together.

Mid-February arrived quickly, and it was time to say goodbye. The farewell sendoff was the last loose end to be tied.

Joint Mok-Brohmann gatherings had always been favorites for everyone in both clans, especially when they were festive occasions such as Uncle Rudolph's fall celebrations or Hans's homecoming from the war. This get-together was different. Without anyone having to say it, Magdalena's farewell party didn't fit that description. Saying goodbye to someone who shouldn't be leaving was hard to celebrate.

Since Magdalena told them she was leaving, Papa and Hans had fenced their emotions. Tonight, the gate broke open, not by force of anger, but by uncontrollable sadness.

Tears, hugs, and lots of stories filled the evening. Magdalena learned that when the chips were down, her loved ones stood behind her all the way. If and when she needed them, she knew now they would always be there—no questions asked.

The guest of honor had carefully chosen gifts for each of them, crafting most of them herself. The old tailor must have been guiding her from above, because they were all of exceptional quality.

No one forgot Magdalena, either. Grandpa Mok parted with the wooden trunk he had owned since his years at the university in Stuttgart. He even had it specially refurbished. Little sister Elsa Emma had been lost in youthful romance and such things, so she hadn't really grasped that her big sister was actually leaving—maybe for good. Tonight, when she handed Magdalena the travel journal she'd bought for her, the kid broke down under the weight of that realization. When Hans gave her the compass he'd had inscribed with, "To help you find your way," he also cried and nearly broke his sister in two with a fierce hug.

Papa gave her a set of butchering knives, complete with protective sheaths. A family bible inscribed with her name, along with a few pieces of the fine china Magdalena cleaned so often, came last from Mama.

No girl on the face of God's good earth had a better family, she thought. So why was she leaving? She refused to entertain that question again—it had already been asked and answered. Magdalena was unable to see any other alternative.

When she brought her gift for Papa in from the barn, the room went silent. Everyone knew that father and daughter had been at loggerheads over her decision to leave. No one was sure how the butcher would react. Her gift box with the pretty red bow wouldn't stop moving as she placed it on the floor in front of him and stepped away.

"Open it quickly, please," she asked her father.

He only got as far as the red bow when an irrepressible black puppy popped out and into his arms. The butcher needed this from his daughter. The *Riesenschnauzer* lifted his spirits. Magdalena was happy to see him smile. It had been a while. Max's little brother would keep him that way, she hoped. Papa started to cry and left the room, but came back quickly and hoisted his beloved daughter into the air. "We'll call him 'Lonesome' 'cause that's what we'll all be until you come home," Papa said.

The second week of March, Magdalena took the train to Hamburg with Papa. During the ride, he considered the incongruity of it all. He found it baffling that he was accompanying his daughter some 700 kilometers in order to make certain that she was safely on a ship that would take her several thousand kilometers farther away on a journey he did not want her to make in the first place.

That night in their shared hotel room, Papa handed Magdalena an envelope containing one hundred thalers. "Here, I don't want you to run short," he said.

Although the Mok family was considered relatively well-to-do in Willenstat, cash was never in great supply. Magdalena knew what it meant for her father to give her that amount of money. She also knew taking it would ensure she could travel by wagon train. Keeping it, however, would mean compromising Fritz's hope that they finance their adventure themselves.

83

"No, Papa. I won't take your money. I have enough. This trip is my doing, so I should pay for it myself."

Proud of her at that moment, he answered, "Know that if you ever need this, the money is yours. You don't have to go, you know," her father added, hoping for a change of heart.

"I know, Papa, but I feel like I must. I still can't explain why. Please try and understand."

Papa hugged his little girl before he turned down his covers and blew out the lamp next to his bed. He didn't sleep much, hoping his daughter might bend a little and change her mind by morning.

She didn't. He left the ship's deck with a broken heart. A piece of it was sailing into the distance. "I hope she finds whatever she's looking for," he mumbled, not knowing exactly what she sought.

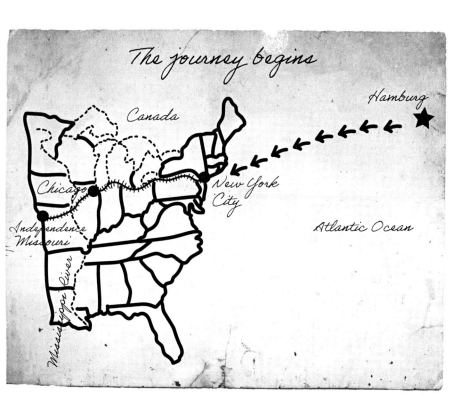

PART TWO/TEIL ZWEI

CHAPTER 14

SS See Falke
16-29 March 1871

As she watches the land become more distant, Magdalena knows now she's not dreaming. She doesn't yet appreciate the reality of being aboard a magnificent gift of the Gilded Age. The floating city, like its landbound cousins, features both perfumed promenades and tattered tenements. Nibbling epicureans are safely walled away from the gobbling sorts, as always. For the next two weeks, Magdalena will straddle these two worlds traveling at previously unimaginable speeds.

Cold, she realizes the sea wind is biting her. The throngs of people that stood beside her waving goodbye are gone. Only a couple of ship hands remain. She's pretty much alone, and that makes her shiver. Coming aboard, Papa had carried her trunk and found her berth in the mysterious labyrinth below. That won't happen anymore. She's on her own now. There's no Fritz, Papa, Mama, Hans, Grandma, or Grandpa Brohmann—none of her family are there to hold her hand. She knows she's brought this on herself. The wind is chilly, but not as cold as that reality.

At the bottom of the first staircase, nothing looks even remotely familiar. She hasn't the foggiest idea where her cabin is. The hall is dark and scary. Halfway down a second flight, it's darker still. Repulsed by a powerful stench, she bolts topside for the safety of light and fresh air.

She asks the first sailor she sees how to get to the second deck cabins. He doesn't speak German. A second crewman is heading her way. He obviously doesn't want to be bothered by another lost passenger. He tries to avoid her but she steps directly in front of him, hoping he understands Deutsch.

"I'm lost. Can you show me how to get to the second deck cabins?"

Obviously understanding her question, the sailor impatiently points her toward the staircase she had just come up from.

"I've already been down those. Please just show me the way."

Resigning himself to the inconvenience, he says, "Follow me." Halfway down a different staircase, he points to a landing and a dark hallway. He doesn't stick around to see if he can be of any further assistance.

Turning as directed into the shadowy passageway, Magdalena can barely make out the "1" on the first cabin door. "I'm just nine doors away," she mumbles to herself. Five doorknobs down, she notices a hulking form that seems to want to remain in the shadows. He takes up all but a few inches of the narrow hallway and doesn't move when she asks to get by. Shifting his weight instead, he presses his body hard against hers. He reeks of sweat and rum.

"Can I be of any help?" the malinger asks, drooling and pushing against her harder still.

"No! Please just let me pass," she pleads.

"Why not stay and talk with ol' McGee?"

Pushing with all her strength, she slips through the gap she's created and darts toward the safety of Cabin No. 10, staying one step ahead of the disgusting laughter trailing her.

A Long Road There

After bolting the door with shaking hands, Magdalena collapses on her bed. What in the world have I gotten myself into, she wonders. Without answering, she quickly gets Fritz's revolver from her trunk and puts it under her pillow. She feels safer at once—like Fritz is standing guard. Exhausted, she falls asleep for the first time on top of an ocean.

The *SS See Falke* was christened in September of 1870 in the Hamburg shipbuilding yard. The iron-hulled leviathan cuts through the sea at an astounding twelve knots. Ironically, she retains the relic of an eleven sail, double mast. This ensures mobility in the event her two 2,200-horsepower engines fail. Blackening the sea's sky with smoke, a single steel stack rises between the soaring masts. The new mistress of the sea eats seventy-five tons of coal a day, shoveled by glistening bodies into her four flaming mouths— around the clock. The "black gang" never rests.

One hundred and ten meters stem to stern and fifteen port to starboard, the floating city can slash through a resistant sea. 130 crewmen—captain to deckhands—wait upon her residents. Fifty gilded guests are served; fifty middle inhabitants are managed, and 600 bottom dwellers are policed. Each of the denizens has a story. There are golden tales, modest dreams, and lots of souls trying only to survive. 830 lives will unfold and intertwine atop and beneath her decks over the next two weeks.

Magdalena wakes with a start to the sound of insistent scratching. "Who's there? What do you want?" she demands, reaching for her revolver.

The scratching stops. But in the blink of an eye, the hideous sound returns. Cocking her revolver, she demands again, "Who's there?"

There's still no answer. Swinging open the door, she leads with her pistol into the hallway—nothing but emptiness. Whirling back to her room, she finds only the specters of her fright. Now, the scary quiet hangs like a fog until the scratching resumes. Frantically, she points her pistol at the air, but it's too late. The intruder's staring her in the eye. The mouse seems surprised by all the commotion. Magdalena falls on her bed and laughs, choosing not to fire at the diminutive trespasser.

Beginning to unpack, this is the first time she's taken note of her quarters. They're spartan to say the least. The room is smaller than her half of the bedroom she shared with Elsa Emma. A narrow single bunk follows the outer wall and sits high enough to slide her trunk underneath. A mirror badly in need of re-silvering hangs over a chipped pitcher and washbasin on top of a worn vanity. On the wall opposite the bed are a number of hooks.

I'm hungry, she decides before finishing either her survey or unpacking. Magdalena hasn't eaten since she and Papa had breakfast. "What time is it?" she asks herself. "Half past one," she answers. "Oh, my," she says, sprinting in the direction of the second deck saloon. An oddly named eating area, she thinks, following her reliable nose toward lunch.

The place is all but empty. "Lunch is over, lady," a busboy barks in German from the back of the room.

"But three squares is part of my package," she protests. This, apparently, is no concern of the busboy. The kid and his dirty dishes leave the room.

Only a few laggards remain at long rows of wooden tables and benches. Alone at one sits an older woman, adjusting her shawl. She seems to be smiling up at Magdalena.

"You've missed lunch, my dear?" the woman says sympathetically in perfect Deutsch.

"Yes, I guess I did. Do you know when they'll be serving dinner?"

"Not until six, I'm afraid, sweetheart."

A Long Road There

"It was my own fault. I fell asleep," Magdalena says.

Pointing to a small cart across the room, the fragile figure beneath the shawl suggests, "There might be some tea left in the pot over there in the corner, honey."

"Thank you so much," Magdalena replies, heading in that direction.

Starting to fill a tin cup that's seen better days, she remembers her mama insisting, "You pack yourself some tins of biscuits and sausages. You'll be glad you did somewhere along your way."

Racing for her cabin, she yells back, "Thanks again," to the kind, now puzzled, woman on the bench. Mama's goodies are immediately under siege. Restraint, never one of her strong suits, nearly eludes her before she manages to stop eating. Mindful of her rodent roommate, she seals the tins tightly just as the fellow saunters in, twitching his nose as if to say, "Am I too late for lunch?" Still a soft touch, Magdalena drops a small course of each of Mama's delicacies on the floor, politely suggesting her uninvited guest join her.

The old pro approaches the Willenstat cuisine with only a modicum of caution; after all, he's not new to panhandling. Finishing his fare, he casually sashays to his very small adjoining quarters.

The young hostess reflects briefly on the temerity of her guest before beginning to arrange her cabin. He certainly must have been a first decker at one time, she thinks, picturing the obvious sense of entitlement with which he left. His exit gave her an idea. As she chuckles to herself, she stops housekeeping, almost before she started, to peer at the ocean out of her porthole. "The sea is certainly bigger than I thought," she mumbles in disbelief, still tickled with her plan.

———

Having weathered a drunken sailor, sleuthed a monster mouse, and missed a much-needed lunch, the landlubber has two hours to kill before dinner. Undaunted and determined, she focuses on solving the riddle of the below deck catacombs. The mysterious mazes can't be deeper or darker than Uncle Rudolph's woods, she thinks. Unfortunately, without her trusty canine compass, the comparison feels flawed to her.

About to begin orienteering, she spies Fritz's revolver peeking out from under her pillow and briefly considers taking it with her. After a hands-on appraisal, she decides the weapon's too big and heavy. Mama had stitched her dresses with large pockets, but the gun is a stretch. Still, wanting some insurance against hallway demons, she remembers Papa's knives. The smallest seems lethal enough and fits perfectly in her pocket—sheath and all.

Not being too bold, she manages only to re-walk the hall directly to the stairs. The top deck in both directions is busy with passengers. Most of the activity seems to be toward the back of the boat. Midway down the flat expanse, about where the smokestack emerges, she steps directly over a bold red line, with this ominous warning below it:

HALT! ZWISCHENDECK PASSAGIERS VERBIETEN

How strange, she thinks.

On the third deck side of the line, even with the cold, hundreds of people are out in the wind. Many of the adults are wrapped in blankets. The older children are roughhousing and running to stay warm. Why don't they just go below to their cabins, she wonders. Turning and heading back toward the other side of the line, it occurs to her that none of them has a cabin.

A few steps over *VERBIETEN*, a crewman shouts, "Stop," as he grabs her arm from behind. When she tries to jerk it away, she stumbles. Papa's knife clangs to the deck. She puts it back in her pocket as quickly as it fell out. The deck cop didn't expect a weapon to spill from the dress of the pretty young trespasser.

A Long Road There

"You were instructed not to cross the line," the patrolman says with a little less vinegar, before stepping back and blowing his whistle for assistance.

"What are you talking about? I'm a cabin passenger. Keep your hands off me," Magdalena says.

As they continue to argue, an officer approaches in response to the sailor's whistle. He politely introduces himself as First Mate Hauff, then questions the crewman about the controversy. When Magdalena produces her cabin key, the officer begs her pardon and dismisses the sailor with a mild rebuke. Walking with her a short way, the young first mate strongly advises, "Confine your walks to the cabin portions, please. You never know what you'll encounter over the red line. Good day."

Safely on her side of the line, she comes upon yet another staircase. The descent is much wider than the others, with a gentler slope. The risers and the stair walls are both finished in oak. As the explorer continues, the distinctive descent opens to a spacious hallway. The thoroughfare is adorned with hanging paintings. Magdalena has only seen such appointments in Stuttgart. Stopping to examine a canvas of a large sailing ship, she's shocked that the light is good enough to easily see its intricate details.

"Fraülein, are you lost? Can I help you? This area is for first-class passengers only. Didn't you see the sign at the top of the stairs?"

"No," Magdalena answers honestly, trying to place the hallway monitor. "There are sure a lot of rules about who can go where on this boat," she remarks sarcastically.

Diplomatically couching his directive in a request, the young officer suggests he accompany her to the upper deck.

"I'll find my own way, thank you." Still, the officer insists. Halfway up the staircase, she remembers him as the mediator of her earlier boundary dispute. He disappears at the top as quickly as he'd materialized at the bottom.

Obediently, back where she belongs well within the second-

93

deck boundaries, she walks into a salty breeze toward the bow. The immense iron "V" seems to be plowing effortlessly through the ocean. Captivated, she turns to look back at the full length of the vessel and becomes freshly amazed, though the lifeboats remind her that this wonder of the sea is ultimately vulnerable.

Magdalena is front and center in the saloon by 5:30 p.m. The older lady who had been so kind to her earlier sits at a table by herself. Magdalena asks to join her.

"Please do. My name is Frau Hoffmann. I'm from a small village outside Berlin," the woman volunteers. "I'm traveling to America to visit my son. He owns a general store in Pennsylvania, you know. My son assures me many of the folks there are from *Deutschland*. I must confess I'm a little nervous to be making such an adventure."

Magdalena can't help but be taken with her pluck and assures Frau Hoffmann that her journey will be all that she's hoping it will be.

"Thank you, child. You know, I've never seen my grandchildren."

"You will before long."

Their table fills quickly with other passengers. Tin plates and cups, as well as worn eating utensils, are placed at the end of each table to be passed around. When the bowls of steaming ham and potatoes, crocks of applesauce, and baskets of bread arrive, each slowly moves around the table—not always in the same direction. Two pitchers of beer are set at each table by a brace of cabin boys with too many people to serve.

Magdalena hopes the bowls still have food when they get to her. The containers are large, and fortunately, they mostly arrive half-full. The petite fräulein scoops an indelicate pile onto her plate as her tablemates gawk in amazement. She snatches a pitcher of beer and pours for herself, wishing she had one of Papa's liter-sized steins. Shoveling supper into her mouth as quickly as it'll go down between gulps of beer, she scours the table for seconds. Two men at the other end have beaten her to the punch, draining the pitchers and emptying the bowls. Finishing her last bites of potato, she resolves in a low whisper, "That won't happen again."

The sunset on the ocean is enchanting. The wind has died down; only mist remains of a full ocean spray. She happily accepts it as she watches the sun dip below the horizon in a burst of color. The sky gradually darkens. Eventually, old friends begin to pop out. Being in the company of stars she'd visited so often from the porch roof at home makes her feel as though she hasn't left. She gradually becomes lost in the celestial mystery as if she were lying on her back just below her bedroom window.

"Good evening, Fraülein. Beautiful, don't you think?"

Irritated at the intrusion, she turns toward the voice of the first mate and returns a tepid, "Good evening, sir. Yes, absolutely gorgeous. I've always enjoyed marveling at the night sky alone."

The officer quietly watches the sky for a few minutes before making another of his purposeful suggestions. "May I escort you to your cabin? Without a lantern, it's difficult to see where you're going. I'm not sure it's a good idea for you to be by yourself out here after dark. We wouldn't want to lose you over the railing."

"Thank you, but I don't intend on falling overboard. I can find my own way."

Stepping away from the bow and heading toward the stairs, she smacks her shin on a hatch sticking out above the deck. It hurts like the dickens, but she doesn't want to let on, saying, "Oops," and forcing a smile.

Stifling his laughter, the officer steadies her. "You stay right here. I'll be back with a lamp in just a minute." With the aid of a lantern, the two quickly reach her cabin without incident. Too stubborn to admit that she needed the beacon, Magdalena offers a mildly genuine "thank you" as she enters her quarters.

Closing and locking the door behind her, the sound of

scampering paws across the floor immediately greets her. She'd temporarily forgotten her roommate. Striking a match, she lights her candle and breaks off a piece of the bread she'd stashed in her pocket at dinner. Placing it in front of her perfectly poised guest, she says, "The rest is backup." Having ruled out seconds, she stores the remaining bread in Mama's tin with the second half of her biscuits. Outraged at such rationing in cabin class, the seafaring rodent pounds the table with his paw and leaves in a huff.

By the light of her candle, she begins the first journal entry of her trip. So many things have happened, she doesn't know where to begin. After a few lines, she decides to finish in the morning. Magdalena blows out the candle and drifts off to sleep.

CHAPTER 15

On Top of an Ocean

A long buffet table at the far end of the saloon is filled with breakfast fare. The choices are porridge, bread, cheese, milk, or tea. The girl is hungry; everything smells delectable.

The weather is sunny and calm on top today. The promenade reserved for pretty people is nearly deserted, so the two snappily dressed older gentlemen near the bow catch her attention. They're trying to fire an old *Windbuschse*, fussing over it in both English and German. After walking past the odd pair a couple of times, she can't restrain herself from offering her services. "I'm helping you now," she announces in tortured English.

Flabbergasted by her presumptiveness, the shorter of the two men indignantly replies, "Thank you, but I doubt you could assist us." His handlebar mustache and red-feathered black fedora suggest a station uncommon in Willenstat.

Magdalena good-naturedly switches to German, "I've been using *Windbüchses* for target practice with my older brothers and cousins since I was about nine or ten. I can take a look at it if you'd like."

The taller gentleman, wearing a short leather jacket and a

97

Herringbone flat hat, seems ready to accept her offer. His German is impeccable. "If you think you can be of assistance, young lady, then by all means, proceed."

Taking the gun and pointing it out to sea, Magdalena pulls the trigger, getting the same results as the men—nothing. After carefully examining the air reservoir, she asks in German, with a degree of technical confidence, "Do you have a hand pump or a spare reservoir?"

"No. I haven't used the thing in years," the fedoraed fellow admits. "I brought the contraption along, thinking it would be a sporting diversion. My man was to have checked it over. He obviously shirked his task."

To Magdalena's delight, the conversation is now exclusively in German. Removing the air reservoir, she immediately sees that the connecting leather sealant is dry and shriveled. "The gasket is withered. It has to stay moist, or the air leaks out, and the gun won't work," she says with humble expertise.

"Good morning," the first mate offers, coming upon the trio in the course of his rounds.

Introductions, including titles, are immediately made, with Magdalena and the officer acknowledging their prior acquaintance. She has correctly surmised that the lineage of the two older gentlemen wouldn't be found around Willenstat. The man with the leather jacket is Lord Rutherford, the Marquess of Derbyshire, England. The second gentleman is Baron von Brunn from just outside Berlin. He's married to the marquess's sister. The three are traveling to America to visit the lord's brother in New York, Magdalena learns in the course of the extended introductions.

"May I assist you?" the officer asks in perfect English, directing his remark to the peers only.

"Absolutely," the baron responds with Oxford polish, relieved to have a man check the rifle. "The old thing won't function," he adds, handing it to the officer.

Replacing the air cylinder Magdalena had removed, the chief mate gets the same result as everyone else. Flummoxed, he hands the rifle to Lord Rutherford, "I don't know why it won't fire. Seems to be in order to me."

Catching only bits and pieces of the discussion in English, Magdalena reiterates, in German, that the desiccated gasket is the problem.

With his credibility at stake, the officer meticulously re-examines the gun. "Turns out the young lady's right. The gasket is shot. Do you have a second reservoir?" he asks in German, in recognition of Magdalena's correct diagnosis.

"No. My man has apparently failed a second time," the baron laments in his native tongue.

"I'll go check the ship's weapons cache. We might have one in storage," the humbled first mate says, heading for the ship's magazine. Returning in short order with an air reservoir, he attaches it to the weapon.

With a degree of flair, the baron accepts the rifle and successfully fires. Gracious applause follows. The royal twosome then magnanimously insists that Magdalena stay for a friendly twenty-shot competition, confident Magdalena will learn a thing or two. Never shy about showing off her marksmanship skills, she permits the pair to twist her arm.

Chivalrously, the gentlemen defer to the lady for the privilege of shooting first. Tradition dictates that on command, one of the non-shooters tosses a glass ball full of feathers into the air, while another scores the shot as a hit or miss. Twenty pulls of the trigger later, no bauble has escaped Magdalena's fire. The astounded royal marksmen respond admirably, each finding eighteen of his targets.

With their shooting dignity permanently at stake, the deflated gentry invoke the right of a rematch. Magdalena is delighted to oblige.

Searching for a strategic advantage, the baron claims the loser's privilege of choosing the weapon for the second go-round. "My *Dreyse* needle gun will replace the aging *Windbüchse*," the baron devilishly discloses.

"As you wish," Magdalena says, remembering her many hours behind the *Dreyse* under Fritz's tutelage.

Leaving their ocean range behind, the bested duo is eager to hear the story surrounding Magdalena's sharpshooting skills. They pester her for a detailed history, curious how she came to be shooting with them this morning, alone on this ship to America. Despite their elevated lineage and strange clothes, she's enjoying their company and senses two good hearts underneath their aristocratic airs. So, she begins long ago in Uncle Rudolph's woods, recounting the episode with the unfortunate farmhand and the *Windbüchse*. Touched and tickled, the baron gently requests, "Continue, my dear. How did you come to leave for America, alone?"

Skipping the most painful details, she tells them generally of Fritz's death and his uncle's invitation to America. "So here I am, obviously needing to speak better English," she says in German.

Both gentlemen find the young girl refreshingly direct, unadorned with the flummery of court ladies. They're puzzled that such an intelligent, pretty girl would make this perilous journey by herself. "What pluck," the marquess mutters quietly to the lord.

After a brief sidebar, both men agree English lessons are in order for their intrepid young foundling. The two believe Baroness von Brunn will be the perfect tutor: fluent in both German and English and in possession of a hopelessly big heart. They inform Magdalena of their plan as a *fait accompli*, not having the slightest notion she might decline.

"We will breakfast at 8 a.m., shoot at 9 a.m., and turn you over to the baroness for burnishing at 10 a.m.," the baron directs.

"Marvelous!" the marquess chimes in. "Excellent schedule, von Brunn. Please inform the baroness accordingly."

"Indeed, I shall, Rutherford."

A Long Road There

Momentarily delighted at such good fortune, the reality of having been booted out of first class intervenes. "Thank you so much for your wonderful offer but remember— I'm a second deck passenger. Many of your privileges are off-limits to me. I'd still love to meet you at nine for more shooting, especially with the *Dreyse*. I'll plan on it, if that's okay."

"No. I'm afraid that is definitely not okay, my child. This exclusion business is utter nonsense," Lord Rutherford declares.

"But I've already gotten kicked out of one of your hallways."

"That's pure hogwash," the baron allows. "I'll speak to that nice young chief mate today and make the arrangements. We'll expect you for all three activities. No further arguments."

Amazed the baron holds such sway, she isn't going to argue, intending to be there promptly at 8 a.m. As the ship leaves Willenstat further behind, the ocean's coaxing more smiles from the unlikely immigrant than she thought were left inside her.

Back at her cabin, she's so delighted with the morning's developments she can barely concentrate on the induction ceremony. Since her quarters will serve as the sacred venue, she tidies up a bit. She doesn't know how many tiny guests to expect; they'll just have to squeeze in. Time is running short. She smooths her hair, washes her face, and fastens her cloak as she lays out a crumbed feast.

Ignoring social graces, the guest of honor arrives early with the first whiff of a biscuit. Withdrawing Papa's largest knife, she solemnly reenacts from memory King Arthur's induction of Lancelot to Camelot's Round Table.

Clearing her throat and mustering her finest stentorian delivery, she begins, "I, Lady Magdalena Mok of Willenstat, Kingdom of Württemberg, of the long and distinguished Mok and Brohmann lines, do hereby dub thee Sir Biscuit Bottom, Duke and Grand Protector of the *SS See Falke*. Your floating domain shall extend from stem to stern and port to starboard. As Grand Protector, it is your sacred duty to guard and defend all inhabitants of the *SS See Falke*—especially me."

As Sir Biscuit Bottom devours the last crumbs from Mama's fare, Magdalena breaks into full-throated laughter before pausing. She realizes she'd almost forgotten the joy of pretending and the bliss of silliness. Almost. As the squire retires to his estate (in a dignified manner, of course), Magdalena begins gliding around the room.

Once again a commoner, she enjoys a lunch of cheese and sausage in the second deck saloon. Chipper and full as she begins to walk to her cabin, a familiar voice finds her from behind.

"Good afternoon, Fraülein Mok. If you're conducting any arms maintenance classes today, I think I need to attend," the first mate teases, revealing for the first time a frivolous side.

"None today," she says. "Though when I do, I agree you should attend," Magdalena offers with a wide grin.

Caught without a comeback, he hands her a small blue card outlined in gold trim. "The baron asked that I make arrangements for you to join them for breakfast each morning and that you have free access to their stateroom for English lessons with the baroness. This pass will allow you both privileges. Please keep it with you when you're in any of the first-class areas."

Magdalena is freshly amazed that the young officer takes even the smallest rule so seriously. She thanks him, nonetheless, as she puts the gilded pass in the pocket of her very ordinary dress.

"Good day and good shooting, fraülein," he says, whistling as he continues on his way.

"Thanks for your help!" Magdalena shouts. Despite her best efforts not to be, she's drawn by the fellow's sincerity.

CHAPTER 16

The First-Class Saloon

The next morning, Magdalena searches nervously for the first-class dining room. She has a pretty good hunch the hallway she was thrown out of—the one filled on both sides with the magnificent paintings of ships on the ocean—finishes there. As she pauses to admire the seascapes again, she expects a worker to pop out from behind a corner and apprehend her at any moment.

Eventually, as she suspected she might, Magdalena comes upon a large room with finely paneled walls. Inside are several leather couches, mostly bookended with exquisite lamp-topped end tables. The section furthest back is the dining area, with still more fine furnishings. Not seeing her hosts, her anxiety level rises beneath the gaze of the privileged. She's about to leave, when a steward appears. "Fraülein Mok, please come with me. Your party is waiting," he requests.

Following the tuxedoed waiter across the room, Magdalena is self-conscious about her clothes for the first time in her life. Spying her hosts, she breathes a sigh of relief. The two gentlemen rise to greet her as the steward pulls out her chair and hands her a menu.

103

From out of nowhere, a second server appears with juice, tea, and champagne. "Just tea, please," Magdalena cautiously requests.

"Nonsense! Give her all three," the baron says. "The orange juice is freshly squeezed, you know. Quite good, considering how late it is in the season. Order adequately, my dear. You'll have your work cut out for you this morning. Yesterday's easy pickings, I dare say, are gone."

The leather-bound menu seems to go on forever as Magdalena starts to scan the unfamiliar litany of choices.

"And a bit of the bubbly, dear?" the baron interrupts. "Steadies the trigger finger, you know."

"Absolutely," Lord Rutherford assures.

Laughing, she accepts half a glass. Sipping, the bubbles tickle her nose as she settles for Mama's reliably delicious but simple breakfast of sausages, cheese, and freshly baked bread.

Her tablemates talk in friendly jabs and predictions for the upcoming match. Magdalena thinks how much the two gentlemen remind her of Grandpa Mok, even though they are aristocrats. She hadn't expected that similarity and hasn't yet figured it out.

Finishing, she nudges the marquess and whispers, "Would it be terribly improper if I took a menu to send my parents?"

Whispering back like a co-conspirator, his lordship says, "I should say not." He delights in watching the menu disappear into Magdalena's oversized pocket.

Removing the needle gun from a crested leather case, the baron announces with great ceremony, "I now ask the faint of heart to hobble below before the intrepid begin competing."

Magdalena and Lord Rutherford hold their ground. "Beauty before experience," the titled German suggests, handing the rifle to Magdalena.

Thinking of Fritz, the shooter's eyes get misty, and she misses both practice shots.

A Long Road There

"A bit worried, huh, my dear?" Lord Rutherford asks rhetorically.

The older marksmen, in contrast, enjoy perfect preliminary rounds. Magdalena quickly corrects any misconceptions that she may be off her game; she misses only once in the first round of actual competition. Unfazed, the elderly shooters answer with two perfect scores. Each competitor then misses once in a tense second round.

As they start their third and final turns, a first-class deck crowd, including the chief mate, has gathered. They're cheering and clapping with each shot, especially for the young fraülein. With remarkable poise and to the crowd's delight, Magdalena is perfect in the final round. Only one feathered ball evades both royal shooters as they answer in succession.

"The match is tied," the baron announces. Then he continues on, as much for the crowd as for the competitors. "We will alternate shooters, each firing once until the tie is broken and only the champion remains."

The crowd erupts in cheers. Four tie-breaking rounds pass without a miss. After a brief conference, the baron informs the gallery, to their great dismay, "Our needle nose is overheated. The match is declared a draw. "

As the cheering section disperses, the wily German quietly pulls Magdalena aside. "I dare say the rifle may be exhausted, but Rutherford and I certainly are. Three great shooters shall share the day's crown. That is, if you have no objections, my dear."

"None, Baron. None at all."

Checking his gold watch, the baron notes with some urgency, "I'm afraid your English tutorial is at hand, my dear."

"You're right. I've got to hurry. I don't want to be late," the pupil says as she scurries off.

Quickly retracing her steps down to the well-decorated hall, Magdalena searches for cabin number five in the first adjoining

105

passageway, as instructed. Arriving at the royal threshold, "a little faint of heart" as the baron might say, she knocks.

An attractive, stately woman greets her. She appears not much older than Mama. "You must be Magdalena. Please come in. I trust you put my marksmen in their place again today."

"We tied, Baroness, in a very exciting match."

"That certainly must have saved their egos, my dear."

"They're very good, Frau, really very good."

"And, you my dear, are exceedingly humble.

"Come, let's sit," the baroness says, motioning to a wooden reading table with two straight-back chairs. Magdalena's eyes sweep the room as her teacher opens her lesson plan. The cabin is twice as big as hers. There's space for the table and the two chairs, a sofa, and still another upholstered chair. Again, the walls are finished oak. Realizing this is the stateroom only and that a bedroom adjoins, she's freshly reminded of the hundreds of passengers traveling as *steers*.

After the lesson, Magdalena feels puzzled. As she had watched and listened to her royal instructor, the teacher seemed down to earth—like Mama—yet she lives in an unearthly extravagance. Magdalena decides she'll have to think on that for a while.

———

Back in her own quarters, she treats Sir Biscuit Bottom to an extra ration—giving it to him a little at a time, hoping he'll stay around to visit. Overflowing with excitement from the morning's activities, she decides to share them with the royal mouse while practicing her newly acquired English. The knight is unimpressed but stays to enjoy his additional crumbs. Finishing, he looks up at her and wiggles his nose, obviously bargaining for more. She laughs at his brazen tactics, as well as her own indecipherable English. "Get out of here, Biscuit Bottom. I won't be bribed," she says, drawing a line in the sand in a mixture of German and English. This doesn't seem to bother Sir Biscuit Bottom—perhaps because he's bilingual.

106

Good to his word, the rodent lord repairs for a nap.

Magdalena decides to do the same. Drifting off quickly, her last thoughts are soothing. The magic of the sea settles her.

After supper, ignoring the chief mate's earnest concerns, Magdalena heads for the open air to again enjoy the exploding colors of the fading horizon and to await the twinkling majesty of the night sky.

The moon is larger tonight; its light gently bathes the deck. Magdalena suspects the scene never gets old.

"You must like the night sky," comes the now familiar voice of the first mate.

"I do. I've always enjoyed being outdoors," she responds without looking in his direction.

"My caution the other evening, about being out here alone at night, still stands. Have you always been so strong-willed?" he asks.

Warming to the intruder despite her best efforts, Magdalena laughs, thinking back to the battles of wills she had with her family members, particularly Hans. "Probably so. I think my papa and brother Hans would definitely say yes."

"How about I escort you back to your cabin?"

Surprising herself, she accepts the invitation. "Thank you. That would be nice."

At that moment, the ship rolls, sending her tumbling into the officer. "Ow!" he yelps, as he breaks her fall.

"I'm sorry. I didn't mean to hurt you."

"You didn't. I cut my arm on a splintered plank. I'm certain there's a piece of something still in there. The slightest touch will set me to yowling."

"Sorry I'm so clumsy," she offers, noticing that the officer is sweating in the cold night air.

"Do you want me to have a look at your arm? I've helped my mama doctor my papa and my brother with many infections from meat bones."

Virginia Pickett

"Thank you, but I'll be alright. Let's get you back to your cabin now," he requests.

CHAPTER 17

Troubled Waters—Above & Below

On her fourth day, breakfast in the first-deck saloon is again an experience. Magdalena chuckles as she eats, thinking how quickly she's becoming accustomed to the silver spoon in her mouth.

"I daresay, you do seem to enjoy your breakfast, my dear," the baron marvels as Magdalena shovels the last delightful bites into her mouth. After her first breakfast, the shy guest began to treat the offerings on the menu as a smorgasbord, much to the delight of her hosts.

Leaving, the conversation switches to the shooting match at hand. The baron had chosen his Bavarian *Werder M1869* for today's match, hoping his competitors had never fired one.

"I'm no stranger to the *Werder*, brother-in-law, as you may have hoped," his lordship says. "You've obviously forgotten we used it last fall while stag hunting on your estate."

Walking to the top deck in between the royal marksmen, Magdalena admits to a distant memory of the weapon herself. "I know I've used one. I just don't remember where or when."

On deck, black clouds are churning, working the sky into a rage. Once more, the first mate appears from out of nowhere. "Looks like we're in for a pretty good blow. You may want to cut the competition short." Sweat pours from his face, and his left hand is badly swollen.

"Splendid idea, my boy!" the marquess acknowledges, taking no note of the officer's condition. Turning to leave, the sailor collapses. Magdalena rushes to help. Her shooting companions seem paralyzed by the body lying on the deck. A very pregnant woman is leaning against the railing on the less fortunate side of the red line.

"Can you please come and help me, Frau?" Magdalena asks.

Without hesitation, the woman obliges.

"Please rest a moment," Magdalena pleads with the first mate.

"I think I'm okay now," he says, trying to get to his feet, before falling back hard onto the deck.

"We need to get you to your room," Magdalena tells him.

"Just down those stairs," he says, trying to motion toward the entryway. "The cabin is marked *Chief Mate*."

Still discombobulated, Lord Rutherford has composed himself enough to place his royal services at Magdalena's disposal, while the baron has left seeking the succor of his wife's decisiveness. Somehow, Magdalena, the very pregnant stranger, and the aging marquess manage to get the seaman down the stairs.

Reaching his cabin, Magdalena asks, "Where's your key?"

"My jacket pocket."

She's uncomfortable frisking the officer but has no choice. Unlocking the door, the three volunteers wrestle the seaman onto his bed. Together, the two girls get him out of his jacket and blouse.

"Good heavens, my man, that's a wretched wound," Lord Rutherford observes, discarding normal bedside manners. Heading for the door, he shouts, "I'll get the doctor."

"No, please don't do that. He's an incompetent lush that

hasn't been sober for a long time. He lost his credential at home in Hamburg for a while. His uncle was an original investor in the line, otherwise he wouldn't be here. Please don't go for him," he pleads, breathless from asking.

"What in heaven's name would you have me do then? You'll lose that limb if nothing's done."

"You said you've helped your mama treat infections," the officer says, looking directly at Magdalena.

"My mama knew what to do. I just helped. I don't have any medical supplies."

"What do you need?" the officer groans.

Aware now of what she might be getting herself into, Magdalena answers anyway. "A scalpel, tweezers, bandages, and hot water."

"There are a couple of bottles of brandy in the bottom drawer. Take the unopened one and give it to the doctor. Ask him to report me as sick. He'll be happy to give you the supplies in exchange for the bottle. The way his mind works, he'll conclude we want the time together in my cabin and be only too pleased to help."

"I'll set him straight!" Magdalena says to everyone in the room.

"No, don't do that, please. He can't suspect I actually need medical attention. If he does, he'll try to give it to me. Then, either me or my arm won't be here long."

Magdalena doesn't have much time to think about it, so she reacts on instinct. "Lord Rutherford, try to find a large basin and have it filled with boiling hot water."

"I'll get someone in the galley on it at once," he says, heading in that direction, happy to leave the room.

Turning to the girl she shanghaied, Magdalena introduces herself, feeling bad she's put the pregnant woman in such a spot.

Extending her hand with quiet confidence, the expectant mother introduces herself. "I'm Rosa. How can I help?" There is strength behind the girl's eyes. Her face and clothes may be tuckered, but perhaps not her spirit.

111

"Would you please stay here in the cabin, Rosa, while I find the doctor? Make sure he doesn't get up," she adds, pointing to the patient.

"I will," Rosa says, sitting down next to the young officer and taking hold of his good hand.

———

Two bloodshot eyes on top of a dirty white smock answer the door. The doctor reeks of rum. Extending the bottle of brandy, Magdalena begins, "First Mate Hauff asks that I give you this."

Taking full measure of Magdalena's attractive young body, the physician slurs, "Thank you, my dear."

"He also asks that you inform the captain he's ill and will be confined to quarters for the next few days."

Opening the bottle, the doctor takes a discriminating pull. "Very fine! Our officer must be in great need of rest if he's willing to part with such nectar." With a wink, he adds, "Is there anything else I can do for you and the first mate? Please attend to his every need, little miss nurse. I'll inform the captain as requested and note my file appropriately."

Fit to be tied, Magdalena bites her tongue, saying only, "I need some medical supplies."

"Ahh, playing the part so well, my dear," the doctor applauds, pointing to a cabinet with an invitation to "help yourself."

Shooting him a nasty glare, Magdalena grabs her supplies and slams the door behind her.

———

Lord Rutherford has returned with hot water, and Rosa has settled the patient by the time Magdalena gets back to the room. The time for backing out has passed, so she drenches the wound and the borrowed instruments with brandy. Handing the bottle to the injured officer, she's frank. "This is going to hurt." As he finishes a very long pull, Magdalena starts to probe.

Outside, the storm has begun to toss the ship. The rolling vessel isn't making matters easier for the surgeon. Magdalena knows she has to find the splinter the chief mate insists is still in his arm. "Please hold him steady," she asks the quaking noble, as if he were a common attendant. "Rosa, can you get a better grip on his legs?" she pleads, probing still deeper. The officer mercifully passes out, the splinter still missing. After what seems an eternity, Magdalena pauses to wipe her brow and sigh—just a minute into her quest.

Beginning to hunt again, Magdalena directs, "Rosa, bring the light closer."

"There it is!" the doctor exclaims, grabbing the lumber with her tweezers and hoisting it into the air.

"Good show, my dear," his lordship exclaims, taking his Paris linen handkerchief from his blazer pocket. It's no match for the sweat on his forehead.

Still focused on her job, Magdalena doesn't acknowledge the compliment. "Rosa, fold some more cloth together, then get that empty bowl and hold it under the wound." She begins to cut with no attempt to accommodate sensibilities. Yellow poison erupts as she does. Laying her knife aside, she grabs the folded bandages, places them against the incision, and gently pushes—trying to void the remaining pus.

Before her instrument finishes clanging in the first mate's battered bowl, Lord Rutherford, who had turned away from the last revolting procedure, tries to buck Magdalena up a bit, "Well done, my dear. The court's surgeon couldn't have performed better! I daresay we could all use some medicinal fortification about now." Drawing his monogrammed silver flask from the inside pocket of his tweed jacket, he offers it to the surgeon first. She takes a sip and passes it to Rosa, who defers, offering it to her barely conscious patient. He's not ready for refreshments, so Rosa enjoys a yeoman's pull—to the amazement of her colleagues. By now, his lordship is in need of his own elixir. He drinks, then permits himself a gratifying "Ahhh!"

Virginia Pickett

Giving the wound another dose of brandy, Magdalena begins to bandage, when she feels a gentle touch on her arm and a squeeze of her hand before the patient slips away again. Collapsing in the bedside chair, she lets her staff know the job's not done. "We've got some long, difficult hours ahead. I could sure use your help," she says, looking at the strange pair fate had sent her. Each pats her on the shoulder.

"Let's all get some rest while we can," Magdalena suggests.

"Just what the doctor ordered. I'll bring some lunch for everyone after my nap," the marquess says, as the first mate's wall clock strikes twelve.

"Please let the baroness know why I missed our class," Magdalena shouts after him.

"Indeed I will."

Not long after that, Magdalena and Rosa, like the officer, are sound asleep.

CHAPTER 18

The First Mate's Cabin

At half past one, two waiters arrive with a pair of silver trays. Neither girl has to be encouraged to eat.

Sitting cross-legged across from Rosa on the floor, Magdalena wonders why this pregnant young woman would make such a journey alone. She's fully aware that her family and friends have asked that same question about her many times.

"Rosa, how'd you ever end up on this boat all alone and pregnant?"

"It's a long story," the dragooned nurse begins, almost as though she's been waiting to tell it to someone. "I grew up near Hamburg, the fifth child of a tenant farmer. Now, I know we were poorer than most. At age twelve, I began to work as a servant at the estate nearby. Eventually, I became a kitchen maid. When I was seventeen, I fell in love with a stable groom. His name was Theodor. When I turned eighteen, we got married. Both of us hoped for a better life from the beginning. My grandfather had gone to New York City years before and was prospering. He was going to help us get started in America. We scrimped and saved every extra penny so we could sail as soon as possible. That was before I got pregnant,

115

and Theodor was drafted. We knew then we'd have to wait until the baby was born and he was discharged, but we never wavered from our dream. He was killed in action three months later."

With her eyes filling with tears, Rosa takes a moment to gather herself before finishing. "I didn't know what I was going to do until my grandfather insisted I come ahead. I knew if I stayed at home, it would be a terrible struggle. I wanted to give my child a chance at something more. Now, here I am sitting with you."

With tears rolling down her own cheeks, Magdalena realizes that she hasn't been dealt the worst cards.

When the patient begins thrashing in his sleep, Magdalena gets up to wipe his face with a cool cloth. "Well, you and your child are going to get that better life you dreamed about," she says, sitting again. "Your grandfather will see to that. You need to get some rest now. Use my cabin. You won't have to go out into the storm that way. I could sure use your help for another day or two. I hope he'll be much better soon," Magdalena says, looking at the young officer.

"I'd be happy to stay and help, Magdalena. Sharing your cabin would make it easier."

"I better warn you. I do have a small, four-legged roommate. I call him Sir Biscuit Bottom. He's a royal mouse that only shows himself when he smells food. You'll have to introduce yourself." Rosa laughs, and her eyes twinkle through the teardrops. As Magdalena describes the antics of her four-legged knight, both girls are soon giggling, their spirits lifted.

Taking Rosa by the hand, Magdalena says, "Come on. My cabin's not far. I'll show you the way." Opening her cabin door, Magdalena says, "Sleep tight," trying to make Rosa feel at home. The barrel of Fritz's pistol is peeking from under the pillow. Without a word of explanation, Magdalena puts the weapon in the pocket of her hanging bathrobe. Rosa doesn't ask any questions.

The patient is awake when his surgeon gets back to the room.

A Long Road There

They begin to talk for the first time like two young people together on a boat.

"How in the world did you come to be on this ship all alone?" the first mate asks.

This time, Magdalena's telling is more emotional than the story she shared with her shooting partners. The officer is visibly moved by her story and pats her hand. She feels his empathy and blushes, quickly seeking the sanctuary of her own inquiry.

"How is it that you're an officer on this magnificent boat at such a young age?"

"Well, it's pretty simple. The water has been a part of my life since the day I was born just a hundred meters off the coast in Hamburg. My father and grandfather were seafarers. I started as a cabin boy on my uncle's freighter at ten. I guess I don't know how else to live but on the water," he says, trailing off and closing his eyes.

Magdalena has never known a sailor. Thinking of the life he just described and trying to picture her patient as a ten-year-old cabin boy, she watches him fall asleep. As her own eyes close, she feels good that she decided to help him.

It's nearly 3 o'clock when a knock on the door startles Magdalena. "Baroness, what a surprise," she says, only half awake but genuinely glad to see her teacher.

"My brother told me why you missed our English lesson. What a ghastly situation. You must be done-in, my dear."

"I just hope the officer gets better," Magdalena replies.

"I brought you a pillow and blanket. I can see there's not a lot of room, but maybe these will help make you a little more comfortable. Would you like me to stay, or do you want to sleep some more, my child?"

"Oh, please stay, if only for a while. I just woke up. I'd love to have your company."

"I was hoping you'd say that. I brought some port to help you relax. May I join you in a glass? We can sip and talk until you fall back to sleep or shoo me out."

"*Wunderbar!*" Magdalena responds, grabbing two tin cups. The baroness pours.

As they visit, the patient's in and out of febrile sleep.

Sitting on the floor, the two talk as an older and younger sister might, without the constraints of station or age. Since this seems to be a day for stories, Magdalena asks the baroness how she came to marry the baron. After several sips of port, the baroness warms to the telling, and Magdalena isn't disappointed.

"I was a very difficult teening miss for my parents. I was not much younger than you when I decided to have an absolutely torrid love affair with the most forbidden man I could find. I found the maneuvering exciting and hadn't the slightest regard for appearances. After that, I overindulged, you might say. I became bolder in my pursuit of daring encounters. I wasn't picky about my Romeo's station either. I'm afraid I may have contributed to more than one soldier being transferred to a remote outpost or a few handsome young servants being summarily dismissed. Over time, my parents were beside themselves—desperate for any means of controlling their scandalous child."

"That sounds exciting and dangerous at the same time," Magdalena interjects.

"It was both and much more, my dear. I'm afraid I was a bit of a brat—in over my head, unwilling to admit I was drowning. In the end, it was my older brother, John, who you know as Lord Rutherford, who came to my rescue. 'Enough is enough' he told me in no uncertain terms. I was to act as a proper young woman—at once. I wasn't sure that was what I wanted, but I began trying—for his sake. I trusted his judgment then, as I do now."

"I have an older brother, Hans, who would have done exactly the same thing."

A Long Road There

"I'd keep him around then," the storyteller suggests.

"John wasn't content with reformation. He began playing cupid. He and my husband had been hunting companions for some time. A recent widower, Viktor, was in the market for a new wife. To my astonishment, I found this older man attractive and sincere. I came to appreciate his *vintage*, shall we say. In time we were married, and I've never regretted my decision for a moment. He's a very good man that's grown cautious with age. But beneath all the absurdities of title, he has a generous heart."

"I suspected as much," the beguiled listener muses.

"My life has been much better than the brat I told you about deserved. I wouldn't change a thing, though, even if I could."

"My story is much different," Magdalena says, anticipating her ladyship's question.

"Everyone's story paints a picture of themselves, my dear. I very much want to hear yours."

With that invitation, Magdalena tells her story again, this time pouring out every loss and detailing every frustration.

"My goodness, you've been caught in some awful rain for someone so young," the baroness says. "From the sounds of things, Herr Diller and the others were not the ones for you. Your time is ahead of you, my dear. Gaiety and true love will find you again.

"I've enjoyed our talk," the baroness adds, taking note of Magdalena's drooping eyelids. "You need to get some rest now. I'll be by tomorrow for a regular lesson if you think that'll work."

Already half asleep, Magdalena confirms their lesson (in English), "Oh, I'd be to love that."

"I daresay we have some work to do, child. I'll see you tomorrow," the baroness assures her pupil, quietly closing the door behind her.

Watching the baroness leave, Magdalena thinks about how there are big hearts and wise people everywhere—you just have to look for them.

119

Virginia Pickett

Past 4 o'clock, the patient is wide awake as Magdalena sleeps. He watches quietly, wondering why she's chosen to help him.

———————

That first night is a very long one. Burning fever and freezing chills torture the patient. Magdalena cools him with moist towels, then wraps him in warm blankets hour after hour. Just before dawn, the fever leaves. The doctor and her patient sleep deeply.

After ten o'clock, Magdalena comes awake. She leaves directly for broth and hot water. Returning with both, the patient is playful. Wonderfully playful, Magdalena thinks, sure for the first time he'll keep both arms.

"I wondered if you'd retired," the officer teases.

Magdalena smiles and prepares her poultice—Mama Mok style, while the sailor demolishes his broth.

"That sure makes it feel better," he says, enjoying the warmth of the poultice. "My thanks to your mama."

"She's used them ever since I can remember. It'll draw the infection right out of that wound."

"Thank you, Magdalena," the first mate says. This is the only time she can remember him using her first name. Sleep again comes easily for both of them. Rosa has slept these many hours, warm in Magdalena's real bed. The marquess has also been out to the world in his gilded four-poster. Both had intended to stand their watch.

Over the next forty-eight hours, with the help of his medical staff, the sailor recovers, seemingly more at ease by the minute. The ocean has finally calmed, and the crew has returned to their normal rhythms. Only a small scar will remind the officer of his harrowing experience, though he'll wonder until the day he dies how three unlikely angels from across the spectrum of life came together to save him.

CHAPTER 19

The Zwischendeck

Rosa comes bounding into the recovered sailor's cabin. "The third deckers are celebrating tonight. I've gotten special permission to ask Magdalena, even though she's a deck above. No officers, I'm afraid—sick or well, Mr. Hauff. This is a closed party," she adds, giggling like a schoolgirl.

"That will be your loss," the patient assures her.

"Where and when?" Magdalena asks.

"The fiddlers start at eight. The ballroom is being cleaned as we speak, but I still think you'll easily find it by following your nose."

As Magdalena reaches the bottom of the stairs, the people seem ready to leave their troubles behind for the next few hours. No one is worried about how they're dressed, only about having a good time. The traveler from Willenstat is hoping to do the same.

"Magdalena, this is Anna Marie and Ida. We call them the 'Mail Order Bride twins' down here. The three of us share a sleeping commons with a few other selected guests," Rosa explains, displaying a playful side Magdalena hasn't seen before.

The twins blush and, unprompted, begin their story with the

polish of many tellings. "It all started, you know," Anna Marie begins, "with those enticing recruiting flyers. I mean, how could a young girl resist?"

"Couldn't," Ida says. "So, the correspondence courtship begins, and before you know it, you're engaged to whoever's putting that pen to paper in another country across the sea."

"Then," Anna Marie chimes in on cue, "if you're as lucky as us, you shove off for America in the luxury of third class." All four girls giggle, as Ida adds, pointing at Anna Marie, "She'll have the short fat one, and I'll get the rich, handsome Romeo." Along with Anna Marie's mock resignation, three belly laughs draw the curtain on the pair's performance.

Magdalena's eyes become fixed on the walls filled with small-knobbed doors just large enough to squeeze through.

"Those are to the luxurious sleeping suites we share," Rosa says with the twins giggling, enjoying her sarcasm. "Behind each are six to eight bunks. Quite glamorous, really," Rosa insists. "Ladies at the front, single men at the back, and married couples in between. This ensures no hanky-panky, hey ladies?" The twins squeal like little girls.

"I hope so," Magdalena says. The twins nod *yes* to assure her of their rectitude.

Rosa shushes her friends with her finger to her lips, whispering, "Listen. The music is starting."

An accordion and two squeeze boxes that have all seen better days come to life between two fiddlers. Pairs of every sort swarm the makeshift dance floor. Four single fellows eventually muster the courage to ask the girls for a turn. Protruding stomach and all, Rosa becomes lost in the music. Spinning toward her partner's beckoning hand, she suddenly winces and grabs her belly.

Magdalena immediately helps her to a chair. "Let's get you back to your suite now," she says. Rosa chuckles at her friend's borrowed expression but agrees.

Crammed into the small cubicle are four sets of narrow bunk beds. Belongings clutter a dirty, uneven floor. Despite Rosa's humor, there's nothing funny about the place. Magdalena has already seen enough of her friend's quarters to extend an invitation for Rosa to move in with her and Sir Biscuit Bottom. No baby should have to come into the world down here, she thinks.

Rosa knows this is the right decision for her unborn child and accepts without hesitation. "*Wunderbar*! And, thank you."

"I'm glad that's settled. In the morning when you get up, pack your nightshirt, and I'll see you before lunch tomorrow. We'll come back later for the rest of your luggage."

Rosa smiles at the thought of packing her luggage, glancing at her lonely, worn travel bag.

"Stop," the duty seaman shouts. Raising his lantern to Magdalena's face, he immediately apologizes. "Oh, you're the first mate's lady. I'm sorry. I thought you were a third decker. May I be of any assistance?"

Magdalena shoots him a daggered look and a brusque "no thank you" before hurrying on her way to second deck number ten. The label *the first mate's lady* is stuck in her craw. That sodden ship's doctor has obviously been spinning yarns about me, she thinks.

She can't fret over her tarnished reputation long. Her roommate is demanding a midnight snack before she can close the door behind her. Devouring the crumbs of Mama's biscuits, her diminutive royal again lifts her spirits.

The hour is late. The hostess and her tiny guest agree to retire. Both are fast asleep in their bunks long before the smell of smoke from the extinguished candle disappears.

CHAPTER 20

The Bowels of the Ship

Magdalena wakes early. She wants to remind Rosa that she's moving to the second deck this morning, never giving a second thought to the fact that she could still be asleep.

Everyone in the small dormitory is sawing logs when Magdalena arrives. Her pal is still packing a partner, so she doesn't disturb either of them, hoping Rosa will remember that she's moving. Her next preoccupation is checking on the first mate. He's equally out to the world. Now she can enjoy what it is that she really got out of bed for.

The sunrise at the bow is beautiful. Magdalena wonders if the day has broken as well for Mama and Papa. She misses them terribly.

Breakfast is just being served in the second-deck saloon when Magdalena arrives. The old lady with the shawl smiles and pats the bench beside her. "I'm glad to see you, dear. I'm feeling as anxious as a small child waiting for Father Christmas at *Weihnachten*," she says, giggling.

"We'll be there soon. Don't you worry," Magdalena assures.

124

A Long Road There

After breakfast, Magdalena joins her royal friends for more target practice. First behind the barrel, she doesn't hear the first officer over the rifle fire until he shouts, "good morning."

"Up and around, huh?" Magdalena asks with some degree of pride as her glass pigeon explodes.

"Yeah, I have a good doctor, but I'm having trouble with my medicine. The soaking isn't going as well as when she was doing it."

"After my English lesson, I'll come by and help you," she says matter-of-factly before firing again.

"Thanks, doc," the officer yells, whistling as he walks away. The royals turn and chuckle with delight. They can smell romance in the air.

Before a word of English is spoken, the baroness pries in German like a curious schoolgirl: "I heard you went dancing last night. You must tell me all about it. Did you have fun? Did you dazzle any handsome young men?"

But Magdalena only describes Rosa's labor pains and their early departure from the party.

"Shucks," the deflated royal says in uncharacteristic vernacular. "I'm not sure this baby will wait for America."

"If it doesn't, I've already decided that Rosa won't have it down there in that dungeon. She's moving in with me today. I've helped my mama birth babies before," Magdalena says.

"If the child can't wait, I'll help you. The two of us can manage," the baroness says, trying to convince the both of them she's right. "Now, I do believe you're here to learn English."

"You betcha!" Magdalena responds in newly acquired deck lingo. The baroness chuckles as she opens her lesson notes.

Still whispering conjugations to herself, Magdalena the doctor heads off to make her cabin call.

125

"Come in," the patient yells, jumping onto his bed. "I do believe you're the best doctor on the Atlantic Ocean."

Giving him a gentle shove backward on the bed, she says, "If you don't lie down and let me soak your arm, you'll be doing it yourself, buster."

"I'm reformed. I don't want to rankle my healer," he says, lying perfectly still while stretching the truth.

"You seem to be doing a fair job of it," Magdalena teases, wringing her compress and placing it over the wound.

"When I was sick, I noticed you looking at my books. I was wondering if you would read to me while you soak my arm. I'm sure it'll relax me. I put *The Three Musketeers* on my desk. Have you read it?" he asks.

"No, but I think my brothers did at the university," she answers.

"Ah, good. Taste runs in the family. I'm all ears," he says, adjusting his pillow as Magdalena begins to read. Both get lost in the adventure in no time. They remain immersed in the story until a knock at the door punctuates a drawn sword. "Come in," the mate calls out.

A cabin boy enters carrying two trays of breakfast food.

"Just put one on the table, son," the seaman says. "Then take the other to Second Deck Ten. When you knock, let her know the food is from me. She may not open the door otherwise. Her name is Rosa."

As the lad turns to leave, the first mate calls out to him, "Hold on a minute." Then, looking at Magdalena, he asks, "Do you have your key?"

"Yes, but I left my door unlocked so Rosa could get in."

"Well, then, problem solved. Get going, Franz, and remember what I told you."

"Didn't want you to miss breakfast, doc," the first mate says, gesturing toward the tray of food.

"Miss breakfast! You're way behind. I ate over two hours ago."

A Long Road There

"How about we call it an early lunch, then?"

"How did you know Rosa was going to be in my cabin?" Magdalena asks.

"Just a hunch. Good spies. Besides, that's my secret." Turning serious, he raises himself onto his elbows. "You know I owe you both a great deal. I'll never figure out how I got lucky enough to have you two around when I hit the deck."

"You owe me nothing."

"I disagree. A lot of the ladies on this ship wouldn't have done a thing but scream. Fixing my arm was way beyond kind."

"We're good friends. How could I refuse? You'd been telling me where to go and what to do since I came aboard," Magdalena says with a straight face—for about a second.

"Say, I've got a break from my duties for a while this afternoon. How would you like to see the ship?"

"I'd love to!"

"Only if you think I'm well enough," the patient says, falling back onto his bed.

"I'll show you just how sick I think you are," Magdalena replies, hitting him over the head with his pillow.

"Careful, or you'll be tending my skull next. I'll see you at your cabin at half past two."

Shaking her head at the clown on the bed, the good doctor confirms their appointment. She's glad she was able to squeeze him in.

It's late when Rosa wakes lazily. Yawning and stretching, she freezes. It's moving day, she remembers.

Dressing, she talks to her baby. "I'm glad you decided not to come aboard last night. I would have liked to stay and dance, but I suppose you were tired." Not waiting for an answer, Mama grabs her luggage and chuckles.

Running, she reaches Magdalena's door on a collision course

with the cabin boy who is just trying to deliver his silver tray of food as ordered. He pivots; the tray sways. Rosa turns the doorknob, and she and her belly dart through the shrinking clearance into the room in the nick of time.

"Are you Rosa?" the cabin boy asks.

"Yes."

"The first mate sent this for you," the young fellow manages. He sets his tray onto the vanity before hightailing it, off to more familiar duty.

The tray is empty before Magdalena or Sir Biscuit Bottom arrive.

———————

As promised, at 2:30 sharp, the patient raps on his doctor's door. Having missed lunch, the royal mouse immediately appears from under the bed even before the door latches shut. Magdalena handles the introductions. "Chief Mate Hauff, allow me to present Sir Biscuit Bottom."

Still irate that Rosa had finished eating before he had even arrived, the mouse manages only an irritated nod.

"Nice to meet you, sir. I suspect we may have had the pleasure previously."

Having evaded the authorities since the ship's christening, the royal mouse looks away, hoping not to be recognized.

"Perhaps not," the mate concedes.

"Let's go see what makes this ship move, Magdalena. These two can stay and fight over these," he says, laying his pocket delicacies on the bed.

A mother eating for two pitted against the best beggar on the boat promises to be an exciting match.

———————

The first mate's tour begins through a maze of corridors and catwalks. Eventually, they descend a steep, narrow ladder into the bowels of the boat. The guide stops on a steel platform overlooking the fire room. He warns Magdalena: "Hold onto the railing. I don't want you falling if the ship pitches."

Enthralled, the fraülein is so taken with the action below, it doesn't occur to her to disobey. The fiery netherworld she's staring into has a pair of open furnaces facing each other on opposite sides of the room. The furnaces are fixed to metal walls that run port to starboard. Magdalena's face is beginning to burn, but turning away isn't an option. She's transfixed by the sooty men below, wielding iron scoops feeding the voracious hot mouths in front of them from black piles of coal. All the while, other glistening figures keep the coal hills replenished by constantly pushing overflowing wheelbarrows from larders in the next room.

Intruding on this otherworldly scene, the officer explains, "The men that you're watching form what we call the 'Black Gang.' The group consists of four three-man crews whose job is to maintain the furnaces. Each group has a trimmer. He distributes the fuel stores to the passer who delivers them to the firemen, who then stokes the furnaces."

As she watches, the black-gang members perform their jobs in a marvelously rhythmic cadence. Magdalena is struck not only by the hellishly hot conditions they endure but by the pride they seem to take in their toil. Just as the first mate is about to ask her to climb the ladder to the engine room, he notices the entire gang doffing their caps and bowing toward their admiring audience of one.

"Look, Magdalena. They're thanking you for coming to watch them."

"It should be me bowing to them," she says, letting go of the railing. Her guide tries to grab her as she curtsies in reply. He's too late. The officer can only watch as her leg hangs perilously over the edge of the platform for two pounding heartbeats.

"You could have been killed. Please hold onto the rail."

"But they were wonderful," Magdalena responds with absolutely

Virginia Pickett

no idea how close she had come to disaster.

Climbing to reach a narrow catwalk in order to descend another ladder, Magdalena's confused as they come to an open door. The room is filled with magnificent, humming machinery.

"This is the engine room. I'll check with the Chief Engineer to see if we can take a look. The place is his domain. Stay put."

Moments later, the officer returns with a sturdy-looking older sailor. His hat is perfectly cocked above the wrench in his right hand. He grips a greasy rag in his left.

"Magdalena, this is Chief Engineer Meyer."

"Nice to meet you, Herr Meyer."

"The pleasure is all mine, Fräulein. Usually when the chief mate asks me to show someone around, an unruly child or a crotchety old aristocrat is my lot. His choice of guests today is a pleasant surprise."

Magdalena blushes, then thanks her host as he shows off his bailiwick. The room is enormous, crammed with shiny, sweating boilers, each with a glass-encased gauge monitoring its blood pressure. After trying his best to explain his mechanical realm, the host finishes by placing his right index finger on top of one of the glass gauge covers, pronouncing, "When the black hand enters the red space, we go topside and pray."

Laughing, Magdalena answers, "I'm glad you're in charge and not me."

"You're too kind, my dear. A good day to you both."

Arriving back at her cabin and grasping her guide's good arm, Magdalena says, "Thanks for the tour. I'm glad you were well enough to take me."

Gently, the officer pulls her a little closer, then kisses her tenderly on the cheek. He whispers, "I hope you know how much I enjoy being with you."

Magdalena is quick to change the subject. "I better check on Rosa." Twisting the knob to her cabin door, she turns and teases,

130

"Haven't we known each other long enough for me to know your first name?"

"I suspect we have. My mother christened me Wilhelm after my grandfather. My friends call me Will. I hope you'll do the same."

"Wilhelm? That's a fine name, Will."

For the rest of the voyage, The Three Musketeers travel back and forth between Magdalena's room and Will's. Reading to Rosa seems to take the expectant mother's mind off her predicament. Mama likes to listen in the sunshine when possible. Most days when they're outside, a crowd of third deckers comes to listen as well. Magdalena reads from a chair that straddles the infamous red line.

When darkness comes, Magdalena still can't resist stargazing alone. Tonight, she's actually hoping to be shooed away. Gazing at the moon, she laughs at life's little contradictions. When she wanted to avoid the young patrolling officer, he always appeared in the blink of an eye. Tonight, he seems to be taking forever to come and scold her away. "Go figure," she muses, continuing to enjoy the moon. Finally, Will appears.

"What do I have to do to stop you from coming up here by yourself?" he asks in greeting.

"I love it out here. Besides, when you join me, I'm not alone."

Grasping her chaperone's good arm, Magdalena stands on her tiptoes and gives him a kiss on the cheek. He slips his other arm around her, pulls her close, then kisses her on the lips. The man in the moon seems to be smiling down. He approves of the new couple.

Papa does not look at many night skies these days. He's sad a lot. He thought losing a child was the hardest thing he and his family had ever gone through—if you can say they're through it. No words can describe the pain they felt losing a son. Today as Papa tussles with his new pup, Lonesome, he's just that. He misses his oldest daughter. She's still on the boat taking her further away from home, so he's wrestling with more than his dog. His family hasn't been forced to break up and scatter to the wind after failed crops, wars, and the hard times that followed. Still, he feels loss all the same. When he looks at Magdalena's picture on the mantel and realizes she's probably never coming home, he shivers. Mama, meanwhile, won't let those kinds of thoughts escape from the deepest closet of her mind.

CHAPTER 21

A Maternity Ward

The next day as Magdalena reads to Rosa and the *Zwischendeck* crowd in the sunshine, D'Artagnan is acrobatically escaping an inescapable peril when Rosa grabs her belly. Interrupting Magdalena, she whispers, "I think it's time."

"It looks like another Musketeer is joining us," Magdalena lets the other third deck listeners know as she and Rosa head to the maternity ward at Second Deck No. 10. Acting as a young midwife, Magdalena is already frazzled when they arrive. "Lie down, Rosa. We're going to start timing your pains. That's what my mama always did. There's no need to panic." This advice, though, is more for herself than Rosa.

Grabbing a pencil and tearing a piece of paper from her journal, her heart's motor is racing at thirty knots as she jots down a plan of attack.

1. Get plenty of clean linen and hot water.

2.

Drawing a blank at number 2, the midwife suddenly orders, "Stay here, Rosa," as if her friend were going anywhere. Running down the hall to ask the baroness for help, she's frantic, thinking about the responsibility she's taken on.

"Baroness, oh, I'm so glad I found you at home. You were right. The baby isn't going to wait for New York. Can you please come and help us?"

"Certainly, my child. Where's Rosa?"

"In my cabin."

"I'll meet you there in five minutes. You settle down. Things will be fine," the baroness assures her young friend.

"I'm already glad I came to get you," Magdalena says, walking instead of running out of the royal suite.

"Viktor!" the baroness calls out to her husband. He is immersed in the bloodlines of several hounds he is considering for his kennel. Removing his monocle and shaking his head, he dutifully responds, "Yes, my dear?"

"It looks like Magdalena's friend is going to have her baby. I'm heading for her cabin now. Please find my brother. Get plenty of hot water and linen, then join me there."

Moments later, the baroness arrives at Magdalena's cabin.

"Hello, Rosa. I'm Elizabeth von Brunn. Magdalena asked me to come to help take care of you. I have a little experience in these matters. How are you feeling, my child?"

"I think my baby is coming."

"Don't you worry. Everything's going to be fine."

After a few hours with no progress, the baroness makes a cursory exam. She's convinced the baby is breech. "Magdalena, go find the first mate, please."

When Will arrives, the baroness pulls him back into the hall. "I'm afraid the child is breech—coming feet first. This is very dangerous for the mother and baby. We need a doctor."

"The ship's doctor is a hopeless lush."

"Is there another physician on board?"

"I don't think so."

"Then, we have no choice."

"How long have I got to get him here?"

"We need him now, but the Good Lord willing, you might have an hour or two."

Things are more cheerful at the galley. After all, ignorance is bliss. Lord Rutherford and his brother-in-law are following their orders to the letter: retrieving linen and fetching hot water and taking their own sweet time about it. They're waiting to get their wagers into the birth pool.

A wee bit of a gambler, the big Scot galley boss had immediately launched the customary birth pool not five minutes after his two royal petitioners arrived. "All right, lads, put your silver in the hat and pick the day and time the happy event will happen," he tells his culinary staff. Word spreads quickly, and the deposits grow like a brushfire. "Remember, the third-deck lass who's bringing the young fellow into this cruel world will take half the winner's trove," the Highlander reminds each treasure hunter as he plops his coin and guess into the big seaman's cap. Von Brunn and Rutherford take three guesses each, tickled with the sporting nature of the tradition.

Certain the ship's doctor will be at least half in the bag, Will stops at the galley for a large pot of coffee before making his way to the sickbay. Knocking, he enters without waiting for a response. An unkempt, white-jacketed body is sprawled out in a chair, with a half-empty bottle of rum sitting on the desk next to him.

Looking up through bloodshot eyes, the doctor slurs, "Good evening. Have you come for another extended medical leave? I dare say that sweet young tart played her role as a nurse magnificently."

The doctor is a large man. Much bigger than Will. But his suggestive words anger the chief mate. Will picks him up by his jacket collar and rams him against the door, shouting, "God help us! We need you to be a doctor tonight!"

Throwing the sot back in his chair, Will sprints for the galley.

Returning quickly, he kicks open the door. The whimpering soul knows what's coming and curls into a ball. The full force of the icy water hits him broadside. Pulling the shivering physician upright, Will tries to force a cup of coffee down him. Gagging, the doctor rushes to the empty bucket and begins to vomit.

"You start drinking coffee and lots of it," Will growls. "I'm heading back to the galley for more water. Stay put!"

"No. Please don't. I'll be fine," the saturated fellow insists to no avail.

Within a couple of minutes, the mate's back, with two buckets of water, this time—one cold and one hot. Without discussion, he begins dunking the doctor's spinning head in the cold water. Begging for mercy, the Hippocratic charlatan seems to be reaching a level of sobriety he hasn't seen in a long, long time.

"Please, just let me sit. Tell me what it is you need me to do," he implores.

Straightening the derelict doctor in his swiveled chair, Will pushes another cup of coffee in his face. "Drink this and listen. There's a third-deck woman who's in labor, but our midwife says the baby is feet first and needs to be turned. Can you do it?"

"I haven't delivered a baby, let alone a breech one, in a very long time. Isn't there anyone else?"

"No. If there were, I wouldn't be here. We've got no more than two hours to straighten you out. The first thing you need to do is clean yourself up."

Behind his exam curtain, the doctor removes his wet clothing and, for the first time in days, gives himself a scrubbing. The hot water Will brought and the bar of soap on top of his cabinet feel foreign. "If the baby is breech, I'll need to consult my medical texts. I'd like to try and help this woman—if only God will help me." The doctor looks skyward from behind his curtain.

Sympathetic for the first time, Will says, "Keep drinking the coffee, Doc. As soon as you're done dressing, you need to start

A Long Road There

studying. I'll be right here. You're stuck with one damn determined guardian angel."

Bare-chested and wobbly, he tries to shave in a dirty mirror with a dull razor. His hands are shaking. "Can you help me?" he asks, sober enough to be embarrassed. Placing him back in his chair a little more gently this time, the first mate grabs the razor. With each stroke, he realizes this broken man may be Rosa's only hope.

"God help me, I can't stop shaking," the doctor mutters.

"We're going to pull this off, Doc. Somehow, we're gonna do it. "

"Goddammit, you can see my hands. What can I do like this? Tell me in the name of heaven, what can I do in this condition?"

"Not much, but you're not going to be in this condition for long. You're going to snap out of it. Where's the medical book you need?"

"The large, gray volume on the second shelf."

Pulling out the treatise, Will exhorts the doctor: "Keep drinking coffee and start studying. You're gonna be okay. I'm gonna get you something to eat."

"Maybe some broth and bread. I'm afraid my stomach has become unfamiliar with food."

"I'll be right back; just keep studying."

At the stroke of 10 o'clock in the evening, Will and the reconstructed physician knock on Magdalena's cabin door. Taking Rosa's hand, the officer says, "This is Dr. Gottfried Hauptmann. He's here to help you, Rosa."

Hearing Will announce him with the respect the title implies, the healer straightens. "I'm here to try." After washing his hands, he begins his first thorough examination in a very long while. Then, in a halting voice, he resurrects a long-departed bedside manner. "Things will be fine, my dear."

Over the course of the next two hours, the doctor labors over his patient without a break. Finally, the baby does a half-somersault. Rosa bites her lip in pain while welcoming the acrobatics. For just a moment, the doctor's found a renewed sense of dignity.

At 12:20 a.m., a healthy baby boy is born. He's welcomed aboard with a slap on the rear and lets out a cry worthy of a young salt. The good doctor cleans and swaddles the new sailor before handing him to his mother. Turning to her physician, she asks, "How can I ever thank you, doctor?"

"You already have a thousand times over, my dear."

Right about then the door cracks open. "Is it okay for me to come in, doctor?" Will asks respectfully.

"You may, and thank you. No one has called me that and meant it for years. I think I'll go up top and enjoy the night air—sober for once. Then, I'm off to a good night's sleep. Call me at once if I'm needed. I owe you all a great debt of gratitude."

As the door closes, Magdalena, Will, and the baroness share an embrace. "I'm going to bed," an exhausted chief mate informs his comrades. He's paced for over three hours.

The baroness is right behind him. "Good night, Magdalena," she says. "We managed—with a courageous doctor and the help of heaven. Sleep well, my child."

"Good night and a thousand thank you's," Magdalena sleepily adds. She can barely muster the strength to spread her pallet on the floor next to the new mother and her baby boy. Before her head touches the wadded cloak, she's already romping in a snowdrift with Max.

Waking with the sun, Will dresses, then makes his way to the ship's purser, who answers his door half-awake—at best. "Is Second Deck 12 still empty?" Will asks the night-gowned officer.

Trying to shake the cobwebs out, the keeper of the kingdom replies, "I think so."

"I need it," the first mate says, adding, "I've been thinking you could use a couple extra days of leave."

"Cabin boy," the purser shouts, coming awake with Will's carrot. "Get Second Deck 12 ready. Now."

"Yes, sir!"

With a wink and a nod, the first mate heads off on his next mission.

Dr. Hauptmann is sound asleep in his quarters, so Will scratches out a note for him,

Your patient is in Second Deck No. 12 for the remainder of the voyage. Thanks again.
Will

Almost before finishing his second 'L,' Will is already running for Magdalena's cabin. After a soft knock on the door, he slowly opens it. He finds Rosa wide awake on the bed. Quietly, he announces, "You're moving next door into your own room, Rosa. It'll be ready at noon," With that, he kisses the mama gently on her forehead as she reaches up to give the officer a heartfelt, one-armed hug. Her new son sleeps in her other arm. With a peck on Magdalena's lips, Will is out the door. She's not quite done playing in the snowbank with Max.

CHAPTER 22

Aloft

Woken for the first time by the sound of a crying baby in her room, Magdalena tries to shake the cobwebs from her head. That's not easy; the world has been spinning so fast lately.

"Sorry we woke you," the new mother says. "I was trying to keep him quiet, but he seems to have a mind of his own."

"I'm sure glad he finally got here. It wore me out waiting for the tiny sailor to finally come aboard on his own," Magdalena says, stretching and yawning as she tries to fully wake up.

"You missed Will early this morning," Rosa tells her. "He'll be back at noon. Guess what? Theodor and I are moving into cabin 12—right next door—for the rest of the trip. Can you believe that? I don't know what Will did to make it happen, but I sure hope he doesn't get himself in any trouble."

"I don't think he will. He's pretty savvy."

"Handsome, too, huh?"

"I hadn't noticed," Magdalena says, nearly choking on her fib as she laughs, hiding her head in the pillow.

"Denials won't do, my friend. I saw that kiss on the lips he gave you this morning."

A Long Road There

Magdalena quickly changes the subject asking, "So you gave your son a real name besides the new Musketeer? Theodor, is that after his papa?"

"Yeah. I'm thinking about giving him some middle names—like a rich man. How about Theodor Wilhelm Rutherford?"

"That's a mouthful."

"But he'll be a fine man if he combines the qualities of his namesakes."

"I think you're right, Mama," Magdalena tells her, finally getting out from under the covers and up off the floor.

Pouring a basin of lukewarm water, Magdalena begins to sponge off. The same sharp who'd been dealing from the bottom of the deck seems to have given her two aces to begin a new hand. Will and Rosa are more than she could have hoped for when the *SS See Falke* powered away from Papa. Two special friends from home. They talk, laugh, and cry—all in German. English has no *persönlichkeit* yet, and personality is important.

———————

Precisely at the stroke of twelve, Rosa and Theodor open the door to cabin 12. Mama begins to cry. She's never had a room of her own. Now, she does—to share with her new son. Opening the porthole, it seems as though the entire ocean is part of her suite.

"Well, what do you think, Rosa?" Will asks through the open door.

"It's *wunderbar*, Will!"

"It doesn't come with a royal mouse," Magdalena adds, poking her head around Will.

Rosa ushers her first visitors inside. Closing the door, she hugs both of her friends. Their embrace is interrupted by a knock on the door.

"Did you order room service already?" Will asks. "Well, you've got to tell them to come in."

"Oh, Will," Rosa says, before granting permission to enter her

141

cabin for the very first time. It's a strange and exciting feeling.

"You asked me to come by at noon, sir," says the sailor standing in the doorway.

"That I did, Mr. Tieck. Ladies, let me introduce *heizer* Tieck. He's a proud member of our Black Gang and the winner of half of Theodor's birth pool." With that, Will hands the new mother her fifty-five-thaler haul. "That works out to about forty of Uncle Sam's greenbacks in New York, Rosa. You worked a lot harder for your share than old Tieck. Maybe you should demand 60-40," he jokes.

As Tieck begins to stammer "okay," a blushing Rosa saves him from himself. "Absolutely not!" she says.

Wringing his hat in his hands, the fidgety stoker stammers, "I picked a later time 'cus my wife took pretty long with our first." With that, he vanishes with his fifty percent of the pot, happy to escape the limelight and his commanding officer.

For the first time in a while, both the day and the night pass quietly. Magdalena never expected that twiddling her thumbs on top of an ocean could be so satisfying.

At a quarter to six as the sun rises, Magdalena does the same. Last night had been calm under a red sky. The sails hung loose. "They'll be shortened tonight, but when the wind returns—maybe by dawn—the men will make sail again," Will had told her in the moonlight. "That's a spectacle that never gets old."

Magdalena is up and dressed, racing topside, hoping for a breeze so she can catch the show. When she arrives, the acrobats are just beginning their ascent up the rope ladders to the top of the masts. As if they were summoned, the course sails seem to shoot from the deck, traveling up the poles. Nimble, fearless, and nearly sixty meters nearer heaven, the tars move like dancers upon a stage, unfurling the topsails and topgallants. For generations, they've waltzed with the wind.

Will spots her. Sneaking up from behind, he whispers *good*

A Long Road There

morning in her ear, but her eyes stay riveted to the high-wire performers. She and Will watch the ballet together in silence, leaning against each other, as well as the ship's last barrier before the sea. The spectacle never gets old for Will.

"I have something to ask you," the mate says, interrupting the last act.

"And what is that?" Magdalena asks coquettishly, feeling buoyant after witnessing such an inspiring aerial extravaganza.

"The captain's ball is tomorrow night. By tradition, he hosts a dinner and dance for the first-deck passengers. Everyone dresses for the occasion. I'd like you to come as my guest," Wills says nervously.

"Oh, I'd love to. But remember, I'm not a first decker."

"It doesn't matter. You'll be with me," Will says, buoyed by her acceptance.

"Oh, Will, it sounds fabulous. But you said everyone dresses up. I don't have a fancy dress."

"Talk to the baroness. I already took the liberty. She has a solution."

"You're a pretty confident sailor," she says, giving him a hug.

"There's one catch," he adds, dampening the moment briefly.

"And what's that?"

"Well, as part of the senior staff, I have certain obligations. First, I have to stand in the receiving line. Then, I'm supposed to dance with a number of ladies in attendance. I simply won't be able to be with you all the time, but I think I've come up with a solution. I went out on a limb again and asked Lord Rutherford to act as my second. He readily agreed. If you give the okay, we're all set. You'll meet in the von Brunns' suite, and the four of you will go to the event together."

"I can't believe you've thought of all this. What if I'd said *no?*"

"Then I'd have hung you from the yardarm," he says, having gained a little swagger.

"Still a silly goose, huh? Well, you're stuck with me because I'm

143

saying *yes*." Magdalena gives him a second hug and a quick kiss on the cheek. "Thank you so much, Will. I can hardly wait."

"I may be silly, but I'll be taking the prettiest girl to the dance."

Tonight, it doesn't take much of her mouse's magic to have Magdalena floating on air. The knight's been by her side through the difficult challenges of the past several days. She wonders if she's grown up too soon as she imagines Sir Biscuit Bottom leaving on a great crusade with only a piece of Mama's biscuit to sustain him.

CHAPTER 23

First Deck Ballroom

Cinderella starts to scurry at once. Preparation for the ball must fit in between her first-deck breakfast, shooting, and, of course, her English lessons, not to mention *The Three Musketeers*. "Goodness gracious," she thinks out loud, "there'll never be enough time to get ready."

As the clock ticks down, the baroness provides a gown that will dazzle the men and irritate the old biddies. The slippers aren't glass, but they fit perfectly. Lord Rutherford tosses in a diamond necklace for good measure. Rosa masterfully styles the debutante's hair and gently defines God's gifts with sparing use of the baroness' royal makeup.

As the sand continues to slip through the hourglass, the reality of mingling with these privileged people, as if she belongs, begins to weigh heavily on Magdalena. She tries to focus. Bathing and assembling herself in the borrowed attire, she stews in front of her clouded mirror. Something is missing. Glancing down at her open trunk, the formal white gloves Grandpa Brohmann had made for her sixteenth birthday are in plain sight, peeking out of their tissue paper. After pulling them on, she can look the mirror square in the eye.

Almost convinced she can do this, she summons Sir Biscuit Bottom with a morsel of cheese, shopping for his approval. He appears in an instant and, after a brief inspection, gives her a regal nod.

She hears a knock at the door. Her knees buckle. It can't be time, she thinks. But it is. She takes a deep breath and swings open the door. "Good evening, Lord Rutherford," she says, avoiding his eyes and the disappointment she expects to find in them.

The old gentleman is fittingly regal. He's wearing a gray formal coat—cut at the waist in front with tails in the back, augmented by a matching waistcoat and trousers. His white formal shirt is topped with a standing collar and black puff tie —all perfectly situated.

Still dodging her escort's gaze, Magdalena worries, what does he think of me? Finally, the moment of truth can't be avoided any longer. The nobleman's eyes sparkle as he admires the astoundingly beautiful young woman standing before him. The pastel pink silk gown gently outlines her form. It features a low-cut, off-the-shoulder neckline adorned with white lace. The diamonds around her neck are glimmering, but not as gloriously as her eyes. With a short bow, the marquess signals his absolute approval.

The von Brunns are waiting for them just outside the first-deck saloon. When they arrive, the baroness grabs both of Magdalena's hands and signals for a pirouette. "My, I'm glad we chose that gown. You look radiant."

A junior officer announces their arrival as they begin down the receiving line of the ship's senior officers. Magdalena is relieved to see that three of the four men are familiar faces. All are impeccably attired in their dress whites and matching gloves. They greet each guest with all the warmth they can muster.

"Herr Meyer, it's nice to see you again," she says, greeting the officer who had so kindly explained his mechanical kingdom to her.

"The pleasure is all mine. You brighten the prospects of this dreary event. When the Black Gang heard you would be here, they insisted I give you their regards."

Magdalena blushes and moves forward to the next officer, extending both hands this time. "Dr. Hauptmann, I'm so glad you decided to come. Will and I were hoping you would."

"I decided to only after he assured me I'd be seated at your table."

"Doctor, have you met the marquess?" Magdalena asks.

Extending his hand, the physician greets the lord humbly, introducing himself by his given name, "Gottfried Hauptmann."

The nobleman, in turn, extends his hand, man to man, using only "John Rutherford" to identify himself.

As Magdalena steps forward to greet Will, he takes her hand and bends at the waist to kiss it, softly whispering, "You're absolutely beautiful tonight."

Finishing with a perfunctory exchange with the ship's captain, Magdalena and Lord Rutherford join his sister and the baron. Sipping his champagne, the marquess devilishly suggests, "I daresay, the gossips are already in full force this evening wondering who that stunning beauty is hanging on my arm."

Laughing, his sister pokes back at him, "Let their tongues wag, dear brother. You haven't been the center of intrigue in years. Enjoy it. The first mate will steal your thunder momentarily."

"Indeed, I'll again be as interesting as yesterday's *Times*."

As the royals continue their small talk, Magdalena scans the room. The dining area has been completely rearranged from breakfast. All the leather couches and accompanying end tables have been moved to the sidelines. In their place sit several round tables impeccably set with white linen, fine china, and crystal goblets. The far end of the saloon—where they're standing—has been cleared for use as the dance floor. Off to the left are four tuxedoed musicians—two on the violin, one on a viola, and one with a cello. They're playing a sedate dinner overture.

A delicate mixture of newly starched shirts, behind-the-ear fragrances, and freshly laundered table linen perfume the air. The room is lit gently enough to be romantic but light enough to observe the details of a gown. There's no similarity to the third-deck frolic, Magdalena thinks.

Guests continue to wander past with nods and smiles as Magdalena watches and surmises. The men appear to be completely comfortable sipping champagne and swapping outsized stories. The experienced ladies seem interested mostly in the impression they are or aren't making. The younger women all seem to be suffering. Magdalena guesses their corsets are laced too tightly. What will they do after they eat a full dinner, she wonders. I'm glad the baroness felt my dress fit nicely without a corset. I can't imagine spending much time in such a painful contraption, she thinks, shuddering. Her attention is drawn away from strangled waistlines when a nice-looking, middle-aged gentleman approaches.

"Good evening," he volunteers with great ceremony. "May I join you?"

The baron, who obviously knows the man, seems left without a choice. "Most certainly, Duke. Have you met Fraülein Mok?"

"No, but I have been admiring the marquess's good taste from across the room," he says, scanning Magdalena from head to toe. Uncomfortable with the inspection, Magdalena clenches her teeth and stands her ground.

"Magdalena, may I present Christoph Görgi, Duke of Steiermark, Austria?" the baron says.

Making a bow with great pretension, the Duke extends his hand. Blushing and not certain what to do, Magdalena offers her right hand as she had done in the receiving line. He accepts it, planting a slow and deliberate kiss upon Grandpa Brohmann's snow-white glove.

"What a pleasure to meet you, Fraülein. I don't think I've seen you in the saloon before."

"Oh, I have breakfast with the marquess and the baron almost every morning before we shoot. But you wouldn't have seen me here any other time. I'm a second-deck passenger, so I eat the rest of my meals there," she says with an honesty uncommon to the occasion.

The circling wolf seems emboldened by her diminished station. "Interesting. May I have the pleasure of a dance after dinner?" he asks, desire oozing from the request.

"I'm afraid my promises may have outpaced the orchestra's program, sir," Magdalena says, aching to escape the lurid scrutiny.

The baroness soon comes to the rescue with the skill and style of experience. Gently clutching Magdalena's arm, she suggests ever so gracefully, "Let's leave these men to discuss their exploits and see if we can find where we're sitting. It was good to see you, your Excellency," she adds without a grain of sincerity.

Once they're out of earshot, Magdalena whispers, "Thank you so much for getting me out of there. He may be a duke, but he gives me the *willies*," she says, managing a perfectly apropos English idiom she's acquired, oddly enough, from the Three Musketeer listeners who are rapidly learning the language themselves.

"You're not alone, my dear. You handled yourself well. You notice his wife isn't with him. He prowls when she's not around. He thinks of himself as a roving Casanova, though, for the life of me, I can't figure out why women are attracted to him."

Magdalena is seated between Will and Lord Rutherford, opposite the baron and baroness.

Dr. Hauptmann is on Will's right. The gold placards at the two remaining seats indicate they're reserved for Mr. and Mrs. Rosenstein. They haven't arrived, and the baroness isn't sure they will, but she warns Magdalena, "They speak only English, so you'll have to pay close attention."

"I certainly will," Magdalena says, responding in English to the delight of her instructor.

Dr. Hauptmann arrives at his seat like a released prisoner. Sitting down, he ponders out loud: "I wonder how many of those people would have been so eager to shake my hand if they'd known I'd spent most of the day treating third deckers." After a pause, he begins to relax and then adds, "You ladies look radiant this evening."

"I wholeheartedly agree!" Will volunteers, approaching his date from behind.

With everyone seated, Magdalena notices for the first time the fancy sheet of paper sitting on top of each plate. The handwritten, powder-blue calligraphy is in perfect contrast to the menu's gold-hued backdrop.

SS See Falke
Captain's Dinner and Dance

Creamed Carrot Soup
Beef Broth
Salmon Croquettes – Sauce Rémoulade
Baron of Beef — Truffle Sauce
Mirabelles
Chicken a la Marengo
Stuffed Goose
Asparagus – Sauce Mousseline
Lobster in Aspic
Pudding a la Diplomat
Pastries
Fruit
Coffee, Tea

As she finishes reading, her empty stomach grumbles. I hope there's plenty of something I like, she thinks, unsure if she needs to choose only one of the selections.

Abandoning any veneer of sophistication, she goes directly to an expert with her question. "Baroness, are we supposed to choose just one item from this list?"

"Heavens, no, my dear," her ladyship explains. "The listings are courses served in succession to each guest." Seeing that Magdalena is still foundering a little, Dr. Hauptmann adds, "Any course may be declined, nibbled at, picked upon, or devoured--all without feeling awkward."

"Oh, good. That's what I was hoping for," Magdalena says, not afraid of showing where she and her healthy appetite are from.

In due course, the stewards come around to fill the water goblets and to offer champagne, red wine, or both. Magdalena chooses the wine. Tonight, the bubbles remind her of Fritz and the champagne he brought home from France. She reaches for his broach instinctively, disappointed to find only diamonds. Home— that seems so long ago, she thinks.

When each course is presented, Magdalena declines, picks, nibbles, or devours, without the slightest concern for propriety. As everyone sips more champagne, the people at the table bubble with conversation. Even the good doctor has an effervescence with only his coffee. His bubbles are coming from within.

Magdalena is lost in her thoughts as the orchestra starts to tune their instruments. The food was sinfully delicious and abundant, but Mama's biscuits and familiar apron were missing. They will always be missing in rooms like this, she thinks. Although she's grown quite fond of several people in this strange floating city, she knows that soon she must leave and step back into her own world. She's ready.

As the black-tied quartet continues tuning, a junior officer comes over and discretely says something to the first mate. Will turns to Magdalena apologetically.

"Duty calls, my dear, the aristocratic two-step. Don't promise all the waltzes to my rivals."

"You may count on one turn around the floor, mister," she says with a smile. "That is if I'm still of interest to you after you're done gliding with the more fashionable sorts."

With a playful flick of her nose and a large smile, Will excuses himself.

The doctor knows he, too, must walk the plank. He can't avoid his social duties any longer. "A painfully weary obligation," he mutters. "The older women complain about real or imaginary maladies, expecting me to diagnose and cure them on the spot. Like a good soldier, I graciously assure each of them they are beautiful and robust. If ever a drink was in order. . . ," he says, with no intention of indulging.

By custom, the ship's captain and his partner are first to the dance floor. After an appropriate delay, other couples of all shapes and sizes join them. Magdalena looks on until her royal friend clears his throat. "May I have the pleasure, young lady?" a bowing Lord Rutherford requests.

"Yes, you may," she says with a curtsey. The two join the throng and manage to gracefully move among them. Next, the baron cuts in and proves to be especially spry. They dance to a raucous polka before the chief engineer re-invents a Viennese waltz with the young Cinderella. From then on, Magdalena doesn't miss a dance. Even the junior officers are obliged. To her great delight, the Duke of Wolves has chosen not to come prowling.

"Did you think I'd forgotten you?" Will says, cutting in halfway through a waltz.

"Will, I've missed you."

"But you haven't missed a dance."

"I've still missed you. Are you done welcoming dignitaries and charming the ladies?"

"I am, except for one last beauty that I'm hoping to charm for the rest of the evening." The song ends, and the first notes of her cherished *Harvest Waltz* flow gently into the air. Will takes her hand and guides her across the dance floor.

What happens next is hard to explain. She knows that she is waltzing with Will, but she can only see herself in Fritz' arms, floating across Uncle Rudolph's humble dance platform. She's in love again for the first time.

"Please hold onto me tight," she whispers to the handsome young Hessian.

In her mind, he answers back, "For only a second. This isn't our time or place,"

Suddenly, she can only see a frayed letter spinning wildly toward her from a dark place. She tries to make it go away, but the yellowed news won't vanish. "Lieutenant Fritz Strasse was killed in action 6 August 1870."

She's crying now.

"Why the tears?" Will asks.

Forcing her mind back to Will and the ship, she answers, "Because I'm lucky to be here with you." She has finally said *goodbye*—not to her Central City mission, but to the specter of her first love.

As the music stops, Dr. Hauptmann requests she remain and give him "the very distinct pleasure of a dance." The doctor looks like a new man in his formal attire. He dances elegantly. "May I say *thank you* once again and ask your forgiveness, as well?" the doctor says. "I hope the scoundrel you met some days ago is forever gone. I will try my best never to walk again in his shoes. I will always be in your debt, Magdalena."

Touched, she realizes that perhaps two new beginnings are unfolding tonight. She's played a part in the doctor's, as he has in hers. Perhaps for the first time since Fritz's death, the young girl from Willenstat sees that life will always shuffle and deal again to anyone willing to stay in the game. As the orchestra takes a moment to relax, Will slides into Magdalena's arms again as Dr. Hauptman

153

graciously bows to his partner. In an instant, a seductive South Sea number fills the air.

Eye-to-eye, they move to the pulsating rhythm. Will steers them straight for the foyer and up the stairs. The deck is bathed in moonlight. As the last insistent notes thunder, they kiss as if they were marooned on a desert atoll.

For better or worse, judgment rides to the rescue and puts a lid on their simmering desire. "That piece is dangerous but certainly gets the blood flowing," Will mutters, trying to regain a modicum of composure with his partner still in his arms.

No less dispossessed of her bearings, Magdalena makes a feeble but valiant attempt to change the subject as she pulls away. "The sky is glorious tonight." Exhaling and clasping hands, they enjoy the silent heavens together, both lost in their thoughts of what might have been—until Magdalena shivers.

"Cold?" Will asks.

"All of a sudden," she says with a second shiver. Will puts his dress-uniform jacket around her shoulders and draws her close. "Tell you what," he says, "I've got to check to make sure the duty change went smoothly on the quarterdeck. It'll just take me a few minutes. What if I take you to your cabin so you can warm up? I'll come back quickly to get you for a second dose of this sky. It'll be a perfect ending to an enchanted evening."

"Sounds wonderful, Mister Will."

With their arms around each other's waists, they slowly make their way to Magdalena's cabin. Lighting the candle just inside the door, Will pulls her close again. "I'm not sure I should leave. You might disappear."

"You're such a silly goose. I'll be right here waiting for you."

With a quick peck on her chilly nose, Will leaves, taking the stairs topside two at a time. After watching him disappear, Magdalena closes the door and wraps herself in her cloak, almost gliding around her cabin, humming to the music in her head.

A Long Road There

Nearly on cue, Sir Biscuit Bottom appears with his nose in the air, smelling for his midnight snack. Magdalena grabs Mama's tin and serves up a double portion. She wants an extended audience tonight with the temperamental lord. He graciously chooses to stay for some late-night chitchat about her evening.

CHAPTER 24

Second Deck No. 10—with an Open Door

In between the waltzes she performs for Sir Biscuit Bottom, Magdalena notices her cabin door has come open. She reaches to close it, but a large hand comes out of the dark hallway and grabs her arm. When she starts to scream, another hand clamps over her mouth. She can feel the cold, sharp edge of a knife against her throat.

"Don't tell me ya don't remember ol' McGee from the hallway. 'Twas I that showed ya ta yur room," he slurs, putting his wet lips to her ear. "Ya listen lass and listen good. If ya scream, I'll start with yur friend next door. Ya can watch the tyke. Am I clear?" he says, flicking his knife blade hard enough against her skin to draw a trickle of blood. She caught enough of his brogued threat to know she'd better keep quiet, or Rosa will be in harm's way too.

"I won't scream," she promises in English.

"Well, okay, missy, that's a bargain," he slurs, slamming the door shut. "The word on the deck is ya carry a wee dagger. I'm just gonna take me a little check—to make sure ya ain't hidin' it under all this fanciness," he adds, beginning to slowly grope.

Magdalena's mind races. *Somehow, I've got to survive long*

enough for Will to get back, she thinks as McGee throws her on the bed. Right then, Sir Biscuit Bottom rolls across the floor inside of one of Mama's open, empty tins that Magdalena had forgotten to put away. Startled, McGee looks toward the sound. When he refocuses on his prey, he's staring down the barrel of Fritz's revolver.

"Lay your fat belly down on the floor, or so help me God, I'll shoot you," Magdalena says, the pistol in her hand trembling as much as her voice.

The pistol is still leveled at McGee when Magdalena hears a knock, then the opening of Second Deck 10's door. "Ready for the . . . ? My God!" Will shouts, grabbing the shaking pistol from Magdalena's hand.

"He tried to . . . . "

Before she can finish, Will yanks McGee to his feet, spins him around, and delivers a straight right-hand. Unconscious, the hallway snake crumples back to the floor, unable to slither away. Will takes Magdalena into his arms and squeezes tightly. "You're okay now— you're safe," he soothes. She grips him with all her might.

Jerking the now half-conscious body up from the floor, Will pushes the gun barrel hard against McGee's greasy hair and walks him toward the door. "We've got a problem down here, Schmidt," he yells to the deck watchman at the top of the stairs. "Grab some cuffs and leg-irons!"

Cuffing McGee's arms behind his back and slapping the irons around his massive ankles, the guard powers him down the stairs into a closet-like room they call the brig. The cell is pitch black and cold, but the rats don't seem to mind McGee joining them. They can always smell one of their own kind.

"He's gone and won't be back, Magdalena," Will assures the quivering girl in his arms. He's never before seen Magdalena afraid.

He sits with her on the bed, holding her close for some time, before asking a single question, "Are you alright?"

"Yes, I think so. I don't know why I can't stop shaking."

"Looks like you've got a small cut under your jaw."

"He put the blade to my throat and threatened to go after Rosa if I screamed."

After wiping the blood from her neck with his handkerchief, Will holds her tight enough so she'll stop trembling.

"I'm sorry this happened to you. You won't be staying here tonight. Get your nightgown and clothes for tomorrow. You'll sleep in my bed, and I'll bunk on the floor. That way, we'll both know you're safe. I don't give a damn about proprieties."

Magdalena smiles for the first time since she was attacked.

As Will pulls the covers on his bed close around her neck, Magdalena's body has finally quieted.

"I'd like to show you and Rosa New York for a few days after we arrive. What do you think of that?" Will asks, trying to get her mind to a different place.

"That'd be wonderful," she whispers.

"I'll take care of everything. That's the least I can do for you two."

"I'm so exhausted, Will. I think I'll try and sleep."

"That's what I want you to do. I'll be right here if you need anything."

When Magdalena comes awake yelling and kicking, tears running down her cheeks, it takes her a minute to realize McGee is gone and she is in Will's room. He's not in the crumpled floor pallet next to her. She shouts his name. When she doesn't get an answer, she curls into a tight ball and begins to cry again.

Sobbing, she hears a familiar voice in her mind. "Come on, daughter, get up," it says. "You're okay. You've got a long trip ahead of you." It's the same deep, comforting voice that has propelled her for so much of her life.

"I was so scared, Papa," she whispers as though he were next to her, holding her in his arms.

"I know you were," she imagines him saying. "You handled yourself well. I was proud. You're okay now." Her father's voice has always possessed the kind of conviction you can't argue with. "Bad things happen to good people. The best get up and go on."

Walking into the crowded first-deck saloon for breakfast takes a little sand. She knows the ship is no different than any place—gossip and rumors travel at lightning speed. Lord Rutherford meets her halfway to the table, offers his arm, and begins with, "As always, you look beautiful."

She can tell by his tone that the rumors have beaten her to breakfast. She hugs him and cries right there in the middle of the restaurant.

"There, there, my child. You cry it out. We heard about your hand-wringing encounter. I do hope you're alright."

Settling a little, she stammers, "I am. But it scared me. Still does. I know I'm so lucky that nothing truly awful happened."

"I'm increasingly impressed with your courage, my dear," the nobleman says, guiding her to the table.

"What's all this, Rutherford? These tears won't do," the baron says with genuine warmth, patting Magdalena on her shoulder.

She smiles at both men. "I'm sorry. I don't know why I can't stop crying."

"A good breakfast will help," the baron says, fumbling for a way to soothe the girl. "I daresay the people in Willenstat are made of sturdy stuff— the sturdiest," he adds, stilling her trembling hand.

The morning's weather is glorious—appropriate for the last shooting competition, though no one's thinking much about the event. After the final shell explodes some distance from an escaping glass fowl, Magdalena and the baron exchange a teary farewell. As he hugs her, she's still quivering ever so slightly. "This will pass, my dear, sooner than you think," the baron says before turning and pretending to inspect his rifles. His aching heart makes Magdalena understand why the baroness loves him so.

Handing her his formal introduction card, Lord Rutherford suggests they walk to her English lesson together. "I'm afraid this may be the last time I shall have the pleasure of your company. You are very special, my dear, and don't ever forget that. Keep this, and if your Colorado adventure proves unsatisfactory, please wire. You'd be welcome for as long as you like in Derbyshire at any time." Having a hard time bearing up, the old gentleman pats Magdalena on the shoulder, turning away to compose himself.

"Thank you with all my heart," Magdalena says. She is beginning to genuinely feel safer and stronger. She gives her friend a long bear hug, one like he's probably never gotten at court. With tears rolling down their cheeks, the nobleman leaves before his sister can answer the door.

The baroness begins tenderly but directly, "I'm sorry you had to go through such an ordeal last night, my child."

"Thank you," Magdalena says, hugging her teacher almost without shaking. "The evening was wonderful—the gown was perfect. I was afraid all evening I'd lose your brother's necklace. Now I've forgotten them both in my room. I'll get them to you later this morning."

"Nonsense, my dear. I'll send a cabin boy. I've never seen that jewelry sparkle as it did on you last night," the baroness adds, kissing her on the cheek.

The last English lesson is their best, even if they don't get around to much grammar.

"I'm so proud of you, my dear," the baroness says. "Now go live your life fully. Have no regrets when you look back on it."

"I will," the pupil assures, embracing her teacher for the last time.

A Long Road There

At lunch, Will can see Magdalena is doing much better, though her leg won't stop shaking under the table. He wants to lay out their New York rendezvous plan without focusing on last night's darkness, so he asks simply, "Are you okay this morning?"

"I'm better. I want you to know nothing bad happened, Will," she says, looking him in the eyes. He smiles. Her foot stops tapping as she hugs him and adds a long kiss on the cheek.

"Good," he says, pecking her on the nose and switching subjects. "We'll take Rosa and Theodor to see her grandfather the day after you arrive in New York. The city is too dangerous for her and the boy to try it alone. I'm having all the luggage delivered to the shipping company's baggage booth at Castle Garden. Immigration will take it anywhere in the city for next to nothing. I'll be at the inn after finishing my duties—probably late tomorrow evening. Any coachman at the immigration center will know the way to the *Gasthaus*. You girls must have your things outside your doors by 6 a.m. Do you have all that, kiddo?"

"I hope so," she says.

When Rosa opens the door and embraces her friend, it's clear she doesn't need to be told about last night. Taking the measure of her pal, Rosa quietly asks, "Are you okay?"

"I'm getting there. He didn't accomplish his purpose," she says, hugging Rosa back hard.

"Is there anything I can do?" Rosa asks.

"You've already done it."

Both girls need to pack. It won't take Rosa long. When they're finished, they'll visit the Musketeers one last time in the sunshine.

Turning to leave, Magdalena says, "Will wants to show us New York City before he takes you to your grandfather's."

"*Wunderbar*! I was so afraid of being all alone with Theodor in the vastness of New York," she says.

Opening her trunk, one of Mama's empty tins rolls across the floor. Watching it, Magdalena wonders how so much could have happened in two weeks.

Racing topside with the *Musketeers*, she's almost feeling confident for the first time today. The deck is bathed in brilliant sunshine. There's quite a crowd for today's farewell adventure. Magdalena's delivery is spellbinding. The suspense builds from her first words until the audience becomes hushed—then breathes a collective sigh of relief with the last thrust of d'Artagnan's blade into his foe's bosom.

With that final triumph, a lone third decker stands and hands Magdalena a large patchwork purse. The possibles bag has a shoulder strap and two inner pockets, both large enough for a pistol. Magdalena manages a heartfelt, "Thank you, my friends."

Four o'clock has come and gone by the time Magdalena gets back to her cabin. Exhausted, she falls on her bed. Just five minutes before the ship's clock strikes six, she wakes. Sprinting for the saloon, she can hear the last dinner call being made. She's hungry for the first time today. The meal goes down easily. McGee has nearly been evicted from her thoughts. Her body and mind are quieting.

Back in the fading light of her cabin, Magdalena lights her candle. Taking her pen in hand, she begins to write:

Dear Mama, Papa, Hans, and Elsa Emma,
Tomorrow morning my voyage ends. Our ship will dock in New York Harbor. When Papa went ashore, I became frightened, almost like a small child left in the dark for the first time. I became deeply cold when I could no longer see his face on the shore. I cried.
Between then and now, something unimaginable has occurred. I feel that all of you have been with me, especially

when I needed you most.

I have met a very special young officer. He's from Hamburg. Wilhelm is his name, though he goes by Will. He wants to show me New York City before I go on to Colorado. What, if anything, will come of us after that is a question only the stars can answer. In fact, my entire journey on top of the sea has been so unreal, it must have been fated.

I'm no longer frightened of being alone, though I still get lonely.

I do love you all terribly.

Magdalena

Sealing the letter, she begins a final entry in her journal.

I have been remiss in chronicling my journey so far. So many unimaginable people, things, and lessons. I'm not sure what changes, if any, have been wrought in me. I've been at the door of disaster, and yet I'm happy. Inconceivably, I find myself on the brink of falling in love. It's hard to know what's real or lasting in this floating world. I need to think. I know I must continue this journey that I've undertaken. What tomorrow will bring is uncertain. I'll try and be ready for it.

28 March 1871

Closing her little sister's gift, she reflects on her words for a moment. Then Magdalena decides to see if the harbor lights are flickering in the distance yet. Grabbing her cloak, she quickly seeks out the stars.

"Thought I wouldn't catch you?" Will teases, creeping up on little cat feet. He pulls her close and kisses her hard.

As Sir Biscuit Bottom finishes his late-night snack, he lingers without inducement. Maybe he feels a little sad. He and Magdalena

Virginia Pickett

visit awhile like old friends until the knight begins to nod off. After blowing out her bedside candle, Magdalena quickly falls asleep on top of the sea for the last time.

CHAPTER 25

New York City, New York
29 March, 1871

At last and already, there will be no more floating tomorrows. Magdalena wakes and pushes back the covers to greet her fourteenth consecutive day atop the ocean. Her teary goodbyes were said yesterday. Today, it's time to leave. The knock she's been waiting for comes precisely at 6 a.m. Two seamen take her baggage before collecting Rosa's single, worn bag.

In a final farewell, Magdalena puts the last two crumbs of Mama's biscuits on her knight's breakfast table. He's strangely hesitant to his meal. Grabbing her hand-stitched shoulder bag, she takes in her room one last time. When her eyes meet those of her tiny nobleman, she whispers, "Goodbye, gallant sir. I shall miss you." He twitches his nose and walks slowly away.

The past two weeks have raced away. They're gone forever. The paradox is that Magdalena feels like a year or two has passed, as though she's been in a magical cocoon. It was a place where things like falling in love and growing up unfold at dizzying speeds but are perceived at a normal pace. She doesn't fully trust this world.

She walks out of Second Deck No. 10 for the last time and shuts the door behind her as if she's closing a chapter on her life. Magdalena doesn't know how she feels. Heading toward the staircase, she can't explain why she's thinking of the *Zwischendeckers* starting a new chapter in their lives. She's confident their trip wasn't magical in too many ways—except maybe for the gift of a new opportunity. "Oddly," she whispers to herself as she walks up the risers to the top deck, "maybe I've been given the same fresh chance." The idea of this kinship feels good.

As the first-class gangplank touches land, Magdalena leans against the same section of railing where she watched Papa go ashore. Today, she's watching with Rosa and Theodor as the hierarchy of passengers leaves the ship.

The process is a rigid one—the first deckers promenade and wave to exquisite coachmen in fine livery. After the last of the privileged have stepped onto terra firma, the second deckers begin coming ashore. Magdalena can't help but speculate about the kindly old lady with the shawl. She hopes she'll get to see her grandchildren soon. Continuing her descent, she watches her three royal guardians find their carriage among the long line of gilded, horse-drawn conveyances. Magdalena also spies Dr. Hauptmann and Chief Engineer Meyer bidding the dandies a final farewell—as required.

Finally, looking back at the throng of third deckers waiting to deboard, she wonders about the mail-order bride twins—Ida and Anna Marie. How will their relationships unfold? Which one will marry an older balding groom, and which will take prince charming to the altar? She smiles at the conjecture.

The harbor reception crowd is immense, filled with the curious, the fashionable, and the gainfully employed, such as longshoremen and coachmen. Watching the miracle steamships dock has become the latest fashionable thing to do. Assorted shadier types are also taking the opportunity to make a buck. Many of them have only

A Long Road There

recently stepped ashore themselves. The iron-hulled wonders have not only become attractions; they're putting bread on the table for a lot of people.

Stepping ashore, Magdalena glimpses Will waving goodbye and throws him a kiss. So many memories in such a short time. Standing on New York City soil for the first time, she's certain that she's left nothing aboard—except maybe a piece of her heart.

CHAPTER 26

Castle Garden Immigration Processing Center
29 March, 1871

It's inconceivable to Magdalena that she's falling in love, but she wrote just that in her journal only twelve hours earlier. Maybe that explains why she's already missing Will after only two steps ashore.

The doors of Castle Garden Immigrant Center are immense. As they're funneled inside with the crowd, Magdalena's glad Will gave her a little head's up of the place. Still, the enormous, high-ceilinged room is overwhelming, filled with hundreds of arriving immigrants and dozens of serpentine screening queues. The thought of navigating the chaotic scene is daunting.

The strength Magdalena normally sees in Rosa's eyes has turned to apprehension. Rage lurks just behind them, should something or someone threaten Theodor. Everyone seems uneasy—afraid they'll lose their tenuous grip on America. Magdalena is no exception. One foot or the other is tapping incessantly, but she's got to drive the coach.

"We'll get through all this official rigmarole quicker than it looks like we will, Rosa. Theodor will be resting his head on a pillow in a quiet hotel room before you know it." Rosa tries to smile while clutching her son a little closer.

Second-deck status is proving to be a blessing. They're only behind the first-class immigrants—and there aren't many of them. Across the way are hundreds of *Zwischendeckers* struggling to stay formed in something resembling a line.

Reaching the rigid-looking processer, Magdalena gives her name, place of birth, and the inn where they'll stay. The German-speaking registrar doesn't look up. Impatiently, he waves Rosa forward. She's trembling but manages to give her information. The gatekeeper abruptly points to Theodor, "Is this your child? Name, please."

Almost inaudibly, Rosa responds, "Yes. Theodor Bauer."

"He's not on the manifest," the bureaucrat announces with obvious suspicion.

Now, fear grips Rosa.

"The baby was born on the ship two days ago," Magdalena says, summoning an authoritative voice but miscounting the days in the process.

"He's not on the manifest," the implacable clerk repeats.

The line behind them is bunching up, and the punctilious civil servant can't stand getting behind. "Herr Theodor Bauer, born 1871 March 27, U.S. waters. Added to manifest," he jots on his ledger before ordering, "Now, get moving." He angrily waves the next passenger forward. Having cleared the first hurdle, the girls are fully inside the processing maze. Confused people clog the floor, standing in long lines to sundry service stations. Eventually, the trio winds their way to their luggage. Will was right; Uncle Sam will send it directly to the inn for ten cents apiece.

After a long wait, Magdalena is able to post her letters home. Then she finds the money-exchange line. Once that's done, they're finally funneled into a crowd being pushed toward the gaping exit.

Everyone is still afraid their second chance will be taken away before they can step outside.

Once through the door, new opportunity begins to feel real, though fear and disorientation linger for the arriving flock without a shepherd. Magdalena hails one of the more humble-looking carriages and rushes to get her companions aboard, afraid the processor's long arm will snatch them back.

The cab driver is from Ireland and doesn't speak a word of German. Magdalena's Gaelic is about as good as his Deutsch, so she can only hope he finds the *Gasthaus*. He doesn't seem worried.

Though the city is immense, it feels narrow and closed in as they bump along the winding side streets. Magdalena hopes their cabbie isn't lost and that the four-leaf clover embroidered onto his hat isn't merely there for show. Her foot starts its incessant tapping again. When the coach's two gargantuan draft horses turn into the circular drive of the *Gasthaus*, her foot goes quiet on its own accord.

Much-needed good news greets the travelers at the front desk. They do have a room, and yes, their luggage will be delivered directly to their suite. Both girls think they must be dreaming as the German-speaking desk clerk lists the inn's amenities. "Indoor water closets, bathing rooms with hot water, laundry services, and a dining room," the clerk recites as if they were commonplace. Ready to leave for their room, Magdalena offers to pay.

"The bill has been taken care of, Fraülein."

"Will, my dear Will," she whispers below her breath.

Up the stairs and a few steps down the hall, the travelers find their room. They can't believe their eyes. They're standing in a small anteroom with a sofa, chair, and a table. "For afternoon tea" Magdalena says, gesturing to the furniture and mimicking a proper lady. A double door, next to a window, invites them to peek inside. Magdalena takes the plunge and turns the knob. Two single beds with lovely quilts greet her. Rosa lays Theodor down on one of the

A Long Road There

bunks and accepts Magdalena's invitation to join in her jumping up and down wildly on the other. Silliness is good for the soul.

"Heaven can't be any better than this," Magdalena says.

"It sure can't," Rosa concurs, appearing unafraid for the first time since she came ashore.

The bed-jumping frivolity comes to a screeching halt when Theodor lets out a thundering wail, instantly bringing his mother back to reality. Picking him up, she guides him to his lunch, settling in comfortably on the settee. Looking out the window at New York City for the first time, the thought that her grandfather is out there waiting for her is comforting. Rosa is beside herself with excitement waiting to see him and their new home. She'd written before leaving—so he'll expect her—but his great-grandson will be a surprise.

As Theodor eats and Rosa dreams, Magdalena is taking a closer look around the place. It's her first stay in a grand hotel. "Look. Theodor has his own bed!" she shouts, holding up a small cradle for Mama to see. As her treasure hunt continues, Magdalena finds an unclouded mirror on the wall above an uncracked pitcher and basin that rests on a waist-high mahogany dresser.

"Well, I'll be. I think we are in heaven!" she shouts.

"I wasn't sure I'd ever reach it," Rosa teases.

———

Theodor is full and, in the best tradition of his namesake Lord Rutherford, appears ready for a snooze. In fact, in no time everyone is asleep—each on a separate cloud.

Just before 5, Magdalena wakes first and remembers that in heaven, people can take long, luxurious baths. Asking the desk clerk for an extra towel and directions, she makes her way toward the smell of steam. The room is empty except for the bathtub and the maid. Climbing into the warm water, she asks the bathhouse girl to make certain the door is locked. "Ahhh. Fit for a queen," she whispers, submerging herself beneath the bubbles. Coming up, the attendant is pouring the last of the hot water supplement into the tub. Magdalena begins to hum.

"Let me know if you need anything, miss," the maid says as she retires to the anteroom.

"Oh, I will," Magdalena answers, resubmerging.

After an appropriately celestial soaking, Magdalena returns to their room and wakes her friend. She reminds Rosa that there's a tub with her name on it just below. Then, like a friend you can only find in heaven, Magdalena volunteers to watch Rosa's little angel.

The *Gasthaus* threesome nearly floats to the dining room beneath them. You don't eat in heaven; you dine. Over the next hour and a half, the ladies do just that while Theodor takes in the sights, sounds, and smells around him.

Floating up the staircase after dinner, the girls stretch out on their separate clouds and gab.

"I wonder what New York will be like, Rosa."

"Spectacular, I suspect. I hope Grandfather is ready for Theodor and me," Mama adds anxiously.

"Oh, he'll be so happy to have you two join him. He and his great-grandson will get along famously. You'll be the lady of the house," Magdalena says, imagining her friend hosting a party for her grandfather. "I can't wait for Will to get here," she adds, with her happy thoughts going a hundred miles an hour.

Theodor is wide awake, listening to the ladies as 10 o'clock approaches.

"Is anyone going to get up and welcome a sailor?" Will shouts through the closed door.

Magdalena is. She hugs him hard enough that he nearly drops his bucket of beer before he's done asking the question. Will pours for everyone but Theodor. The girls have a million questions about the city.

"All of your queries will be answered tomorrow," their guide assures them. "We're going on a grand tour before we take Rosa to her grandfather's." Both ladies give the seaman a hug and a kiss on opposite cheeks at the same time. This is one time Will doesn't mind getting caught in the middle of a storm.

Before long, Theodor lets Mama know it's time for his bedtime snack. They retire to the privacy of the bedroom, leaving the sailor and his girl to snuggle on the settee. The spooners talk until well past midnight. Out the window, the lights of the city still flicker.

"I love you, Magdalena."

"Will, you're a silly goose."

"No. I mean it. I love you."

Kissing the seaman and nestling against his chest, she falls asleep in his arms with that thought. Will watches her for a while before slipping out of her arms undetected.

Not much after eight the next morning, Will yells through the door, "Time to hit the deck, girls. We've got a whole lot of city to see. I'll meet you in the dining room in an hour."

After breakfast and a nonstop volley of questions from the excited tourists, Will suddenly announces, "The coach leaves in five minutes," then walks out of the dining room. He looks dapper in his new touring hat.

After an endless four minutes of fidgeting, Mama takes Theodor in her arms, and the girls run through the lobby and out the wide front entrance. There, in an elegant black carriage pulled by two glistening ebony steeds, sits Will in the driver's seat. "Get in," he says. "What are you waiting for? New York City doesn't wait for anybody, girls."

And so, the tour begins. The guide is a good one— probably as good as any, as a matter of fact. He's seen the sights of the metropolis many times—just never before with the girl he's fallen in love with.

Stopping the carriage, Will says, "This is Trinity Church, ladies. Best view of the city for over a hundred years." He takes Theodor from his mom and heads up the steeple stairs. At the top, the first-timers gaze in silence on at the iconic city, awestruck with the unobstructed view of the harbor. After a while, their guide has to pull them away. "Come on. There's a lot more to see."

Parking the carriage in the grass just off the pathway, Will orients his passengers. "This is the Central Park menagerie, ladies—the perfect spot for the likes of us," he chuckles. "The public began donating a Noah's ark of animals a long time ago, and the zoo's been a hit ever since."

The park is a Garden of Eden, a refuge from the city's commotion and crowds, a quiet place for rich and poor alike. It was a gift from the city fathers. Today, it's also a bucolic sanctuary for three silly young people. For a few hours, they pretend things will be as they are forever—a gentle breeze on a picnic blanket, a deep blue sky overhead, and a carefree, limitless horizon.

After a *Gasthaus* sack lunch and twenty quick winks for the guide and Theodor, the sightseers are off again—this time to the heart of the city. Will wants them to feel it beat with all its force. They stroll from store to store, trying on the latest fashions, always under his discerning eye, waiting for a thumb's up or down before returning the merchandise to the rack in either case. At Tiffany's, the diamond tiara stays under the glass. The clerk knows browsers when he sees them.

"Photo shops are all the rage in New York," Will says when they're finally done with the extended posing process. Accepting the sailor's payment for three copies, the photographer says, "They'll be ready in a few minutes if you want to wait."

"We've got a lot more to do before day's end. Can you just send them to the *Gasthaus* for us?" Will asks.

"I'd be delighted to. That'll be another two bits. I'll have them there before supper tonight," the shopkeeper assures, ringing his cash register a second time.

The foursome heads off again. Will insists they hop on one of the world's only horse-drawn streetcars, which rolls on tracks just beneath the road's surface. Before they've slid a block on the rails, Will and Magdalena are both hanging by one hand from the car's rear platform. They come back inside only to placate Rosa, who is terrified that they'll fall.

Back in the carriage, behind their 1,500-pound shining four-legged engines, they're headed for Fifth Avenue to prance by the recently completed Stewart mansion. "Perhaps we'll stop for tea," Will suggests. "Mrs. Stewart would be delighted," he tells the giggling girls. The surrounding elegant brownstones stand in stark contrast to the enormous marble-faced mansion. "Ladies, take a good look. Now you can brag that you've seen a two-million-dollar home. Real people actually live there," he assures his doubting passengers.

CHAPTER 27

At the End of the Brownstones, New York City
30 March 1871

"Rosa, it's getting late," Will says. "I think we ought to find your grandfather. What's the address again?"

"235 Cherry Street," Rosa recites from memory. The excitement of seeing her grandfather is the only thing keeping her from crying. She knows she has to say *goodbye* to her friends—probably forever.

The horses continue to clop past well-kept brownstones. People and children are coming and going without a care in the world. Gradually, the tidy homes give way to smaller sorts—not nearly as well kept either—before disappearing altogether, leaving only old, rundown tenements and lots of bars where hustlers, thugs, and ladies of the evening are all trying to make a buck.

"235 Cherry Street, are you sure?" Will asks.

"Yes, that's it, I'm sure," Rosa says, fussing over Theodor. She wants him to look his best when he shakes his great-grandfather's hand for the first time.

From the carriage, Magdalena can only see darkness down the narrow alleyways. Will is uncomfortable in this part of town—

176

always has been. Against his better judgment, he stops the carriage in front of a dilapidated old tenement. A few feet away, a young man that seems to have a chip on his shoulder leans against a lamppost.

"I'm looking for Ernst Deutscher," Will tells the fellow.

"What's it worth to you?"

"Two silver dollars. Half now, and half when I'm talking to him," Will says, flipping a silver coin at the kid.

Snapping it out of the air, the young man disappears. No one in the wagon speaks a word while they wait. There must be some mistake, Rosa thinks, holding Theodor tighter in her arms. Soon, the neighborhood kid returns—alone.

"He's dead, mister. Two weeks ago. The old landlady says they hauled him off to the pauper's cemetery. Where's my other dollar?" It clangs at his feet as Will turns the horses around. Rosa is already in tears.

She had only read about her grandfather's success in his letters. She couldn't possibly have known it was an illusion. A dream that never came true. Like so many others, Rosa's grandfather had drawn too many deuces.

From inside the all-black carriage, Rosa feels as though she's in a funeral cortege, a requiem for her dream. The wooden wheels bounce over the pockmarked streets and drum the dark rhythm of a dirge. The girl has only her worst thoughts to keep her company—except for the sleeping bundle lying in her lap.

Nothing is said all the way back to the inn. Each of the mourners dwells upon life's cruel conundrums.

For Rosa, her walk upstairs to their hotel room is long. Theodor feels like a hundred pounds. At the top, Will takes him from his mama and hands the sleeping child to Magdalena. Reaching for Rosa's hand, Will guides her to the couch and puts her head on his shoulder. Long before her tears diminish, Theodor wails for dinner. Life does go on.

"I'm exhausted, Will," Mama whispers almost inaudibly. She

stares vacantly at the city lights as she nurses her son, a small blanket draped over her breast. She's rocking him and herself.

Watching her friend struggle, Magdalena begins to cry. "I'll come get you two for dinner in a while," Will says, turning to leave so the girls can be alone.

"No, please. I just want to sleep. You and Magdalena go see the city at night."

"Alright," Wills says, not pressing the issue. "Magdalena, I'll meet you in the lobby in half an hour."

Magdalena immediately hugs her friend. They sit in silence, looking out at New York City. After a few minutes, Rosa insists Magdalena go with Will.

As the door closes behind her friend, Rosa thinks about how today was supposed to change her life for the better. The dead-end street she'd been on for so long was to become a thoroughfare of opportunity. Theodor's life was supposed to be different than her own. Now, she fears none of these things will happen. At nineteen, the widowed kitchen maid sobs.

Will has chosen one of his favorite eating spots in New York. The day's tragedy was a bad one, but the blow is blunted with Rosa out of sight. Gradually, Will and Magdalena escape the pall. At their table, they are engaged in easy conversation when their server approaches.

"These are compliments of the gentlemen across the way," their waiter says, delivering two steins of beer and pointing to four stout sailors on the other side of the room.

"Those coal jockeys never forget a pretty face," Will says, tipping his cap to four members of the Black Gang.

It's an evening to remember, Magdalena thinks. The couple laughs and dances. They tease and talk—real talk about what they want and where they think they're headed. Will's eyes sparkle as he tells Magdalena about his dream of someday captaining his own ship. She becomes intense, pledging again to get herself to Central City.

A Long Road There

"Why is that?" Will asks.

Caught off guard, she fumbles for an answer, then settles for the truth. "Because that's where Fritz and I were going." Will grows quiet. Magdalena understands. She imagines how awkward she would feel if her sweetheart still grieved a former lover and the life they'd never build. She knows Will is hurting. As much as she would like to, she can't change that right now. Soon, the uncomfortable moment passes, and their evening finishes well.

Walking into the lobby of the *Gasthaus*, hand-in-hand, the couple becomes somber at the thought of Rosa's totally changed circumstances. "I don't want this evening to end sadly," Will says before they go any further. "I've got an unopened bottle of brandy. How about one nightcap in my room—but only if you promise to smile."

"I will. I promise."

In Will's room, the brandy never gets opened. They're in each other's arms even before the door closes. This time, neither makes any attempt to douse their passion's fire.

"Are you awake?" Magdalena asks with the day's first light.

"Have been for a while."

"I can't leave Rosa and Theodor in New York all alone. I just can't. I'm gonna take them with me."

"I've got a better idea. Why don't we get married and the four of us will go home? You'll love Hamburg. You know, it's not so bad to be the wife of a ship's captain."

"I see you've promoted yourself."

"I'll get there. I hope you'll be beside me when I do."

"Will, I wouldn't be here this morning if I didn't think we loved each other. I don't know why, but I've gotta get to Colorado. I'm not asking you to understand, because I don't. Once I've seen the

179

place, maybe I'll be ready to be a captain's wife." After she utters the words, Magdalena is suddenly overcome with the feeling that something wonderful is slipping through her fingers again.

"Have it your way. You're going to anyways," Will says, turning over to face her. "I'll wait," he tells her, kissing her long and hard.

After a few quiet minutes, he asks, "So, just how do you plan to get to Colorado, young lady? You should know by now that there are bad people walking around in this world."

"I've got it all figured out. I've studied up on the whole thing," Magdalena says. "We're going to take the train to Independence, Missouri, like Fritz's uncle suggested. That's where the Oregon Trail wagon trains start— they go all the way to the Pacific Ocean. Fritz's uncle is waiting for me in Central City. He's made the trip and doesn't think I'll have any problem at all." At least, that's the way I read his letter, she silently assures herself once again.

"Magdalena, I don't think you have the slightest idea what you're getting you and Rosa into, not to mention Theodor. At least consider taking a train the whole way."

"Too expensive, too loud, and too cooped up."

"I can help you out with the money."

"That'd be over two weeks inside of a train car. I couldn't do it. I don't like being cooped up. Besides, Rosa is scared of trains. She told me so."

"Two weeks in a railroad coach? You're talking about three months in a wagon crossing some godforsaken country."

"My mind is made up. The three of us will have an adventure. From what I read, we might be able to work our way across for the wagon train boss. Rosa can cook, and I can drive a team as good as any man, that's for sure."

"There's no sense arguing with you. Come over here and give me a kiss," Will says in a soft voice, pulling Magdalena close. They make love again, knowing that all too soon they'll be parting for longer than either of them is willing to consider.

Rosa is already awake when her roommate opens the door. Embarrassed, Magdalena can only manage a sheepish *good morning*. Rosa gets up and gives her friend a hug. Nothing needs to be said. Both girls understand things are different now for each of them.

"What are you and Theodor going to do?" Magdalena asks as gently as possible.

"I don't know. I'm frightened. I've got a son that I've got to take care of somehow. I don't have a choice about that."

Magdalena can see the resolve in her eyes. "Look at me, Rosa. I thought about this all morning. The three of us are gonna go to Colorado. What do we have to lose? We'll be together looking for a new life, and we'll find one. That has to be a whole lot better than searching alone."

Rosa can feel Magdalena's determination. She pauses before asking, "What about Will?"

"I'm not sure," Magdalena admits. "I told him this morning I was going to ask you to come to Colorado with me. After that, I honestly don't know. Whatever happens, you and I are going to stick together."

"*Wunderbar*," Rosa whispers.

With a loud knock, the door flies open. "What'd I tell you, Magdalena? Read this," Will says, handing her a telegram.

First Mate Hauff,
Report to company vessel Wind Vagabund by 15 April 1871 to serve as skipper during Captain Freytag's convalescence. Further orders at vessel.
Johannes Schmidt,
Vice President Staffing & Operations
Deutsche Schiffahrtsgesellschaft (German Shipping Line)

Virginia Pickett

"Your dream has come true," Magdalena whispers, but she can't help but greet the news as bittersweet.

"Well, half of it anyway," Will says. He looks at her expectantly, and Magdalena knows he wants her to shout, *I'm coming with you.* As much as she doesn't want Will to hurt, Magdalena isn't able to do that right now. She and Rosa have a different path before them, one that travels west on solid ground.

———

Will has had the luggage sent ahead, so the carriage is empty as he pulls up to the *Gasthaus*. As Rosa and Theodor step aboard, he's acutely aware this may be the last time he ever sees either of them. Magdalena is lagging behind; she wants one last look at the inn. In that moment, she glimpses all that she might be leaving behind.

As the horses clop away, everyone has the feeling that something is coming to an end—strange for three people all starting new beginnings.

———

As the girls' luggage is loaded onto the train, the first call for boarding fills the station. "Chicago, Illinois, and points west and south."

Will gives Rosa a long hug before she steps aboard with Theodor. The new skipper is a mess. As the second "All aboard!" crackles the air, the two lovers share a kiss, both wishing it could last forever. After helping Magdalena onto the train steps, it's all Will can do to let loose of her arm.

"I'll write to you," he calls out, waving goodbye as she slips further away from his arms.

"Remember, Independence General Delivery!" Magdalena hollers back at him.

"I'll remember!"

The taste of her last kiss and the sound of her final goodbye linger as the train disappears in the distance.

182

CHAPTER 28

Inside a Pullman Car
First Week of April 1871

By 1871, iron horses are running in herds. From New York harbor to the ports of California, rails now connect America. Steel tracks have become the arteries of the nation.

Rosa is grateful the click-clacking rhythm of the train has put Theodor to sleep, though it hasn't done much to diminish her apprehension of the fast-moving giant. Magdalena is knee-high in arithmetic, penciling out how to stretch the bankroll she and Rosa have pooled. The darn thing is not very elastic. By sundown that first day, everyone is tuckered. They get to sleep lying down, courtesy of Mr. George Pullman and Will's generosity. He had insisted on buying the girls first-class train passage, which included Pullman car status much of the way to Independence.

The next morning, the dining car feels more like the first-deck eatery than the second to Magdalena. The snappily attired waiters know their job. They move with great precision and efficiency under their hoisted silver trays. The white table linen and sparkling place settings are equally stunning. The people sitting behind the glistening silverware seem to be cut more from Lord Rutherford's cloth than from the shawled old lady's.

Breakfasts cost thirty-five cents. As Magdalena hands the waiter a silver dollar, she's hoping for some change in return. She recalls the baroness telling her, "You only live once, my child." Magdalena wonders if her ladyship has ever had to count her pennies. Luckily, Theodor has brought his breakfast, she thinks, smiling to herself. She leaves a shiny dime for the old Black gentleman who had tended to them so well.

After dining, the girls are surprised to find that their berths have been converted back to day travel. They didn't have to lift a finger. A kindly, Black middle-aged gentleman that everyone calls George has already taken care of that. When they pass him in the narrow corridor, he asks, "May I be any further assistance, ma'am?" He's polite and accommodating, but proud, in his snappy uniform, answering all their questions with *Yessum*. Magdalena suspects the gentleman's pride was earned, though she isn't sure where this intuition comes from.

As the miles pass by her window, Magdalena decides to write the folks at home even though Will is popping in and out of her thoughts. The letter is long and chatty.

Once she's done, it's time to write Will. "I already miss you," she begins. After several pages on that theme, she closes with, "I hope you haven't forgotten me by the time you get this."

Laying her pencil aside, Magdalena takes stock of herself while watching the landscape go by. When did you stop loving Fritz, she wonders. I didn't. Then how is it that you're in love with Will, and why are you still going to Colorado? The interrogation upsets her, so she stops the questioning—for now.

Rosa is marveling at the expansive scenery out her window. Meanwhile, her son behaves like an experienced traveler. He is, after all.

As the days pass, the unlikely traveling partners turn to sewing. Theodor is going to need baby gowns. The to and fro of their needles remind Magdalena of Mama and little sister Elsa Emma.

A Long Road There

The kid turns seventeen in July, she remembers, shaking her head in disbelief.

It is a blustery afternoon when they roll into Chicago—a city the girls decide to take in only from their train seats. After passengers flow off of and onto the train, they leave the great central station of Chicago. As they gain speed, the porter calls, "Rock Island, Illinois; Independence, Missouri, and points south and west." For the next hundred and fifty miles or so, the girls hear passengers buzzing about the big muddy stream. Magdalena wonders why the fuss. When the track does come alongside the waterway, she understands. The Mississippi has a majesty all its own.

When the porter finally makes his call for Independence, Missouri, Magdalena can't believe they've come over 1,200 miles. New York City, in many ways, is already a blur.

"Colorado is not far now, Rosa," Magdalena tells her pal, with no idea how wrong she is. She's still bound and determined to get there. Once she's accomplished that, what's next remains uncertain. She's leaving that up to the stars.

CHAPTER 29

Independence, Missouri
April 1871

It's twilight when Magdalena steps down from the train in Independence, Missouri. Having someone to defer to would feel good right about now. Papa isn't here to carry the luggage, and Will hasn't made a reservation at the *Gasthaus*. If things go wrong, she'll have only herself to blame. Rosa is sitting on top of Grandpa's trunk feeding Theodor. She trusts Magdalena to be in charge. "One brick at a time," Magdalena tells herself, thinking of Papa's borrowed adage.

Since there's no line of gilded coaches or cabbies of any kind, she has to start somewhere. Making sleeping arrangements seems like a good place.

"I'm wanting hotel," she tells the clerk who's heard it put worse over the years—here at the start of the Oregon Trail.

"There's only four, lady. Are you traveling on the cheap?" the clerk asks, looking the trio over, knowing that most just off the boat are.

The expression puzzles Magdalena, and the man can see it. "Is money important to you?" he asks, rephrasing his question.

186

A Long Road There

"Yes," Magdalena answers honestly.

"Then, it's the Independence Inn ya want. Fifty cents a night is all. Bath in the morning for a dime."

"Could you send please?" Magdalena asks, pointing to Grandpa's trunk and Rosa's dusty bag sitting outside the door.

"For a nickel a piece I can," the clerk tells her.

She finds a quarter and lays it on the counter, hoping it'll do. The honest clerk gives her two baggage claims and fifteen cents change. Magdalena is delighted, dropping the buffalo heads into her purse.

"A mile and a half straight down the road," the agent says, pointing the way.

The walk is dusty. The girls take turns carrying Theodor. When they arrive, Magdalena tries to put on a good face, though she's sweating. "Well, Rosa, here we are," she says, trying to be upbeat. Still, it's clear to them both that the hotel has seen better days.

The Musketeers are all tired even before they climb into bed. Rosa and Theodor double up in the worn, single bunk, and Magdalena curls beside them on the floor.

"We're almost there. Well, we're at the end of the beginning, anyway," Magdalena whispers to herself as her eyelids close.

In the morning, Magdalena goes to the front desk and asks after Robert Douglas, the wagon master Fritz's uncle had recommended.

"Ol' Douglas ain't here," the morning desk clerk says. Taking a sip of his coffee, the fellow behind the newspaper continues, "Buffalo is still bossin' a train. His camp is a pretty fur piece straight down that road out front. Can't miss the wagons. If he ain't around, wait. He'll come rollin' in 'fore long." Though Magdalena doesn't understand all of the clerk's twangy English, she got enough of what he said to start walking—again.

Forty minutes or so down the road, the hoofers come onto a lonely group of wagons. Six or seven are formed into a corral.

187

There's a battered coffee pot hanging over a dying fire that sits dead center in the circle.

"Mr. Bison . . . ." Magdalena calls out— her version of his trail handle. There's no answer, so the girls find a rock beside the embers and rest their feet for a while. Soon, a man rides up on horseback, pausing close enough to cast a shadow on them.

"Howdy. You two lookin' for me?"

"It's the wagon master we want to see," Magdalena tells the mounted cowboy.

"Then ya found him," the fellow on top of the horse says. He dismounts with the skill of 10,000 repetitions, flawed only by the misery of uncooperative bones. "My friends call me Buffalo. Others call me a lot of things. Mortimer Simmons is about the nicest, I suppose." Straightening to his full height, he extends a large, calloused hand in Magdalena's direction.

She is face to face with her first real cowboy. When he speaks, he doesn't seem all that unlike Papa, though the man before her is packaged much differently. He's about Papa's age, wearing a well-worn Texas cowboy hat. His ruddy, wide-jawed face looks honest. It's furrowed but not wrinkled. The eyes under his wide hat brim look younger than the weather lines suggest. There's a leather possibles bag slung over his left shoulder with a strap that runs full across his chest so the pouch can rest on his right hip. The thing looks like a first cousin to the one the third deckers gave Magdalena, except for having been in the elements so long. An oversized revolver is strapped on his left hip, where it stays unless someone's foolish enough to cause him to disturb it. Each trimming seems to be part of the cowboy. In the end, it's the broad smile that puts Magdalena at ease.

The girls see only the man standing in front of them, but Buffalo was younger once—like everyone. He lost a wife to smallpox in '59, just before the war. Still hasn't gotten over losing her. He's been wagon training since 1843, except for the war.

A Long Road There

"You ain't gittin' another biscuit, so no need wastin' yur time tryin', Beau," the boss says, shaking his finger at the rust-and-white mutt that followed him into camp. "This is Beau, ladies, after the late Colonel Beauregard Dixon, proud commander of the Texas Sixth Cavalry, whom I pleasurably served under in the feud between the states. I reckon the old cur is about the best train dog west of the big muddy, 'lessen he's got his mind on the ladies. He ain't been worth much lately, courtin' some town missy. Word has it he's a daddy. Now, where was I—oh—what is it that I can do for you two, I mean three?" he says, pointing at Theodor.

Magdalena is mesmerized by the boss's sidekick, so Rosa pipes up in English. "We want to go west. We can work. I cook good food. She drives a wagon. Do you need us?" she asks.

Buffalo can only smile. He's heard a lot of broken English over the years—all sorts have been aboard his trains. It just so happens, though, that he does need a cook and a driver for this run to Oregon. These two aren't exactly what he had in mind, but there's something about them that he likes. They're young and pretty. That's one strike against them on the trail. He just likes them. During these last thirty years of dealing with people, he's done pretty well following his nose.

"I'll tell you what— you two be here at sunup," the boss says to Rosa. "You can rustle up some grub for the hands, and your friend can chauffeur me around. I've gotta head up the road a piece to get some lumber. We'll see then if she can do more than play with Beau."

Magdalena had heard Buffalo say, "Beau's a daddy" and immediately stopped listening to him, thinking hard instead of puppies mottled white and orange-brown.

CHAPTER 30

Independence Environs

By the time the sun says *hello*, the aroma of coffee, fresh biscuits, and frying bacon already fills the air. Rosa has a knack for cooking wherever her kitchen is—whether an outdoor campfire and chuckwagon or inside the finery of an elegant German mansion. Nobody has to ask the boys twice to *come and get it*. A lot of pointy-toed boots start shuffling in. The cook can't help but notice that each fellow has a battered but, what seems to be, highly valued hat sitting on top of his head.

Once Buffalo gets a taste of breakfast, Rosa has herself a job. "Good vittles," the boss says. "You're spoiling these fellas," he adds before walking away. Beau is torn between staying and begging or starting the day's work. Buffalo chooses for him, "Get on over to that wagon, buster." The dog complies.

"Let's see what you can do in the driver's seat," the wagon master says to Magdalena before jumping aboard shotgun. Beau clambers into the empty bed. The hauling giant is hitched to four, big ornery-looking mules.

The job interview begins. There are no frayed nerves for Magdalena. She is comfortable behind the reins— always has been.

190

A Long Road There

"Are you ready, Mr. Bison?" she asks, cautiously inching out of the campsite. She figures a fishtailing exit might not help her get the job.

"Let her go," Buffalo says. "Take the first right. The yard is a fair piece up ahead. I'm gonna fetch some twelve-footers. Ya can't miss Jacobson's if you can read." After those instructions, the boss slides down in his seat and pulls his hat over his eyes.

When Magdalena turns the wagon at the sign, Buffalo wakes—if he ever was asleep. "Ya made it, huh? Good. Jus' stay here and keep them mules calm. They can git a little skittish when we're loadin'. Twelve footers are a might too heavy for a little lady like you, anyhow."

Magdalena gets the gist of what the boss just told her—the broad strokes are all she's gleaned from her conversations in America thus far. Catching some of what's said most of the time isn't going to get me far in this new land, she reckons. "I've got to start thinking in English—cowboy English," she whispers in German. Stewing in German is easy, she thinks. I'll show Mr. Bison who can lift a twelve-footer soon enough, she vows.

Catching his breath after six rounds with the twelve-footers, the boss hops back aboard. "Ya always wear gloves, kid?" he asks.

"My grandpa was tailor. He made for me. No, no. I work for gloves," she corrects herself, smiling at the memory and her budding English.

About halfway back to the campsite, Buffalo says, "You and your partner got yourselves jobs."

"*Wunderbar!*" the driver replies, pretty sure they've been hired.

Now that she has a job, the kid decides to press her luck. "Mr. Bison, your dog is daddy?" she asks. "I'm pleased to want puppy. Is this possible?"

Showing off his broad smile again, the boss says, "It sure as hell is. Take a left here."

191

"Petro, what in Sam Hill is up in Little Italy?"

"Pasta, lots of Mama's pasta, Buffalo, and there ain't near enough for a chowhound like you," the smithy says, laughing, as he walks over to their wagon. There's almost no vestige of the old country left in the second-generation Italian. The farrier pretty much speaks all Missouri these days. "Mules need shoein'?" he wonders out loud, secretly hoping their footwear is fine since he's busier than he wants to be.

"No, no, ya ain't getting any Buffalo nickels today. Ya got any of Beau's pups left that happen to speak Deutsch? The kid here's lookin' for one."

"None of them listen to anything they're asked to do, so it don't matter what language ya ask 'em in. We got three left. They're drivin' me and Mama plum crazy. She cin have 'em all. They're out back."

Beau's missus is beautiful. The long-haired, black-and-rust-colored dog isn't too friendly though to the strangers trying to kidnap her pups. Mama Petro gets a firm grip on her as she shows Magdalena two of the whelps. They're gorgeous. Magdalena is still shopping when she hears a "yap." About a hundred yards or so out in the pasture behind them, a rambunctious pup wrestles with a leftover snowdrift from the hard winter.

"That one's a little feisty, miss. Always off scoutin' on his own, never mindin'. I'd reckon you'd be best to stick with those two," Mama Petro advises.

But the snowbank cinched it for Magdalena. The oversized outlaw, with a rust hold-up mask on his face, has found a home. She decides to call him Scout since that's apparently what he likes to do. Magdalena scoops the young lookout into her arms. America is going to be a good place for them both, she decides.

Putting the pup in the back of the wagon with his pappy and the lumber, Magdalena asks, "How much?"

"Nothin'. Ol' Petro wanted ya to take all three. I guess we'll see how good a pappy Beau is," Buffalo says. He seems as proud as a grandfather. The mule team, meanwhile, moseys home without much guidance.

Magdalena understands perfectly that she doesn't have to reach into her purse. Her nodded assent is unmistakable in any language.

Even before unloading, Buffalo calls the girls over to the fading breakfast fire. Rosa is just finishing her cleanup. Beau starts showing his kid around the place, letting him know the rules.

"Well, ladies, you got yourselves jobs—so let's talk a little turkey. Here's what I'm offerin'. Dollar a day and keep. You can move into that third wagon over there. Job starts tomorrow at sunup. We're fixin' ta leave close to the end of April as possible. What'da ya say?"

Based on his smile, the girls both figure they've got a job, but the details are all Greek after that.

"We say okay, Mr. Bison," Magdalena says, agreeing for both Rosa and her.

"Good. Now tell me your proper tags—I mean names. I'm Buffalo, not Mr. Bison," he says, pointing at himself.

After nodding *yes*, Magdalena points to herself. "Magdalena," she says, shaking the boss's hand like a real cowboy.

"Rosa," the young mother says. She follows suit and extends her hand a little more delicately.

"And the boy?" Buffalo asks.

"Theodor Wilhelm Rutherford," Rosa says proudly.

"We'll call him Butch around here," the boss corrects. "Maggie, it's gotta be Maggie," he says, pointing at Magdalena. "That handle of yours is too much of a mouthful. By the way, you were pretty fair skinnin' those mules today."

Magdalena smiles broadly, able to sniff out the compliment hiding in Buffalo's strange idiom.

Maggie and Butch—those are odd names, Magdalena thinks. After reaching a cowboy's agreement with their new boss, Magdalena heads back to the hotel with her new pup, Rosa, Theodor, and a little more bounce in her step.

By nightfall, the three new hands are pretty much moved into their wagon. They talked Buffalo into hauling Grandpa's trunk over when they showed up with only Rosa's humble suitcase. The boss had made the mistake of observing, "You two travel pretty light." Magdalena—nobody's fool—responded with her big brown eyes and "We're pleased to have big trunk moved."

That first night, Mama and Theodor take the indoor quarters. Aunt Maggie is under the stars where she'll be from now on, unless the weather turns foul.

The sky is brilliant tonight. Magdalena can't get to sleep, thinking of Will and the star-studded nights on the ship. She grabs her pencil and starts to write.

7 April 1871

Dear Will,

So much has happened since we left New York City. I can't wait to tell you about it, but even more, I wish you were here to share it with me.

We got to Independence fine. Rosa was nervous the whole train ride and glad to be done with it. Theodor mostly slept and ate. We can tell he's growing already. I mostly was just amazed at how big America is. We were on the train for a week, and they tell me we're not quite halfway across it. How big can America be?

Guess what! Right after we got here, we met a nice older man who's been a wagon master for a long time. He's putting together a train for Oregon and needed some more hands. Rosa is the new cook for his crew, and I'll be working with the horses and mules and driving a wagon sometimes. Things couldn't have worked out any better. Everything would be perfect if you were here.

Tonight, as I look up at the stars, I think of you and me

doing the same thing—together on top of the ocean. I miss you terribly.

By the time you get this, you'll be on your own ship. I'm absolutely thrilled for you. I know you'll make a wonderful captain.

Tomorrow is my first day of work, so I'll stop for now. I miss you and can't wait until we're together again.

Love, Magdalena

The women soon learn that the job of preparing to head west is sunup to sundown. Magdalena rides, wrangles, and runs errands with the wagon. The kid is so good with the animals that Buffalo makes her Yancey's first lieutenant in charge of the remuda. Over the following days and weeks, she writes Will often—at least on the nights she can stay awake long enough to scratch a little love talk onto paper.

All the hands are getting fat and sassy on Rosa's cooking. She's getting back her confidence. The kid took an awful bad blow with her grandfather's death, but she's on the mend—being important to people again is getting her there. Both girls are "smart cookies," as the boss calls them, so speaking and thinking in cowboy is getting easier by the day. Scout is trying to find his place in the family. He can't seem to please his pa or his grandpa right now. His new mama babies him pretty good though.

The Harbor of Hamburg, Germany
April 1871

With his official appointment as captain of the *Wind Vagabund*, Will hasn't had a moment to spare. For two days he's been plowing through requisition forms and other official documents in his captain's quarters. His desk is still strewn with papers. He takes a moment to look out of his porthole onto the Hamburg harbor. While he watches the sun slip into the water, he thinks of

Virginia Pickett

Magdalena. He hasn't written her since leaving New York. "The hell with the paperwork," he says to himself. "I need to write my sweetheart." He grabs the captain's quill, honoring a long clipper tradition of the captain working behind a feather, and begins,

16 April 1871

My Dear Magdalena,

How can two weeks seem so long? When you left on the train, I knew I should have pulled you back into my arms or jumped on board beside you. On the crossing from New York, I'd catch myself scanning the top deck—looking for you shooting trap or reading to the third deckers. Each evening I expected to see you at the ship's railing and was disappointed when you weren't there. The night skies just aren't as magnificent without you to share them with me.

I'm now officially Captain Wilhelm Hauff, master of the Wind Vagabund on a run to Hong Kong and back. She's a beautiful vessel, and like me, she's had a long association with the sea. Remember the ships I showed you in the New York harbor—the sleek ones with the tall masts? The Vagabund is a clipper like that.

I'm looking forward to the voyage. Ever since I was a cabin boy on my uncle's clipper, I've wanted command of one of these pretty ladies. I got lucky. With the steam ships taking over, it won't be long before they're all put to rest.

As I write this, I'm buried in paperwork that I've got to finish before we sail day after tomorrow. I never knew there would be so many details that would require my attention. Writing you has been a pleasant break from that drudgery.

Know that I'm missing you and counting the days until you're in my arms again.

Love,
Will

CHAPTER 31

Two Miles South of the Oregon Trail
30 April 1871

As the new day dawns, it's time to leave Independence. The month in Missouri has been a good one. Magdalena is on better terms with life than she's been since Fritz died. Missing Will terribly even feels like a good sign. She writes him a note most evenings. It feels like he's with her when she does, even though she knows it'll be weeks before they get mailed and maybe even months before he gets them. Falling asleep most nights, she tries to picture him in his captain's uniform standing on his bridge.

Rosa no longer wonders what possessed her to follow the lead of a girl she'd only met weeks earlier. She doesn't feel the need for that question any longer because Rosa has become a part of Buffalo's crew—part of a family. She likes that feeling. Theodor, meanwhile, is growing faster than prairie grass.

Both girls have gotten comfortable with the English language—more precisely, with the cowboy dialect. They can get mad and giggle in cowboy English. Most of their conversations are laced with Buffalo's wisdom. Being able to talk with the boys around the campfire makes all the difference in the world. That's not to say a little German, like one of Papa's proverbs, doesn't still find its way into most conversations. It makes the girls seem wiser than their years.

Today, like every year at the start of a new trip taking people on the Oregon Trail, Buffalo sits on his paint at the head of the train. He is about to guide forty wagons of travelers over 2,000 miles through some rough country in every kind of weather. He begins, as he has every journey for decades, by bellowing, "Wagons west!" The wooden wheels start rolling north for the Oregon trail—just two miles up the road.

This year's train is a little smaller. They've been shrinking that way for the past couple of years. Locomotives are to blame.

As always, this year's line of wagon travelers is a diverse mix of folks. A lot are fresh off the boat. Almost everyone is on a shoestring budget. Over the years, these dream chasers have come from a kaleidoscope of countries. Today, the wagons are mostly driven by Germans, though there's a pair of fiddling Irish brothers, two families of freed slaves, and an assortment of other intrepid souls— most of them looking for 160 nearly free acres in Oregon.

These days, the travelers move along the trail mainly in boats— Prairie Schooners, that is. Long ago, the Conestoga went the way of the dinosaur. A menagerie of critters labor to pull the boats-on-wheels. There are mules, oxen, and horses on every trip. Whether they're snapping leather from the driver's seat or ambling alongside their critters, the people cuss and coax or sing and hum. They'll try anything to keep the animals moving along.

The boss has learned that human nature won't suspend itself over the next two thousand miles. These folks will be together for over four months. On the trail, the wagon master has seen the best and the worst of humanity. He doesn't expect any different on this trip. Buffalo is no fool. He's no do-gooder, either. He's not out to save anyone's soul—just to get them to Oregon.

Buffalo knows the cowboys are going to scuffle and chase

women whenever they stop at a fort or in a town, especially after they've pulled a cork too many times. He's learned the hard way that people—whether in wagons or houses—are going to covet their neighbors' wives, steal, cheat, and even kill. Heading west on wooden wheels doesn't make them better people.

A dog gets one free bite, and a hand under twenty-one is permitted two stupid mistakes. A grown man ought to know how far he can go, so if he steps over the boss's line, he's got to face the consequences. If he breaks Buffalo's rules, he's going to feel The Bison's wrath. For Magdalena, that's not too different than Papa's approach, so she's pretty comfortable with the rules.

Buffalo is in charge. Nothing is written down after that as far as the hierarchy in his organization goes. Clint is the trail boss ramrodding the wranglers who'll take care of Buffalo's 500 cattle. The livestock meanders along behind the train until they're sold off at the forts. Old Clint is about as good as they come at punching cows. He can scout, too, and doubles up on his duties most trips. He's been with Mortimer off and on for a lot of years. Each man has the respect of the other.

After Clint, only the bottom of the wrangler's pole is clear-cut. Sitting right there on the ground is Brett. The kid hails from Cincinnati. His uncle, a friend of Buffalo's, convinced his mother to turn him over to the bison for some growing up. He nearly stumbles over his tongue anywhere within ten yards of Rosa or Magdalena. No matter—the boy possesses a good heart and is learning to cowboy mighty fast. Maybe not fast enough for Buffalo, but his harmonica around the campfire goes a long way with the boss.

One rung up the pole from Brett is Yancey. A couple of years back, he came drifting into Independence looking for work. Buffalo put him through quite an entrance exam and kept a close eye on the bronco buster. He liked what he saw. That was that. He's been in charge of the remuda ever since.

A Long Road There

Mitch manages Buffalo's teamsters. He never has had much to say, even when he was a kid, but has always gotten more done than most. Thin as a reed, but birch hard, the former Union sergeant is *cowboy* handsome. He can handle a wagon as well as any man and better than most. Like a lot of the boys, he's a bachelor. The boss doesn't give a tinker's damn that he was a Yankee soldier. He's a straight shooter. He's been pining lately for a life with roots. He wants to settle down and grow fruit in Oregon one of these days—ideally before his hair is as gray as Buffalo's.

The kitchen had always been old Frenchy's. The tough decades and miles finally caught up with him coming home after last year's trip to Oregon. He and the boys were just two hundred miles out of Independence when he passed on. Buffalo drove a marker into the ground that read: "No better biscuits have a man ever made."

On this trip, Rosa is pretty much on her own, making up chuckwagon rules and recipes as she goes along. She figures out quickly that lots of good-tasting hot coffee goes a long way with the boys. Even before they left Missouri, the fellows could taste that the woman could do more with her larder of beans, bacon, salt pork, flour, salt, and sugar than most trail cooks they'd come across. The crew knows that nobody can do much with jerky and hardtack when and if it comes to that. So, Rosa is way beyond what they expected from day one and a lot better looking than Frenchy. They learn early, though, not to push her. She hits hard with that wooden spoon of hers. The thing that cinched the new cook's place in the cowpokes' hearts was the girl talking the boss into dried fruit and molasses. It wasn't like Buffalo to allow such extravagance. The boss did make sure the cook got plenty of canned milk and baby bottles—just in case Butch rearranges his mealtime to when Mama's supposed to be cooking. In that case, the nearest cowpoke will be lassoed into mothering—something they're proving to be pretty good at.

The culinary facilities are top-shelf. Buffalo didn't spare any expense on the chuck wagon. Besides the interior serving as the storeroom for the provisions, the converted hauler has lots of additions just for the cook. Built across the rear is the pantry—complete with shelves, drawers, and a folding lid. An ingenious foldable lid protects the box's contents when traveling and then drops down to serve as a worktable when cooking. The pot rack, larger skillets, and the Dutch ovens are stored in the *boot* underneath the pantry. Water barrels sit on either exterior side between the wheels, with the rest of the lateral panels hosting hooks for hanging things like the coffee mill and toolboxes. Underneath the wagon is the possum belly—a piece of suspended canvas—for storing firewood or animal chips. Rosa will quickly appreciate it when there isn't any other fuel available for the cook fire. Last but not least, when the weather turns wet, the hands will rig up a *fly*—nine feet of canvas tarp—to keep Rosa and the vittles dry, not to mention the fellows chowing down. Quite a complexity of convenience, the old chuck wagon.

No description of Buffalo's crew would be complete without mentioning Beau. The old cur is indispensable. The cattle mind him, and the horses fear him. The mutt's son Scout is on his first trip, so there's no history on the pup. He's half the size of a horse, but green as a celery stalk.

In the end, Buffalo has put together a fine group of shepherds. Whether it's people or animals they're tending, they take care of their flock and look out for each other.

From the first day on the trail, the people start to learn how best to negotiate the diverse terrain and weather of the storied pathway. Rolling along rain or shine, though, come sunset—dog-tired or not—they must circle the wagons—form a corral. More than a few permutations of this have evolved toward the same end: safety. Under Buffalo's method, the prairie schooners circle end to end, slightly overlapping with their tongues sticking out. There's good reason for all the fussiness. The corral's circumference is a fine imitation of a fort and allows for security and quick hitching for fast getaways when circumstances call for it. Over the years, a lot of trains have been attacked. Granted, the Indians are friendlier these days along the trail, but the bandits aren't. The second thought behind the corral is conviviality. A community begins thriving within it from the first night on the trail. Forming the circle will be second nature to the travelers long before they get to Oregon.

On good days the train finds a comforting rhythm. By sundown, the animals and the people have generally lost the cadence. After chow, especially early on until hides have toughened, bedrolls are full before Rosa and the other cooks have finished cleaning up. As days pass, the people find the energy to visit and sing after supper. The young people usually beat them to it by a few days. Indian leg wrestling, matchstick poker, and mumblety-peg top the nighttime diversions, unless Buffalo has been persuaded to spin a yarn. The kids love the way he can tell a tale. After a few weeks, Magdalena can't be beat in the knife-throwing contests. That only drives the fellows to lose more nickels trying to prove she can.

Some nights the whole train listens to Sean and Shamus fiddle a jig and, more often than not, step one while they're doing it. On nights when everyone feels quiet, the gospel tunes of Moses and Isaiah remind them they have a soul.

There have been a few fistfights and some wagon creeping, like all of Buffalo's troupes, although this group has proven to be as hard-working and congenial as any. The Bison is pleased.

That doesn't mean loneliness can't catch up with him or the hands. The youngest are especially prone to the blues. Four months on the trail is a long time for a kid. But the tears can still catch the boss by surprise, like they did on the night before Fort Kearney. Buffalo rolled a smoke and walked the corral before he turned in— as he does every night. It was well after 11. The day had been a hard one, even for the hands with a whole lot of miles in the saddle. As the boss walked, he was exhaling from his first satisfying draw when he heard a low sobbing. Walking in between the wagons, he'd found Magdalena crying in her bedroll. "What's up, kid?" he'd asked.

"Nothing. I miss my family," she'd said.

"You made a choice, Maggie. Every choosin' has a consequence. You gotta carry that water. You're up to it. Ain't no rule against a nighttime cry or two," Buffalo had said, walking away slowly. He couldn't let the girl know just how much he wanted to comfort her—because he needed her to buck up.

———————

As the train nears Fort Kearney on the Platte River, everyone is ready for a change of routine. The fort is the first major milestone of their trip, though Magdalena can't figure why it's called a fort—it doesn't have a palisade. Still, it's a good stop. The travelers replenish their spirits and supplies, and Buffalo sells some of his cattle.

Leaving the fort without walls, the train travels west up the Platte River Valley and will for quite a while. Like most days since leaving Willenstat, Magdalena pulls Hans's compass from her pocket—just to see what direction she's traveling. Today, it's mostly west-northwest. Satisfied, she watches the brown water meander past them, hoping Clint can find some moving springs and creeks so she doesn't have to drink from the chocolate river. The boss says they'll be traveling along the river for over a hundred miles, so the prospect of Clint not finding good drinking water isn't a pleasant one.

Today, a full week out of Fort Kearney, riding herd with Buffalo has gone well, really. But Magdalena still can't erase the memory of six warriors confronting the boss a ways back. They were demanding a toll of sorts for the train to cross their ancestral lands—ten head of cattle. The warriors were gaunt, but their eyes were hard, nothing like their cousins at Fort Kearney. Armed with every sort of weapon, from knives to rifles, there was no doubt in Magdalena's mind that nonpayment would have dire consequences. She knew

A Long Road There

Buffalo wasn't inclined to bend for anyone. So, as she watched his hand slip over the gun on his hip, her fingers found Fritz's pistol in the possibles bag across her shoulder. It was the second time on her journey she knew she would have shot a man if she had to. Will had saved McGee, and Buffalo tendered eight cattle, which the warriors accepted before vanishing into the hills. The thought of killing a man—even being willing to do it—unsettles her as she watches the prairie grasses blow in the wind.

Not more than a mile farther, still thinking deeply, a familiar and penetrating shiver finds her again. It's the feeling she had as Papa and the German shoreline vanished. It makes her cold, even though the sun warms everything on this expanse of the lonely Nebraska prairie. She knows she's not completely alone anymore. Buffalo is only a stone's throw ahead, but the echoes of Papa asking her not to leave are blowing across the plains and making her sad, not scared like she was that day leaving him behind for the first time—just sad.

Somewhere on the Atlantic Ocean
Between Europe & the Caribbean

The moon's playing peek-a-boo from behind the clouds whipping across the sky. There aren't many stars as the new captain of the *Wind Vagabund* surveys the ship's top deck and the sea beyond. He's glad to finally be sailing on an ocean again. Since returning from New York, the skipper has been reading captain's training manuals, processing cargo and supply paperwork, and supervising a crew getting ready to cast off. He didn't know how hard a captain had to work.

Catching one of the few night stars as it falls, he can't help but imagine Magdalena leaning against the railing like only she could do. Soothed and saddened, he walks below, wishing she were with him.

Virginia Pickett

Alone in his cabin, Will stares at the picture of the four of them that's sitting on his desk. My, that day in New York was one to remember—as happy and sad as they come. Rosa didn't deserve to suffer like she did, he thinks again before focusing on Magdalena. He's glad he insisted they get their photograph taken, freshly reminded of how beautiful his sweetheart is. Putting quill to paper, he begins to try and tell her that.

30 April 1871

My Dearest Magdalena,

We're several days out of Hamburg on our way to the Caribbean to unload cargo. Then, I'm off to Hong Kong. From there, I'll point her to San Francisco, where we'll load and unload before heading around the Horn. It'll be a long trip before I next see the German coast. That'll sure be a welcome sight!

As you know, this has been my dream for some time. I count my lucky stars to have gotten this appointment. The challenge is far more than I ever envisioned, but I'm loving every minute.

The only hole in the dream is your absence. When we talked in New York, we said we'd wait a while before deciding if we want to get back together. I don't need to wait any longer. I know I love you and want to spend the rest of my life with you. Since we stop in San Francisco on the way home, let's plan on meeting there. We'll marry, then sail for home. It'll be wonderful being together again.

Your trip to San Francisco should be easy—only two days by train. I'll write as soon as I know when I'll arrive. It should be no later than September. Please come to me. I know we'll be happy together.

I long to be with you. Even though we're thousands of kilometers apart, we'll soon be together again.

Your loving and devoted Will

CHAPTER 32

Nebraska Prairie
Spring 1871

With light barely beginning to show itself, Buffalo is not yet out of the sack. Meanwhile, wind howls through the valley and thunderheads roll in. Prairie storms aren't any laughing matter. Some of the hands, already awake, are pulling out slickers and cinching up saddles. Clint has gone out ahead, trying to get a feel for what kind of a licking is around the corner. Fighting the wind, Rosa does her best to cook breakfast under the flapping canvas fly.

Getting a good smell of the morning, Buffalo finally wakes and immediately starts barking orders. "Git yur slicker on, Maggie. It won't do ya no good once ya git wet. Grab some of Rosa's biscuits for you and Yancey and hightail it to the remuda. Keep 'em quiet. Sing to 'em. Keep 'em away from the herd."

There is urgency in his voice. Buffalo doesn't shake easily, so Magdalena gets nervous.

"If them critters stampede, you get out of the way right quick, missy. That's an order. You hear me?" Buffalo yells after his young wrangler.

Virginia Pickett

"I will," she hollers into the wind, riding off toward her ponies.

With each thundering crack, the sky becomes more of a bully. The tethered wagon teams are edgy, pulling at their restraints. A mile or so out, the cattle are getting the jitters, too, just like the drovers babysitting them.

Buffalo rides the circumference of the corral and warns his charges of what's coming. "Git yur youngins inside," the boss warns. "Stay within the circle. Soothe yur animals. We're in for a drenchin' Noah himself might take note of."

"Git Butch in the wagon, Rosa. Forget them vittles. Tie everything down!" Buffalo screams into the wind at his cook.

"Brett, git out there and help with the herd, and be careful for God's sake."

"Got it boss," the green kid answers, excited to get an assignment from the headman.

About then, Clint gallops in, shouting. "All hell's 'bout to break loose, boss. I'm goin' back with the herd." Buffalo waves his approval.

With the next explosion of thunder, it seems Beelzebub has escaped his netherworld. The cattle start running crazy. The hands try to steer them to a spot where they can't run anymore. That's deadly business.

Old Buffalo stands firm in the center of his wagons, leaning into the wind, answering the sky's roars with some of his own. "Hold steady! Stay in yur wagons, folks!" he yells. Satan's got nothing on the boss.

The wranglers are trying their best to get their crazed herd into the draw. Somehow, young Brett finds himself on the inside lead—directly in harm's way. When his pony gets horned, they both go down, disappearing beneath a flurry of angry hooves. The hands can see them go under, but they can't help. Brett and his animal won't be cowboying together anymore—not on this earth, anyway.

A Long Road There

When the devil broke loose, the horses and mules started a stampede of their own. Yancey and Magdalena were trying their damnedest to steer them to the same draw the cattle were headed for. With the sideways rain hitting them square in the face, the two lost sight of each other.

As quickly as it broke, the world comes back together. It's still drizzling, but the storm is pretty much spent. The tired cattle mill around in the draw just in front of Yancey's remuda.

With the animals quieted, Yancey notices Magdalena isn't to be seen. Quickly, he starts retracing their stampede route. Not too far back, Yancey finds her lying facedown in the muck just a few feet from her downed pony. After firing two shots into the air, he pulls his unconscious partner out of the mud and waits for help. It doesn't take Clint long to get there. When Magdalena starts to come around, the cowboy talks to her softly. "We thought we'd lost ya. You stay still now," Clint orders.

"What happened?" she asks, blood running down her cheek.

"You got thrown in the stampede. Ol' Buster broke his leg. He's gonna have to be put down," he says, pointing to her horse trying futilely to get up from the mud.

Magdalena gets to her feet and walks to her pony. Reaching in the saddlebag for Fritz's revolver, she turns to the cowpokes. "Then I'll put him down." With tears running down her cheeks, she pats her animal gently and fires.

———

Getting out of the slop that afternoon is exhausting. Most of the folks are still grieving for Brett. It takes them hours of digging, pushing, and cussing to get their prairie schooners free.

By late afternoon, the hands have dug a proper place for Brett to rest. They pound a marker into the damp earth that reads: "A good cowboy that could sure play his harmonica." Buffalo says some words before the talented brothers from the Georgia plantation take up their mouth harps. Moses and Isaiah play the kid home to

Amazing Grace. Before day's end, Buffalo writes to Brett's mama. "Your boy did his job," he pens. "One fitting a man."

That night, somber music fills the circle as the fires flicker down. The wake is mighty sad. Brett was just a kid.

Buffalo sits all alone. The boss can hardly take losing a man anymore.

Rosa and Mitch are holding each other a little closer tonight. They've been a pair around the evening fires for a while now. From the beginning, it seemed like they were two souls waiting to bump into each other. The young mother desperately needed someone to anchor her life, and Theodor needed a father. Mitch was ready for a good woman in his life, one that would help him raise a family and share his dream of growing fruit in Oregon. They found each other. Strange how the stars line up every now and then.

Scout and Magdalena are where they always are—curled up with each other beside the fire. Stroking her pup, she sobs loud enough to be heard. The girl is taking Brett's death mighty hard. Scout tries his best to comfort her. The boss doesn't say anything; he just walks over and pats her shoulder for a while.

As the fire burns lower, just two hands remain seated around it. Staring into the shrinking flames, both young fellows are thinking private thoughts. Separately and together, they consider how easily it could have been them and their ponies, instead of Brett and his, left in the Nebraska soil.

Magdalena is still grinding her teeth on dirt and dust as she crawls under the wagon to get out of the drizzle that has come up out of nowhere. She is filthy all over, but even a sponge bath isn't allowed until Clint finds fresh water again. The kid from Willenstat, who had enjoyed a feather bed and a homemade quilt beside a bedroom hearth, is lonely and tired tonight. Sleep comes easily— no dreams, just a deep uninterrupted absence from the trail.

The previous day's struggles or tragedies don't entitle the sad and weary to a long recovery. Everyone has to wake up with the

A Long Road There

prairie the next day. With Buffalo spurring them on, the train pulls out as the sun gets out of bed. Most days, he allows an hour at noon for the animals to rest. A good day doesn't end until the sun says *uncle*. The boss is a hard man in these regards. He has known good folks that were buried in the snow while trying to cross the Rockies too late in the season, all because their wagon master had been a sympathetic soul earlier in the trip.

Tossing in her bedroll just before the sun's up, Magdalena's trying to find a new piece of soothing ground for the last few minutes before this day begins. It hadn't taken the kid too long before she realized that riding and shooting as well as the men is only a small part of doing her job. Making it from one day to the next is the bigger piece. She's come to learn that rolling across America can be a matter of life and death every day—in some way or another. That's one of the hard facts of life on the Oregon Trail, she thinks, as the rude clang of Rosa's iron triangle rattles her senses awake but no longer stuns her sensibilities.

Sitting up and stretching, she smiles, thinking of Buffalo telling her, "It takes a mighty thick hide, missy, to bear up on the trail." He'd asked her then if she thought she could. Her foolish answer was "Oh, yes, I can." That was before she got a little trail wisdom. Now, she tries not to speak until she knows. Standing full into the morning, she wonders why it is she's come to like this wagon training so much.

CHAPTER 33

Along the South Platte River and Ash Hollow Spring on the
Nebraska Prairie
Late Spring 1871

It's a wide and fickle prairie that stretches across the state of Nebraska. The thing can hold you in its arms and whisper softly in your ear, then swat you down without any warning. So, if any of the folks still think Uncle Sam's invitation to come drive a stake for a few pennies into 160 acres you can call your own is a gift, they won't once they've finished crossing the prairie or started farming the piece for that matter.

Magdalena's favorite times are riding herd with Buffalo. Gazing at the landscape and thinking is food for the soul. But she doesn't mind the interruption whenever the boss starts spinning a tale of the old West and wagon training when it was hard. She tries to get him talking as often as she can.

By now, the Platte River has split. The train follows the south fork for a spell before crossing and heading mostly west. The stream looks mighty peaceful. "Is this the river they say is so dangerous?" Magdalena asks, gazing out on the lazy water.

"Don't look like it, does it?"

"No, it's almost putting me to sleep."

"It won't when you're crossin' it."

After making an early camp, Buffalo has everyone working on their boats the rest of the day. Beds are jacked up for blocks to be placed underneath, so the bottoms are as high as the wheels. Watching the boss check the work from wagon to wagon in the last of the daylight, Magdalena knows he's nervous, which doesn't do much for her tummy.

After dinner, by the light of the quickly fading cook fire, Magdalena decides it's past time to write Grandma Brohmann. She hasn't been ready until now.

24 May 1871

Dear Grandma,

I'm somewhere in a place called Nebraska, working as a wagon driver making my way toward Colorado. Many German-speaking people and others from all over Europe are in this train of wagons, trying to get to a place called Oregon. There, for almost nothing, the American government will sell each of them 160 acres to farm. We've been moving across an immense prairie following a river called the Platte for over a month.

As usual, you were right in telling me that I had no idea what I was getting myself into. Now, I know that. I have grown up some, Grandma. I really have. I had no choice.

I love you so much,

Magdalena

By daybreak, Clint and a couple of riders are already out in the middle of the river. They're marking a fording alley.

Not much later, it's time to cross. The folks will go one at a time on Buffalo's command. Today, Mitch is driving the chuck wagon across first, with Rosa and Theodor sitting right beside him. He has made the treacherous trip more times than he cares to remember. But this time is different. His sweetheart and her boy are along with him. He's scared, and he doesn't scare easy. The cowboy sure wants to get to Oregon. Growing fruit and raising a family sounds better to him now than it ever has. At the bank, he snaps the reins to get his animals into the water.

A rider out ahead with a lead on Mitch's mules is there to help the critters stay in the alley or pull them if they get frightened enough to consider stopping. A second rider is positioned downstream with a whip as an insurance policy to keep the team moving. Stopping mid-stream is a driver's worst nightmare. A loaded wagon sinks mighty quick. And people inside can panic quicker. The South Platte is known for its quicksand bottom. It has swallowed more than a few wagons, along with their passengers, over the years.

Despite the chilly morning air, Mitch sweats the whole way across until he has his wagon safely on the other side. Magdalena and Scout are next into the water. She reads her boss pretty well, so this truly "ain't no laughin' matter" as he told her earlier. The man hasn't managed a smile since before supper last night.

Nobody questions her skill or mettle. Still, her stomach is in her throat when her front wheels hit the water. With the beds jacked up, the wagon is top-heavy and has a whole different feel—riding like it'll tip over sideways with the least little breeze or jolt. Magdalena knows she's got a fair piece of work ahead of her, so she starts doing what she does best—talking to her animals. Clint flashes her a big smile as her front wheels come out of the water, before ordering, "Start forming the corral with Mitch, then take care of yur mules and git on back here with your pony."

One by one, the wagons continue fording. Buffalo and Clint cuss and coax each one across. Nothing appears different as Josef Karlsson guides his oxen into the chocolate water. His wife, Agnes,

214

and four children are peeking out of the back of the wagon. About a third of the way across, one of the younger boys pokes his head out of the canvas bonnet—right as the wagon lurches. The kid is suddenly in the river, thrashing to keep his head above water, but not succeeding at it. Clint is on his mount, Frosty, and after him before the boy's mother can start screaming, but not before Beau.

Mrs. Karlsson is frantic. Her husband can't stop, or three more of his kids might be joining their brother. "Somebody save my son! He can't swim. Help him, please!" his father frantically pleads.

"Keep them oxen movin', Josef. Yur doin' just fine. We'll git yur boy!" the boss shouts from shore.

Beau is first to the flailing lad. Before he can latch onto him, the kid starts sinking like a rock toward the quicksand bottom. Beau dives after him, leaving only agonizingly quiet water behind. Everybody is praying—then cheering when old Beau breaks the surface with the boy in his mouth. Clint has the youngster on his saddle right quick after that. The kid spits up a good share of the South Platte by the time they reach the other side. The boy's mother is thanking God before her son is off of Clint's horse.

Magdalena is the only one still watching Beau. He's struggling to get to shore and losing the battle. Her first toss of the lasso doesn't hit its mark. The second does. As it slides over Beau's head, Magdalena starts pulling.

Beau's not moving when he hits the bank. Pumping on his ribcage, Magdalena demands, "Spit it up. Come on, Beau, don't ya give up now. Ya still gotta lot of things ta teach Scout. You ain't done by a long shot. Come on, Beau."

About then, Clint snatches the dog up by his hind legs and shakes him. Beau starts to spit up a little South Platte himself—to a second round of cheers. The mutt is on all fours pretty quick after that. Magdalena bear-hugs him while Scout licks his face.

———

With the fires burning low inside that evening's corral, the boss is smiling now. He couldn't shake the grin off his face if he tried. He's got the same number of people, wagons, and animals he had this morning. The South Platte didn't get one of them. So, along with everybody else, he's clapping, toe-tapping, and singing to Isaiah and Moses's revival rhythms.

Magdalena is lost in the night sky. She watches falling stars, mighty grateful to be sitting next to the fire in one piece on the north side of the South Platte.

———

There's sweet water ahead in Ash Hollow spring. The Plains Indians have relied on the moving creek for survival long before there was an Oregon Trail. The trouble is there's a small mountain between the train and the stream. Windlass Hill isn't the Rockies, but the outcropping will test the mettle of Buffalo's folks yet again.

The order of the wagons to the summit is no different than when they crossed the South Platte. On the boss's command, Mitch starts his mules climbing. The path the wagon trains have carved over the past thirty-odd years is narrow and rocky.

Rosa is out of breath trudging toward the peak with the other walkers. Theodor is a load. Only drivers, the old, and the sick ride. The cattle and the horses blaze their own trail to the top. They don't need much prodding. The animals can smell the hollow on the other side of the mountain.

Sitting in the driver's seat of Rosa's chuckwagon, the Willenstater is up next. Magdalena snaps the reins and hollers, "Giddy up." Before long, the mules are straining hard. They're as sure-footed on this loose dirt and rocks as there is. Magdalena tries to steer the team clear of the biggest boulders. Even that's not an easy job. Her wheels are cracking, creaking, and clunking over the sandstone opposition like they're going to snap at any time. Magdalena winces, then exhales every time they don't. There's no slowing down though—gravity might get the best of her and her rig. The young fraülein is cajoling her mules in English and German with

A Long Road There

her fingers crossed—all the way up.

At the top, their climb feels worth it. There's no view quite like the ones that haven't been messed with much by people. The panorama is unlike anything she's seen so far. Ragged stone outcroppings emerge from rugged hills, all dotted beautifully with scrub cedars and pines about as far as the eye can see. Taking it in full circle, Magdalena ends up looking at the hill she has to go down. That's not a comforting prospect.

———

Buffalo has ordered everyone to tie down their wagon contents; that way, things don't go flying out during the descent. But the drivers won't be tied down. The wagons' brakes won't be of much help in restraining the prairie boats on the way down. A runaway is a mighty dangerous thing. Neither the people in the wagon nor those already at the bottom are safe. Still, there's not much choice about getting off the top of this hill.

The boss's remedy is pretty simple. For those wagons with mule teams, the crew uses lots of rope and manpower. Two lines are fastened to either side of the wagon's rear axle. Several men take hold of each, and the tug-a-war with gravity starts as the wagon is eased down the hill. Sounds easy. It ain't, as Buffalo told every one of his drivers.

The schooners pulled by oxen don't use as much human muscle. Instead, only the wheel pair of the burdened beasts is harnessed to the front of the wagon. The rest of the oxen are hitched to the rear—facing the wagon. Not liking their new spot, the 1,500 pounders tend to protest. This makes a pretty fair braking system.

———

A broken wheel is about the only casualty of the day. That's a fixable problem.

Safe on flat ground, the boss chooses a fine camping spot. He's smiling like everyone else. They'll be staying an extra day beside the spring. He wants everyone to recover from their brawl with gravity. Fort Laramie is a tough 150 miles up the road.

"The rest will do 'em good," Buffalo whispers, wondering if maybe he's getting too soft to do this job. His stomach has been in his throat for a day and a half. Listening to Moses and Isaiah's fine gospel music puts him at ease but doesn't answer his question.

CHAPTER 34

Fort Laramie, Wyoming
June 1871

After their rest, the terrain starts changing. Unlike the Platte River Valley, the ground is uneven and rocky. The long, lush grasses of Missouri and eastern Nebraska give way to shorter, stubbier growth. Scruffy junipers and pines dot the landscape as the wagons bump along. Before they say goodbye to Nebraska, off in the distance the rocks are starting to look like things. They were christened way back when the Trail was young. There's a Court House and a Chimney before Scott's Bluff, where legend has it pioneers left an ailing comrade behind to die. On a quiet night, some say you can still hear his lost ghost roaming the hills.

As she watches Rosa and Theodor bounce next to Mitch, Magdalena misses their close relationship. There's a new trio of Musketeers now. She's learning that parting ways doesn't always mean a death. For the first twenty years of her life, that was the only way she became separated from dear friends and loved ones. She'd always struggled with a passing—kicking and screaming against accepting it. First her brother Kurt, then Grandpa Brohmann, and finally, as if losing those two weren't enough, Fritz. But since leaving home, she's been dealing with partings of a different kind— Magdalena and her friends coming to the "Y" in the road and traveling different paths. It seems like that's been happening a lot these past several months of her journey. She's not sure this new kind of parting hurts any less.

Both Buffalo and Rosa have been begging her to stay on with the train all the way to Oregon. "You can get a new start with Mitch and me," Rosa had said.

"I'd be proud to have you work permanent or until you get hitched," Buffalo had told her.

She's still set on catching the stage to Cheyenne with Scout, just like she'd told Buffalo the morning after she took the job. He thought it was a crazy idea then and still does. "You're chasing after a ghost, kid," he told her. "That ain't too smart. That soldier is dead. If you don't wanna work for me, you outta marry that sailor. I don't like seamen, but the swabbie has gotta be better than a phantom."

Inside Fort Laramie, Rosa and Mitch start a new life together. The wedding ceremony at the little military chapel is short but moving. Rosa makes a beautiful bride. That night, inside the wagon circle, the reception gets trail raucous. The cowpokes aren't going to let Mitch and Rosa get hitched without a shindig to remember. The folks in the train are ready to celebrate right alongside Buffalo's boys. The fiddling Irish brothers join Moses and Isaiah to make music that has everyone gliding to waltzes and high-stepping to sprightlier tunes until the wee morning hours. Even the old bison proves nimble on his feet. You would have thought he was a captain in the Confederate army again, watching him and Magdalena waltz around the corral as if they were at a Dixie cotillion.

Magdalena is done in when she crawls into her bedroll, but the darn sandman won't come to visit. Counting cows isn't working either, so she starts mulling these past few weeks since Brett's death.

A Long Road There

Not much has changed since that night she spent crying over her pal. Tonight, everything has a rose-colored hue. Watching the people laugh and dance, she was convinced that no one who had made it this far could possibly have the same outlook on life as when they first snapped the reins in Independence. This evening, celebrating with Rosa and Mitch, it seemed to her like almost everyone was counting and finding mostly blessings, not burdens.

She still can't come to terms with life's strange reversals. She'd sat next to Rosa not three months ago when the neighborhood toughie told Will, "The old man's dead." It seemed to her then that hope was a galaxy away for Rosa. Tonight, her friend is a bride beaming with happiness, heading for a Shangri-La to grow fruit with her new husband and baby boy.

Magdalena turns over and pulls the cover back that Scout had confiscated. She's cheered knowing how difficult it is to wrestle the human spirit to the ground and keep it there.

The next morning, the wagon train has nearly rolled out of sight when the stage to Cheyenne is finally ready to pull out of the fort. Buffalo stands next to Magdalena with his reins in his hand. "You can stay on, kid," he says, hugging her hard enough to show that he means it. Still, Magdalena steps aboard.

Riding hard to catch up with his wagon train, the boss makes a decision that's been a long time coming. He'll get these folks the rest of the way to Oregon, but this will be the last time he delivers anybody to the end of the famous trail. Over more years than he'd like to count, a whole lot of dreams have come true because he's seen each trip through to the end. His Texas stubborn streak was partly responsible for that. Now, the world is passing him by, and he knows it. So after Oregon, he'll point his horse toward Montana. Maybe he and Clint can finally start that ranch they've been thinking on all these years.

Looking back as the fort slips out of sight, Rosa's lip starts to quiver. She feels a little like a traitor for leaving Magdalena behind. They've forded a lot of rivers together in a short time. Whenever Rosa fell out of the wagon, Magdalena always managed to pull her back inside. Rosa chuckles at herself for thinking so deeply in cowboy metaphors but doing so makes her feel good—a little like she's going home to Oregon, not going there for the first time.

"This won't be the last time I'm gonna see that woman," she pledges, loud enough to be heard.

"What was that, honey?" Mitch asks, coming back from his own thoughts.

"Nothing, sweetheart. Just makin' a promise to myself."

A mile or so up the road, Rosa reaches into her travel bag and pulls out the picture of her with Will and Magdalena in the New York photo shop. Happy tears fill her eyes. Not too far down the trail, she puts the keepsake back inside the new leather suitcase her fellow travelers gifted her. The folks on the wagon train knew the bride's bag was plumb tuckered.

It's hard to beat the odds. Maybe Rosa has.

Bumping along in the coach toward Cheyenne, Magdalena is glad she and Rosa hadn't tried to take a stagecoach west. It's hot, dusty, and uncomfortable. At least Scout gets to ride up top in the fresh air where he can keep watch. She thanks heaven that Buffalo was able to talk the coach dispatcher into letting her dog on board.

Magdalena is sharing a bench with two very large men, both smoking cigars. Being next to the window helps a little. Leaning against the frame, she closes her eyes, hoping no one will intrude on her thoughts as she shepherds them to Will and their last wonderful afternoon together in New York.

They were down by the harbor, holding hands, both completely at ease. Like a kid at a candy store, he was pointing out vessels, describing their smallest details. She knew then that the captain's real sweethearts were the clippers—the sleek ships with so many masts. Tough competition, she'd thought at the time.

Looking out on the tumbleweed landscape dotted with antelope, she wonders if she should have married Will right then. He would have made room for her and the clippers.

Somewhere during the stagecoach trip, she comes to a decision. She's going to ask Will to meet her in San Francisco when he stops there on his way back from the Orient. Being a captain's wife sounds pretty good, even if her husband's mistress is the sea.

———

After a lot of bumps, the stage rolls into Cheyenne. The kid and her dog are stuck with Grandpa's oversized trunk again. Starting to drag it toward the train station, a Cheyenne cowboy about her age drives up in an empty wagon.

"Where ya headed with that thing, ma'am?"

"To the train station."

"That'll be a mighty long block," he says, hopping down and throwing her trunk in the back. "Jump on up. I'll run ya over."

It's a heavy trunk. The cowpoke seems gracious enough, and it's only a block, so when Scout gives him the okay after a sniff or two, she climbs aboard.

"Thank you so much," she says as the cowpoke hauls her trunk inside the depot door.

"No trouble at all, ma'am," he says, tipping his hat and moseying on his way.

"Such nice people out West," she says to herself, smiling. Stepping up to buy a train ticket to Golden, Colorado, she realizes the visored old ticket clerk likely isn't one of them. He's not about to let Scout on board—baggage or otherwise.

"That's against the rules, lady. Thirty pounds or under—reads right here, ma'am," he says, handing Magdalena an underlined page on railroad pet policy.

223

Virginia Pickett

Since Buffalo isn't here to talk him into letting the pooch on board, Magdalena has to get her pal a seat. Thinking on her feet, she pulls Lord Rutherford's card from her possibles bag and displays it prominently. She smiles, with unmistakable insincerity, making sure the old buzzard knows he's about to get put in a vice.

Resurrecting some of the ten-dollar words she'd heard her three royal friends toss around, she begins to turn the handle. "I'm expected to be in Central City, with my dog, today. If that isn't possible, I'll have to wire my benefactor, Lord Rutherford, the Marquess of Derbyshire, at his brother's estate in New York. His brother is a major stockholder in your railroad. Both will be quite upset that Scout wasn't allowed on board. Lord Rutherford is a hopeless lover of animals. I'll wire him now to see what he suggests. What was your name?" she asks, twisting the vice tighter as she turns to head for the Western Union office across the way.

"Wait, lady. I'm an animal lover myself. How 'bout we let the pup go as baggage?" the compromised bureaucrat suggests, obviously willing to stretch railroad policy when necessary.

Magdalena supervises the loading of her luggage—tail wagging piece and all. Scout is not pleased about being tethered, but accepts his fate when Magdalena gives him the bone she had saved from last night's steak dinner, along with a bowl of water. The bowl is courtesy of the now eager-to-please baggage attendant. Lord Rutherford certainly would have gotten a good chuckle at his protégé's arm-twisting—had he been around to see it.

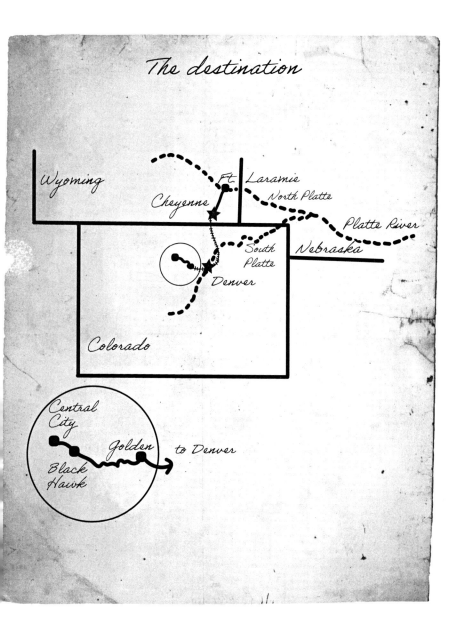

PART THREE/TEIL DREI

CHAPTER 35

Colorado
Late June 1871

When the porter makes his call for Golden, Colorado, Magdalena thinks he has made a mistake. The 130 miles from Cheyenne went by quickly, watching the spectacular landscape change with the ever-ascending mountains.

The depot is unremarkable, other than the beautiful snow-capped backdrop, as she steps foot in Colorado for the first time. She's anxious to get Scout. He's raring to go when the baggage-car door slides open, so much so that his leash slips free before the attendant can get to it. Magdalena is quick enough to avoid a collision with the eighty-pound missile. A reassuring tussle is enough to convince the pup that he's liberated—no strings attached.

Staring at Grandpa's trunk on the ground in front of her once again, Magdalena sighs. "We're almost there, Scout." He has heard that before, so the pup is smart enough not to get too excited.

Sitting on the trunk while taking in her situation, Magdalena can't help but reflect for a moment. "If you're watching, Fritz, you can see we're just a climb up the mountain away. I wish you were here to make it with us," she says, talking loud enough for the soldier to hear her.

227

A brakeman looks over his shoulder at her, wondering if Magdalena is all there. She's wondering the same thing as she gets ready to go into the station.

"We're not quitting now, are we?" she asks her four-legged traveling partner. Inside, they step into the ticket line behind a lady that looks like she's ready to do just that.

"Ain't no track to the top, ma'am," the clerk says to Magdalena after tending to the tattered spirit of the woman in front of her. "There's a stage, though. It should be along in three or four hours," the pleasant clerk adds. "Ol' Stan's outside right now. He's heading up the mountain as soon as he's loaded. You might see about hitching on with him. He'd probably enjoy the company."

"Excuse me," Magdalena says in English with only a slight German accent, interrupting an older gentleman's loading. "Are you Stan? The clerk said you might like some company up the mountain."

"Sure, I'll give a Deutschlander a ride any time," Stan says, recognizing a countryman when he hears one. "Is that your mutt?" he asks.

"Yes, that's Scout."

"Well, he's welcome, too. I just lost my own dog a couple weeks back. The ride is gonna cost you, though."

"How much?" Magdalena asks, suspecting Stan's got himself a pretty profitable partnership going with the railroad clerk.

"A lot. You'll be stuck listening to me blabber the whole way," he says, laughing at his own humor.

Three and half hours is a long time to wait, and Stan seems like a nice man—a nice German man, to boot. Grandpa's trunk isn't going to carry itself up the mountain. She's got Fritz's pistol in her possibles bag, and Scout's wagging his tail, so she jumps on up, satisfied Stan has cleared her version of a security check.

"I'm Magdalena Mok," she says as Stan sits down in the driver's seat. "Some people call me Maggie. That's fine by me," she adds.

"Maggie works for me," Stan says, already comfortable with the new handle. "Gerhardt Stanhauer. That's a big mouthful, too, ain't it? Just call me Stan."

"Stan it is," his rider agrees, thinking someone must be watching over her as she tells Scout to lie down on top of the load.

It doesn't take long for Scout to squeeze in between the old German and Magdalena. When she starts to shoo him back, the driver asks that she let her pup stay. "Like I said, lost my pooch a few weeks back. He and I hauled supplies between Denver and Central City for a lot of years. That's back when the stampede of people would trample you if you weren't careful," the driver says.

"Was Central City much different then?" Magdalena asks, hoping the old-timer will tell her the story behind the place at the mountaintop.

"You can bet on it," he says, warming to his yarn. "Back in '59, Mr. John Gregory—knew him personal I did—struck the yellow stuff on up the gulch. Some say there was no richer strike on earth than the mile between Central City and Black Hawk. Two towns sittin' on either end of the strike—bookendin' the gold, you might say. Wasn't long before we had 30,000 folks digging in these parts. 'Gregory's Diggings' they started calling the place. Like I say, largest lode in the west for a while. Things are settled quite a bit now. We got churches and schools. Now that's not to say there ain't any gold left. A few thousand folks think there is. Yeah, those were the days, kid," he finishes, urging his team on up the hill.

You could have heard a pin drop during Stan's story. Magdalena sat spellbound, imagining the glory of this city she had been seeking for so long.

"What about you, young lady? What in tarnation is a kid like you doing in Colorado by yourself? I can tell you ain't no prospector 'cause you ain't got the fever," the driver says, sizing her up.

Stan can't help making Magdalena feel at ease—that's his

229

nature. He's not a young man. The passenger suspects he's getting close to sixty, though the twinkle in his eye lets her know there's still a lot of youth inside him.

Her story has been told so many times since Hamburg, Magdalena is starting to feel like the narrator of someone else's tale. So, whether it's the warm feeling Stan gives her or that she just needs to talk to someone, she can't say. Either way, she starts telling him her story.

"If I were looking for gold, then my coming here would make more sense than it does. I'm not, so most folks at home thought I'd lost my mind when I said I was coming ahead to Colorado after my fiancé was killed. I'd lost a brother earlier in protests and then a sweetheart in the war. Not long after that, my dog Max got killed protecting me from a wild cat. That's when I got it in my head that coming out here was the only way I could sort things out. Sounds stupid, I know, but that's how it was. Then, I met a wonderful young officer on the ship. In New York, he asked me to marry him. I was still bound and determined to take a wagon train to Colorado, and he had just been appointed to captain a real clipper ship—like he'd dreamed of all of his life. We decided to wait. I'm gonna marry him as soon as he gets back to America from the Orient. He doesn't know that yet, but I am."

"Don't sound so stupid to me. Broken hearts cause people to do some mighty strange things. Falling in love again never hurt nobody."

"Thanks. My family all thought I was crazy. I'm beginning to wonder myself."

"Well, now, both make sense—if you think about it. I'm sure they didn't want you to leave, 'specially on your own. As far as you being skeptical of your bearings, I s'pose when a body gets to looking back on things, they sometimes don't seem as reasonable as they once did."

"Thanks. I hope you're right. I do miss my family, though,"

A Long Road There

Magdalena adds, staring off into the distance. "I'm only going to stay a few weeks in Central City, until it's time to meet Will. He's the officer I'm going to marry. We'll be living in Hamburg, so I'll see my family often. While I'm here, I wanna look up my dead fiancé's uncle, Hermann Strasse. He's sorta expecting me. Maybe you know him."

"He took off some four months ago," Stan says apologetically. "He got the fever real bad again. Just up and left, headed for Nevada."

Four months ago when she boarded the ship, that news would have devastated Magdalena. Today, it feels almost irrelevant to her life. Things are so different now. Last November, she had taken her pen in hand to write to the only person that she thought could bless her heady and confused quest. Her world had been a mess.

Yup, things have changed a whole lot for me since then, she thinks, before suggesting matter-of-factly, "This gold fever must really take hold of a person."

"Ain't nothing worse," Stan confirms. "So ya came across by wagon. Not many folks left that'll try that. I s'pose anybody that's done it won't ever forget it.

"Me and the missus and our boy came across in '58. Gunner and his ma came over on the boat with us. Somehow, we all ended up on the same wagon train. A lotta water over the dam since then. We lost the boy to smallpox in '59. He wasn't but ten. Gunner lost his ma to cholera that next spring. We sorta been a family to each other since then," the driver finishes, getting a little misty-eyed.

"Sounds like you had it pretty tough," Magdalena remarks.

"No more than most, kid."

"I won't forget my trip across, that's for sure. My friend Rosa and I worked all the way for a man named Buffalo Simmons. His real name was Mortimer."

"Well, I'll be—Buffalo Simmons, if that don't beat all! He ran the very train we crossed on. Quite a cowboy."

"He sure is. He believed in Rosa and me enough to give us jobs. I learned so much from him—not just about driving a wagon, but how to handle life."

"So, you can drive a wagon, huh?"

"I sure can. Have been since I was twelve or thirteen. My grandpa taught me."

For the next few miles, the old teamster and young woman turn quiet, digesting all that's been said. Then, Stan says, "If you're fixing to stay a few weeks, I could use a driver. I do hauling, includin' mining equipment. Right now, I've got work up to my eyeballs. Can't handle it all by myself. I'm havin' trouble finding anybody to help me. Most are headed for Nevada. Those that didn't are digging in the dirt here—all excited about hitting a big strike again," he adds, shaking his head at human nature.

"I could use a job. I've gotta wait until I hear back from Will, so I'll be here until I do."

"That's fair. I won't plan on you definite for too long, but I sure could use you right now."

"It's a deal," the new driver says, extending her hand.

Neither one of them knows the other from Adam, but both have the same good feeling about the person sitting next to them. Stan, like Buffalo, has been following his nose concerning people for a long time now. And he's done pretty well doing it—just like the old bison. Magdalena doesn't have as much experience as Stan or Buffalo, but her intuition has served her well, considering her limited practice at using it.

Farther up the road, Stan asks, "Where ya planning on staying tonight?"

"If you could drop me at a hotel, that'd be fine."

"Well, I'll tell you what, if you don't mind roughing it a little, we've got a room off the barn. It's got a bed and such, not fancy, but a place to throw down. You're welcome to it. I usually give wages, plus room and board to my driver, anyways."

A Long Road There

After spending the last three months sleeping under the wagon or beneath a starry sky, a soft mattress with a roof over her head sounds plenty inviting. "Okay, that suits me just fine," she lets him know.

"You'll like the missus. Marta can cook, leastwise most folks around here think she can. She'll remind ya a little of home. Whenever I get to missin' Berlin, she rustles me up a schnitzel."

"*Wunderbar!*" Magdalena shouts, amazed again at just how lucky she seems to be.

Scout starts to bark when it suddenly gets foggy. "Easy boy, them's just clouds," Stan reassures the pup. "We'll be up above 'em shortly. 'Pert near 9,000 feet in spots, old Central City is, kid."

"Wow, above the clouds," Magdalena says, feeling a little like she's ascending into the heavens.

"Giddy up there, now," Stan encourages his mules, as they struggle with a hairpin turn. Then, just as the animals manage the pull, right before Magdalena's eyes is the same brilliant blue sky they'd just left behind.

Marta's dinner that night does remind Magdalena of Mama's and almost everything else she's left behind. Marta could have been Mama's sister. She works with no complaints and enjoys watching folks eat. Magdalena can tell the couple loves each other, not because of what they say, but more because they know what each other is thinking. They seem glad to do something for their partner before being asked.

After dinner, Stan shows Magdalena her room. While unpacking and getting ready for bed next door to Stan's four-legged workers, she starts talking about her journey with Scout. "Well, boy, we finally made it. I guess I've traveled just about every possible way a person can. You weren't on the boat. That didn't really seem like traveling as much as visiting other worlds. Trains—I suppose they're about the same anywhere. You're from Independence, so you probably knew a little more about what we were getting ourselves into taking a wagon train. Maybe you didn't get lonely, having your dad along. I did, especially that first month or so. After that, I felt like America and I were getting to know each other. Your homeland is quite a place, Scout. I couldn't have done it without you.

"Time to hit the sack. We start a new job tomorrow, and we don't want to be late."

CHAPTER 36

Central City, Colorado
Late June 1871

The next morning, Magdalena and Scout sit on the porch steps jutting from the kitchen door, waiting for breakfast. "Come on in here," Marta tells them. "Make yourself at home. Food's just about ready."

The group soon sits down to a wonderfully hearty meal. Scraping his plate like he might find more bacon and eggs, Stan winks at his wife of thirty-five years and teases, "There's no better food in the city. Delicious. She's still the best-lookin' gal in these parts, don't ya think, kid?"

"Stan, you're embarrassing the girl," Marta says, turning red.

"Ya can't hide from the truth, honey."

"Get outta here, you old soft-soaper. Ya ain't getting any cake until lunch, no matter what," the cook scolds, putting a battered plate of scraps on the floor for Scout. It's a hand-me-down. Marta hasn't used it since Kaiser passed.

"The team is already hitched, Stan. I figured you'd want to get going right away," Magdalena cuts in, shining the apple on her first day of work.

235

Virginia Pickett

"Well, I'll be. I don't remember the last time I had a hired hand do something without bein' told. Let's get going."

Most folks aren't yet awake as the pair starts through town. Except for the breakfast diner, the businesses are all asleep too. The saloons, and there's a lot of them, won't get up until after noon. The few people out of bed all seem to know the boss—each waving and hollering *hello*. When two rugged-looking miners come out of the café, Stan tries to avoid their gaze, knowing he's going to get the business for the pretty young driver sitting next to him. One of the miners whistles loud enough to attract attention, and the other yells out, "Hey, Stan, moving up the quality of your drivers?" The old German just laughs, thinking *you're damn right*. Magdalena blushes and gives the reins a stiff flick, trying to hurry the wagon along the road.

"Make a left just past that rock up there. You can see the Breton operation soon as ya turn," the boss says, pointing up ahead.

Pulling into the property, they're greeted by a man fit to be tied. "Stan, it's about time you got that equipment up here. What in the hell took you so long?"

"Now, don't go gettin' all riled up and puttin' the blame on me, Ewen. I can't get it here any faster than they get it to Golden, and you damn well know that. It came in on the train yesterday afternoon, along with my new driver, Maggie," Stan says, pointing to his good-looking new addition.

Spit-smoothing his hair, the miner is down off the porch in nothing flat, extending his hand like a gentleman. "Name's Ewen Pembroke. I'm the Breton foreman. I'll get a couple of fellas to help ya unload," he adds, all smiles now.

"Git on inside, you ol' sandbagger. You ain't been this sweet to a driver yur whole damn life," the German says, shooing Pembroke back into the building like an angry wife with a broom. "There's paperwork that needs to be done," Stan says, giving the miner a mock kick in the pants.

236

A Long Road There

"Nice to meet you!" the foreman yells back, undeterred, as he disappears into his office.

The two dock men that come out of the warehouse are tongue-tied when they lay eyes on the new driver. They move a lot quicker than if Stan had been in the wagon alone. Magdalena never lifts a finger.

After that first day, Magdalena mostly unloads her own wagon. The miners all quickly fall back to old habits. Truth be told, they enjoy watching her move more than helping her out. Right off, Stan begins sending the kid solo whenever he thinks he might be in for a bawling out. Magdalena seldom gets the going over the boss would have taken, but she quickly learns to give as good as she gets.

CHAPTER 37

Stan and Marta's Place
Summer 1871

After a week or so of twelve-hour workdays, Magdalena starts stopping by the post office every day. She knows it's too early to hear from Will again, but she gets excited pretending she might.

"You've got something today, Mr. Reynolds. I can feel it," Magdalena says as she strides into the post office for the seventh day in a row, slamming the door behind her. This afternoon, the postmaster only smiles and nods his head. He likes the kid, despite the danger she poses to his door.

"I do have your letter. Good thing, because my door won't last much longer."

"Oh, thanks so much, Mr. Reynolds," Magdalena says, grabbing her letter and gliding out the door. The letter, however, is from Papa and postmarked over three months ago. Even though it's not from Will, she's excited to get news from home. Sitting in the old rocking chair on the wooden sidewalk outside Stan's delivery service, she starts to read.

Magdalena,

I'd prayed you would change your mind when I blew the candle out the night before you left on the boat. You know the hole in my heart is large, but I know how much you love all of us, so it will heal. This will always be your home—always—whether you are here with us or any place else on God's good earth. I am with you always, wherever you are.

Love,
Papa

Tears are streaming down Magdalena's cheeks as she strokes her sidekick, who has been gnawing on an old bone that had been lying by the rocker. He doesn't understand why she's sobbing. Magdalena explains, "Papa's blessing and forgiveness have made me happy enough to cry, boy. I wish you knew him. You'd love him as much as I do."

On her twenty-first day in town and her fourteenth day in a row bothering the postmaster, the civil servant is finally able to hand Magdalena the letter she's been yearning for. She hugs old Mr. Reynolds, then skins her mules all the way home.

The letter was dated 30 April 1871—the same day she left Independence over three months ago. Will had to have written it before he'd received her letter telling him she was coming to San Francisco. *"My Dearest Magdalena,"* it begins. Will wants her to come to San Francisco. He'll be there by late September and will wire her at once.

When she gives Stan and Marta the good news, it proves infectious. Everyone starts dancing around the kitchen table. Even Gunner, who's sharing dinner that night with the family—as he does most evenings—starts stepping a jig. The powerful miner's fancy footwork is an odd sight.

As Stan had told Magdalena, Gunner had come to Central City with his mom in '58. By chance, Stan, Marta, and their boy were on the same boat and wagon train. When Magdalena met him at dinner her first night in town, he didn't seem old or young. Watching him dance triggers her curiosity. She's guessing he's somewhere between Uncle Rudolph and Cousin Heinrich's age—thirty-five or six, maybe. He's not what most folks would term handsome, but he certainly isn't homely, either. His large gray eyes are wide-set in his broad face. She's always thought that his auburn hair looked like it'd just been mussed, even after Marta had corralled him for a haircut. He doesn't stand much taller or shorter than most men but seems more powerful. Not chiseled-strong, but boulder-like. Stan's told her he's a jack-of-all-trades; best plasterer in the area, he'd bragged.

Still puzzled after her appraisal, Magdalena pauses before the light comes on. "*Vertrauenswürdig*—trustworthy—that's how he looks," she whispers.

As Marta shuffles the cards, Magdalena is still thinking on her canasta partner. He doesn't seem to have any real plans other than striking it rich—which even he doesn't see as a serious possibility. One day at a time—that's how he takes it. Letting her mind travel down this track a little further, she muses that maybe he's not too different than Papa. Anyway, he makes her feel mighty comfortable; Magdalena decides she's glad to have him as her friend. All these fine characteristics don't seem to be helping us get better cards— that's a shame, Magdalena thinks.

The next day, her three Central City friends seem glum. The girl has gotten into all of their hearts. The thought of her leaving for San Francisco in a month saddens her three pals.

The kid can't wait. She is so excited that it's hard for her to concentrate. The girl works every day when Stan needs her, which means almost every day, and then fishes with the men on Sundays. She has trouble baiting her hook and telling the fellows about all her plans at the same time. "My wedding dress will be simple. We'll have a church wedding with organ music," she tells them. Gunner is happy to help her with her hook as she rambles on. He sure doesn't want the kid to leave, but if that's what'll make her happy, he's okay with it.

So, the days pass, and the happy hummingbird doesn't tire. She's in love again.

Willenstat, Württemberg, Germany
August 1871

On a particularly hot, early-August day for the Kingdom of Württemberg, Mama receives the letter to Grandma Brohmann which Magdalena had written two months earlier. Carefully reading her daughter's words several times over, Alexandria begins to cry. She's proud of her daughter and terribly sad her mother isn't here to read Magdalena's words. She had died several weeks back.

CHAPTER 38

Pacific Ocean Between Hawaii and San Francisco
Late Summer 1871

On deck, watching the sea, Will thinks about his first voyage in command, feeling like he's on top of the world. Captaining the *Wind Vagabund* has been a challenge, particularly in the first few weeks. But the crew has come together and has been operating as a solid unit for some time. Rounding the Horn was a test, as always, but they made it unscathed. The unloading and pickup in Hong Kong went smoothly. Hawaii was a welcome paradise. For three days, he mostly lay on the beach and thought of Magdalena. Her letter had finally caught up with him— the one saying she was his forever. "In ten days, we'll be together," he had told himself. He's glad the ship is sailing with the trade winds; they'll get him to California that much quicker.

He has so many plans for the two of them. When they get back to Germany, he'll take a much-needed furlough. They'll spend time together and meet each other's families. He owes Mama Mok a hug, anyway, for helping to save his arm. He's thinking of giving up clippers and going back to transatlantic steamships. Being with Magdalena is more important to him than taking extended voyages to the Orient under the majesty of sails only.

As he watches the waves, he can tell the wind is picking up and not always out of the west. Before going below, he warns the officer of the watch to be particularly vigilant; it looks like a storm's brewing.

In the quiet of his captain's quarters, he writes to his sweetheart. It doesn't matter that he'll hand-deliver it to her in San Francisco.

The ship is pitching so hard that Will has trouble finishing his letter. Giving it one last try, he dips his quill and starts again, just as the vessel lurches violently, causing a black mess all across his desk. His half-finished missive is ruined. Dabbing at the dye, he calls a cabin boy, then rushes toward the quarter deck.

Nerves are snapping, and sailors are praying by the time he gets there. With each mountainous wave, the sea water crashes over the side rails, washing anything not tied down into the deep. Fighting to get to the bridge, Will sees a sailor with both arms wrapped around a railing. The storm loosens his grip with each surge. The lad isn't three meters away, but Will can't get to the boy. The blinding rain and devil's wind are holding him where he stands. Stretching and reaching with his free hand, the captain somehow snags the sailor's belt and shouts to the kid, "Let go." He won't, and the captain can't, or they'll both be beneath the waves. By now, a grizzled tar has made his way to the distressed pair. The old seaman delivers a right cross to the terrified sailor's jaw; the skipper now has the kid in both arms.

"I'll see to him, sir. They need you on the bridge!" the older sailor screams into his captain's ear.

With the aid of a rope line the crew has strung, Will makes his way there. The officer of the watch has already tried to lash himself to the pedestal and is trying his damnedest to keep the ship into the wind. Suddenly, a wave higher than a house tosses the clipper like a kite in a tornado. The lashed officer is blown free. The captain knows it's one minute before midnight and starts shouting orders, trying anything to stop the clock. He dives for the spinning wheel and somehow grabs a handle. Spoke by spoke, he turns his ship into the wind. The mainmast is moaning more with each stronger gust. Suddenly, it surrenders with a final booming crack.

The captain lies buried and broken on his bridge when the first mate and three gallant crewmembers get to him. A long piece of the yard has run him through. The skipper is not yet gone, but he's knocking on heaven's door—and knows it. The storm has started to ease, as if to watch him go.

In those last few minutes when most confront their end, Will chooses to question the dealer and plan for the future. At twenty-six and in love, he feels he's done his part to make the world a better place. Why won't I be around to enjoy it, Will demands without getting an answer.

"Get me to my quarters," he orders before screaming, "Oh, my God!" as the first mate backs out the spar in his belly.

Lying in his own pooled blood in the only captain's quarters he's ever known, Will asks for paper, quill, and ink.

The ship's surgeon hands them to him, along with the nearest book he can find—*The Three Musketeers*—to serve as a writing surface. Will dips his quill, glances for the last time at the photograph of his girl resting on top of his desk, and begins to write,

My Darling Magdalena,

I'm not at my desk, so my hand may be unsteady. Bear with me. I won't be able to meet you in San Francisco as we planned. I've got to check on a very special place on a far-off harbor. I'm in a hurry. I don't want to miss the best spots. If I get the one I have in mind, I'll be able to sail the seven seas every day and still sit beside you each night. They say these spots can only be seen alone, but I don't feel alone at all. I feel like you're sitting by my side right now.

It may seem like I'm gone a long while, but you'll be with

me soon enough. As I told you in New York, I'll be waiting for you when you're done with your trip to Colorado. There's no rush—we've got forever. I'm sure now that I was a silly goose not to marry you in New York, whether I had to carry you to the altar kicking and screaming or not. No worries. We've got an eternity.

See you as soon as you get here. I love you always,
Wil

The captain didn't have time to finish his second "L."

The next day on a calm sea, the first mate delivers Will to the deep as the young captain's entire crew stands at attention. There aren't many dry eyes.

Miraculously, the ship and most of the seamen survive the storm. The first mate mails his captain's final message as soon as they arrive in California.

Halfway through September, Magdalena is just finishing up tending her mules after a long, hot day of hauling for Stan. Marta sticks her head out the kitchen door and hollers, "Magdalena, there's a letter here for you—from New York. Mr. Reynolds asked me to give it to you."

Taking the missive, Magdalena's struck by the flowing penmanship. Quickly opening it, she reads,

3 September 1871

My dear Magdalena,
It is with a leaden heart I write to you today. Brother Phillip received news by wire that Will was killed trying to shepherd his vessel through a nasty storm. Phillip is a major stockholder in Will's shipping line, so I think you can take confidence when he says that the first mate's log recorded thusly,
Captain Hauff stood valiantly beneath the mast, shouting

orders at his crew when the swaying timber finally gave way. It felled the skipper where he stood. He was never to get up again.

I know not of the disposition of your romance with Will at this time, but am certain these bad tidings will torment your heart.

Though it will not relieve your pain, I thought you should know my brother also said that many crew members' lives were saved, along with the Vagabund, due to the singular gallantry of Captain Wilhelm Hauff.

You remain in our hearts and are always welcome for as long as you like at Derbyshire.

Remorsefully, I remain your servant,
John Rutherford
Marquess of Derbyshire

"Oh, God, not again. Please, not again!" she wails.

CHAPTER 39

A Tuesday Quilting Circle
Fall 1871

The aspens that adorn the mountains in golden tones are now dropping their leaves. By late September, Magdalena's tears are spent. Her life has regained a small semblance of rhythm. Central City has had its first snow, and the small miners are starting to shut down for the winter. Their exodus until springtime means Stan's business will be halved. Magdalena is already down to a few days of work each week. Long walks with Scout give her time to sort through everything that's happened.

By the first week in October, Marta is spending every Tuesday quilting with friends. The circle started in '59 when she and Stan lost their boy. He was ten. A couple of the other German arrivals had a pretty tough go of it that year, too. They found solace behind their needles, a lot like Mama had done when she and Grandma began sewing after Hans left for the army. This Tuesday, Marta figures Magdalena needs to spend some time with folks that have seen dark times, a lot of them more than once.

"Ladies," Marta says to the group, "this is my friend Magdalena.

Virginia Pickett

She's come from Germany all by herself—worked her way across on a wagon train from Missouri. She's feeling pretty low after losing her fiancé. He was a ship's captain. Magdalena was to leave for San Francisco this past September to marry him. She came over in the first place after losing a sweetheart in the war at home. I s'pose the same pat on the back we've all needed might do her some good today."

After that, the young woman sitting next to Magdalena introduces herself. "Hi. I'm Myra. Ya thinking of staying on with Marta and Stan?"

"For right now, anyways. I haven't figured out yet what's next," Magdalena answers truthfully.

"Well, if ya can stand the winters here, come spring there'll be a whole passel of single miners comin' back. You can just about have yur pick of a husband," she offers, trying to get a smile. She gets a little one, but Magdalena is not ready to think about that sort of thing. Undaunted, the woman doesn't give up, just changes her tone, sensing where Magdalena's at.

"I found another man when I never thought I could—after I lost my second husband, Albert, down a mine shaft a couple of years back. Wilbur is his name. We have a new little one now. That's him over there with my other two youngins. They lost their pa in the war back home before Albert and me came out with the kids to find my brother. When we got here, he was already gone. Things fell apart again when Albert got killed. Everything worked out, though. I found Wilbur. I'm okay now, if it helps you to know that."

Over the next three hours, Magdalena talks and cries with a lot of women, some not much older than her. They all have two things in common—a history of hard times and resiliency. When she and Marta leave that day, Magdalena is a little ashamed for walking around down in the dumps for so long. These ladies have inspired her.

After that, she becomes a regular at the Tuesday quilting circle.

248

A Long Road There

She enjoys the camaraderie and the support. These ladies have been punched in the mouth and still got up. Some had to mend their lives a lot more than once. This makes Magdalena think that her troubles are no hill for a climber. Ever since that first quilting session, Gunner hasn't had to pull nearly as hard to get a smile out of his pal.

As fall deepens and Stan has less delivery work for Magdalena, she helps him and Gunner build up the winter firewood piles for both houses. On one such day after chopping in the crisp air, Magdalena cleans up for dinner and comes bounding into the kitchen. "Marta, it smells delicious, and I'm as hungry as a bear. What can I do to help?" Magdalena asks as the sun sets on a beautiful mid-October day.

"Nothing, dear. Just relax. It'll be ready in a bit. There's a letter on the table for you. When I stopped by the post office today, Mr. Reynolds gave it to me. Said he'd had it for a few days."

Hesitantly, Magdalena takes the correspondence and stares at the script on the outside. "I don't recognize the writing, and I don't know anybody in San Francisco." Finally, opening it, there are two pieces of folded paper. She begins with the larger of the two—the one that enclosed the other note.

Dear Fraülein Mok,
    Captain Hauff wrote this right before he died.
With my deepest condolences,
    Albert Schmidt, First Mate
    Wind Vagabund

Magdalena grabs the back of the kitchen chair and slumps into it. Holding the other piece of unopened paper, she turns it over in her hands several times before unfolding it. She recognizes Will's handwriting immediately, even though the script isn't as steady as normal. Her hands shake as she starts to read, *"My Darling Magdalena."*

When Marta glances up from her cooking, her young friend's face has lost all color. Before she can say anything, Magdalena is up from her chair. "I'm not hungry, Marta. Please don't delay supper for me. Scout and I are gonna go for a walk. I'll see you in the morning."

All Marta can do is call after her, "Alright, dear. Remember darkness comes earlier now!" As she turns back to her stove, the cook notices a piece of paper Magdalena had dropped on the floor. It's the note from Will's first mate. She sighs deeply, fearing her friend will have to go through the dying all over again. She's been making such progress, Marta thinks. "That don't seem right, Lord," she whispers.

Scout knows something is wrong as he walks along beside Magdalena. Tears are rolling down her cheeks. Coming on to their favorite stand of aspens, Magdalena looks down on the town at gloaming.

When she reads Will's words a second time, she begins to smile, thinking of him shopping for a home on the seashore. The vision is sublime. She can't help herself.

Scout is grinning, too. His tail keeps time to the music in his heart. Magdalena pulls him close, "You didn't know Will or Fritz, did you boy? You would have liked them both. You don't suppose I could spend time with each of them in heaven, do you—that God might be okay with that?" Scout doesn't dabble in imponderables.

Before dark, Magdalena and her pup are home.

"Marta, I hope you saved me some of that stew. I'm awfully hungry," Magdalena says, coming inside and hugging the cook.

Marta is drying her last dish. "Help yourself. What's left is sitting on the table," she says, amazed and relieved by her young friend's resiliency. "Thanks," she whispers toward the ceiling.

CHAPTER 40

In & around Central City
Late Fall & Winter 1871-72

Toward the end of October, Gunner lands a big plaster job. He's under a deadline and hasn't made many dinners lately. Magdalena decides he must need help.

He's surprised when she walks onto the jobsite at 5:30 in the morning. He's also touched by the gesture. He gives her a trowel and a mud board and walks her to a far corner of the room. After a brief tutorial, he says, "Behind those pipes, kid, the water guys left a small hole in the wall. Patch 'er up." She can't mess this up too bad, he thinks.

Trying in vain to fill the hole, Magdalena sighs, watching her instructor as he moves his spreader like a modern-day Da Vinci.

"How's it going over there?" Gunner asks, not looking up from his canvas.

"Not too well!" the apprentice shouts from across the room, tangled in the plumbing.

When Gunner comes to check on her, Magdalena is covered with more plaster than the hole. "Take a break, kid," he says, trying to avoid giving his helper an honest appraisal. Magdalena flips the

251

dollop of mud on her trowel straight at her boss's forehead. Score one for the apprentice. She laughs, until the journeyman loads his weapon to return fire, then she's off running with the plasterer in hot pursuit. Down the stairs, through two empty rooms on the first floor, out the front door, around the building, and back to the scene of the crime she goes. With a mighty leap, Gunner grabs the squealing assailant and fires. Bingo! A direct hit on her left cheek. The combatants drop their weapons and plop to the floor, laughing so hard their sides hurt.

That evening at dinner, when two different versions of the story are told, Stan and Marta can only shake their heads at the children. Now, when Magdalena isn't working for Stan, she's known to devilishly stop by and offer Gunner help with whatever job he's working on. When he sees her coming, he immediately hides his extra trowel and mud board.

The November sun is bright on the new snow. It's Magdalena's twenty-first birthday. Except for her usual job of tending the mules, Stan doesn't have any other tasks for her. She's trying to decide how she'll spend the rest of her natal day.

"Forget those ol' mules, "Gunner says, appearing out of nowhere. "Come on out here. I've got something to show you. Close your eyes. Now, don't peek," he tells her.

Everything is dark, but Magdalena can hear a soft plop-plop in the snow. "Okay, open 'em up. Happy Birthday," her friend says, pointing at the snowshoes lying in front of her. "Are you surprised? Do you like 'em?" he asks, not sure what the birthday girl thinks based on her puzzled expression.

She manages a "*wunderbar*" that doesn't knock him over.

"They'll grow on ya. Wanna give 'em a try?"

"Right now?"

"Why not? It's such a beautiful day. I brought mine and the sleigh. Trust me. You look like a natural shoer."

A Long Road There

Getting the contraptions on is a small victory for the novice. The twenty-yard tutorial to the sleigh and back is cold, difficult, and wet. Scout thinks it's playtime. Smiling, Gunner reaches down to brush off Magdalena each time she tumbles. He's hoping her unpredictable fuse doesn't light.

"Let's go. I think you're ready," Gunner shouts. Out in front, Gunner spots a pair of deer and points toward them. It's a doe with last season's offspring. Magdalena is enthralled.

Somewhere along the way back, the teacher takes a tumble. Magdalena dubs him king of the course, then crowns him with a handful of white powder. Scout pins the old plaster worker right where he sits and wags his tail.

Back in front of a warm fire, hot chocolate in hand, the snowshoers get lost in laughter. From then on, it's hard to keep Magdalena out of her birthday present.

Just a few weeks later, it's Christmas Eve—Magdalena's first one away from home. While watching the candle flames flicker on the tree they'd decorated earlier this afternoon, a warm chill runs down her spine as fond memories pull at her heartstrings. The last few days have been difficult. The holidays at home were always her favorite time of year. Even as Magdalena grew up, she always waited with excitement for *Sankt Nikolaus* to come with presents. For as long as she can remember, the *Weihnachtsmärkte* and all the hubbub surrounding it has swept her up. There's no market in Central City, and Stan and Marta have adjusted to American Christmas customs. After dinner tonight, they'll take a sleigh full of presents to the parish children peeking out of candle-lit church windows.

Without Papa's special sausages and Mama's scrumptious *Weihnachtsstollen*, things don't seem the same. Elsa Emma isn't here to complain about having to help pluck the goose that Stan and Gunner have gotten for tomorrow's dinner. Hans won't be hiding behind the barn door with a snowball when she steps into the sleigh to go to evening services.

"Dinner's ready, Magdalena!" Marta hollers from the kitchen, interrupting the girl's reminiscing. Scout is already begging the cook for scraps. No, it's not the same, she thinks, heading for the table and enjoying the aromas of Marta's oven and Stan's sausages—but it sure is swell.

CHAPTER 41

Down & Up the Road to Golden
Late March 1872

Life is good, Magdalena thinks, as she begins prodding her mules down the mountain. The forty-mile round-trip to Golden this morning should be beautiful under the powder-blue March sky. She'll be home by three—plenty of time for a nap, dinner, and a canasta championship with Gunner.

The mules pretty much know the descent by heart, so the driver can get lost in her thoughts without much worry. Will's death, and even their time together, seems like an eternity ago. Her heart broke in two when she heard the news he was gone, that's for sure, but it seems like a horrible dream to her now. Papa is all but demanding that she come home. In his letters he's even threatened to come and get her himself. She needs to write him and let him know she's staying in America. It'll break his heart again when he reads that, especially when his daughter still can't tell him exactly why. Blowing in the wind and enjoying the freedom of it doesn't line up with the Mok tradition. That bothers her, but not enough to go home and see if Herr Diller will have her.

She could go to Oregon and try and hook on with Rosa and Mitch, she thinks without much conviction, smiling at the irony.

255

It wasn't that long ago Rosa was joining up with her. Truth be told, Magdalena is enjoying the freedom of a clean slate—blowing in the wind for a little while. She smiles as she pictures Papa's scowl. It's just as clear in her mind's eye as if he were sitting beside her.

It's almost one o'clock when Magdalena asks her mules, "Well fellas, it's time to head back to the barn. What do you say to that?" The wind is blowing hard out of the north. Loading had taken a lot longer than expected. Snugging the tarp over the equipment a little tighter than usual, she glances at the sky. Scout jumps aboard, and his driver points the team up the mountain.

The clear March sky is long gone; the ceiling is starting to look a little crazy. For just a moment, she thinks maybe she ought to turn around—but, no, not Magdalena. Snapping the reins, she dismisses the idea. "We should be home by 3 o'clock. That sky isn't about to let loose, is it, boy?" Magdalena takes her partner's silence as a *no*.

Just a mile or so up the road, the snowdrifts are over three feet deep in places. "I can't turn around. Gunner would never forgive me for costin' him the canasta championship," she mumbles. "Ain't that so, Scout?" she asks. The lookout still doesn't answer.

Over the edge of the road on her left, she can still see Clear Creek through the snow—a long way below. The stream isn't frozen, though the water looks frigid. She slows to a crawl around every curve so she and Scout don't end up taking a bath.

"We ain't tipped yet, and we ain't gonna. Right, Scout?" she says to her navigator, letting him answer this time.

His short double bark, at least in her mind, confirms they're not going swimming. Though he's not letting on, the mutt knows Magdalena has their necks in nooses. He gives his pal a nuzzle for luck, knowing they're going to need it. Magdalena lets out a sigh of relief, believing her friend thinks they can make it. Just seven more miles, she tells herself. "Come on, fellas," she urges the team while squinting desperately to see the road ahead of her. The navigation is pretty much up to the mules now.

A Long Road There

The edge of the roadway has vanished altogether. The creek is still down below, but she can't see it anymore. Even Stan's most sure-footed animal, Neptune, has turned hesitant.

Suddenly, the wagon fishtails, and she loses control. Magdalena hears cracking lumber and frantic animals galloping off before everything goes black. When she wakes up, Magdalena is pinned between a demolished wagon and the mountainside's cold, gray rock.

———

At half past three, Stan starts to worry. The snow has been falling hard on the mountaintop since before noon. He expected Magdalena home a couple of hours ago. Before he can get his coat on, his front door swings open. Gunner is covered in snow from head to toe.

"Maggie back yet? Two of her mules are draggin' harness outside."

"Damn," Stan curses, "we gotta find the kid, Gunner."

"Well, what are we waiting for? I'll fetch the wagon. You get a fresh team."

"Get the sleigh instead. We ain't gonna make it far in that wagon."

Gunner has trouble keeping the sleigh on the road. The sun is sinking quickly behind the mountains. It'll be blacker than the ace of spades in no time. The two men are frantically scanning both sides of the road, looking for Magdalena, Scout, or the wagon in the rapidly fading light. Without saying so, both know the chances of finding her are getting steadily worse. It won't be long before they have to give up until morning.

———

In the few minutes between flipping the wagon and waking up, Magdalena has been straddling two worlds. On one side, Papa's dog Abe rolls in a snowbank with Max, whose stomach isn't even scarred

257

by the lynx. "You need another pair of gloves, don't you?" Grandpa asks, looking at the shiny leather palms on the ones she's wearing.

In the other world, Scout is licking her face. She can feel the trickle of warm blood down her cheek, but not much else. The snow buries her up to her waist.

The men have fought their way down the mountain about as far as they can go. Their lanterns aren't shedding much light through the swirling snow. Both know that continuing in these conditions is foolhardy.

"Gunner, we ain't gonna find anything in this snow except maybe graves for ourselves. We've gotta head back. We can hope for a miracle tomorrow."

"Ten minutes, Stan. I've gotta feeling."

"Okay. Ten minutes, and that's it," Stan says, firing two more shots into the night, hoping Magdalena will answer.

Fritz's pistol is somewhere beneath the snow with the rest of her load, so Magdalena can't fire back. Scout hears the shots but won't budge an inch from her side until she orders, "Go get Stan. Find Stan. He's our only hope," she tells her pup as the last corner of the wagon disappears beneath the snow.

Beau would be proud tonight. His pup takes off up the mountain, with Magdalena watching him. She worries that the snow is too deep for him to make it.

"That's fifteen minutes, Gunner," Stan says. "We've got to head back up. I'm as sorry as you are."

Slumping over behind the sleigh reins, with tears running down his unshaven face, the heartbroken driver concedes and turns the sleigh for home.

A Long Road There

Magdalena's still traveling in and out of two worlds. Grandpa's not real hospitable when she's on the other side. "You don't belong here yet. Get on back to where you're supposed to be," he demands every time she shows up to play with Abe and Max.

The sleigh is still upright when Gunner finally gets it pointed back uphill. "Get up, mules," Gunner says, just before yanking on the reins to stop them. "Did you hear that, Stan?"

Putting his ear against the night, Stan yells, "I sure as hell did. That's Scout barking."

Not two hundred yards from where they'd tossed in the towel, Scout pops out of the night demanding they follow him.

"Maggie, Maggie, where are you?" Stan yells down the mountain.

She can't see a face, but knows the voice isn't Grandpa's. She hollers back as loud as she can, "I'm pinned and can't move. Please help me."

Stan can barely make out the sound of her voice not fifteen feet away, but that's all he needs to hear. "You just stay put, Maggie!" he screams, jumping out of the sleigh. "We'll get you outta there." Turning back toward the sleigh, he shouts into the storm, "Get the rope, Gunner, and tie your end to the sleigh, then toss 'er over here!" Stan can't see the sleigh now twelve feet away; he can only hope Gunner finds his voice with the rope. Somehow he does, and Stan begins digging frantically for a wagon part to tie his end around.

"Is that you, Stan? Stan, are you there?"

"I sure am, Maggie. You hold on. We're gonna pull the wagon enough to get you free." As he finishes, Scout's scratching steel. The wagon axle is a beautiful sight.

"Please hurry, Stan!" she hollers, now without as much strength. Half-frozen and buried to her chin, she starts to fade away.

"That a girl, Magdalena. I'll see you later," is the last thing she hears from Grandpa. He always had a sense of humor.

"Gunner, start them animals," Stan orders. He can't see the sleigh, Gunner, or Maggie, but has ahold of the line. He hopes to feel it go taut. It does, but the wagon won't budge. Scout isn't having that. He lets the mules know they don't have a choice in the matter.

Scout is still barking orders to the mules when Stan gets both of his arms around Maggie. He scoops her out of the frozen prison and somehow carries her through the waist-deep snow—all the way to the sleigh. Gunner marvels that the old German still has such strength. Gunner quickly takes Magdalena and puts her in the back of the rig.

When the men come in carrying an unconscious Magdalena, Marta is ready for the worst. "Put her in our bed, Stan. We'll sleep in the spare room. Gunner can have the couch," she says, taking charge.

Looking at her young friend, Marta doesn't hold out much hope. She's seen a lot of people never come to after disappearing in a mountain blizzard. As she piles more covers on Magdalena's shivering body, she looks up and whispers, "Give her a break, Lord, please."

That night, the plasterer doesn't sleep much. He's sending requests skyward himself, pacing around his borrowed couch most of the night. Every hour or so, he pops his head into Magdalena's room to make sure the fire is still going.

By morning, the weather is clear enough for Gunner to fetch the doctor. The mile in the deep snow is slow, even by sleigh. At 6 am, the city isn't moving at all.

"Stan's new driver got the worst of it in the storm last night. She was trying to get back up from Golden," Gunner tells the pajamaed doctor. "We'd sure appreciate it if you could take a look at the kid.

A Long Road There

She's over at Stan's. I got the sleigh."

"Alright. Give me a minute to get dressed and grab my bag," the doctor mumbles, still half asleep.

Arriving at Stan and Marta's house, the doctor disappears into the bedroom, closing the door behind him. A maddening quiet settles over the house for the next half an hour as Magdalena's friends wait. When the bedroom door finally comes open, it's hard to read the physician's face. "The kid's got a nasty gash, a big bump on her head, and she nearly froze to death, Stan. Maggie is young and strong. Let's see how she does the next few days. I'll come back tomorrow to check on her. Keep her warm." Looking at Marta, the doctor adds, "Give her lots of your chicken soup and hot tea. I think that will get her over the hump." The collective sigh of relief is audible.

A week after the doctor's first visit, Magdalena wakes up hungry. When Gunner knocks on the bedroom door to see how she's doing, he finds her in one of Marta's long, flannel nightgowns, sitting up and wrestling with Scout.

"Do you wanna go snowshoeing today? The conditions look perfect," the patient says, looking out the Stanhauers' bedroom window onto a sparkling snow-covered pasture.

Gunner sits on the bed, puts his head in his hands, and cries. This is the first time he knows for sure that his friend is out of the woods. Magdalena leans over to hug him, saying, "You're the best friend a girl could have, Gunner."

CHAPTER 42

A Central City Café
Spring 1872

Magdalena gradually regains her strength over the next several weeks. Convalescing, she wrestles daily with what she's going to do from here. Some mornings, going home seems like the best thing. By evening, it doesn't.

Together with Marta's chicken soup, fishing with Gunner on sunny spring mornings has been powerful medicine for the recovering patient. On just such a day, Gunner looks up from watching his line and says, "What do you say we give these fish to Stan and Marta and go out on the town tonight? We can catch the dinner special if we get to the cafe by six. Who knows, maybe we'll stay for a little dancing."

"That sounds great, but I can't imagine you dancing, Gunner," she says honestly, not intending to throw water on his idea.

"You might be surprised, young lady."

As the waitress clears the table, Magdalena feels swell about life. Gunner is knee-deep in an old fishing story. The sound of his voice is the perfect background for her happy thoughts. Tonight,

A Long Road There

the possibilities for what she is going to do with the rest of her life are still endless. The difference is that now she isn't too concerned. Magdalena loves the mountain and the people in Central City. Stan and Marta have made her feel like she's part of the family. Gunner? He has been a Godsend. "Today is a good day to be alive," he tells her almost every morning. She's starting to believe him.

As the fisherman is landing the biggest trout caught in these parts since '59—and standing up to do it—Magdalena giggles and feels good all over. It has been a while.

"Gunner, I'm gonna request my favorite waltz. Whaddya say?"

Dropping the whopper over the side of the table without even noticing, Gunner can only say, "*Wunderbar!*"

The late summer flowers by the creek are magnificent as Magdalena watches Gunner bait her hook. Four months have passed since her accident. "Smile. The sun's come up, and today's gonna be a good day," Gunner reminds her. They both believe it.

Since that first waltz with Gunner last spring, Magdalena has been hearing a message from her heart. She has started to listen lately. It's a simple message: *You've fallen hopelessly in love with this marvelous man.*

Taking her pole from Gunner as he tries to bait her hook, she lays it on the ground, then kisses him hard on the lips. "I love you so much, Gunner."

Thunderstruck and overwhelmed with happiness, the burley plasterer can only whisper, "You don't know how much I've wanted to hear you say that. I've loved you since the day we met."

Two weeks later, Magdalena is walking down the aisle toward Gunner. It's been a long road. Trying to stay in step with the music, she looks toward the chapel's bow trusses that arch toward heaven. She gazes higher, then whispers to Grandma and Grandpa Brohmann, "You're going to like Gunner."

NACHWORT/EPILOGUE

Magdalena's Front Porch
6 April 1917

Let me live in a house by the side of the road,
Where the race of men go by—-
The men who are good and the men who are bad,
As good and as bad as I.

From "The House by the Side of the Road" by Sam Walter Foss

"Rosa, you're supposed to be helping your mama!" Magdalena yells from her porch to her nine-year-old granddaughter who's romping in the remnant of a snowbank with her new puppy, Scooter. It doesn't seem possible to Magdalena that the pup is Scout's great-grandson four times over.

This morning, Grandma is enjoying the warm April sun from her porch. Her feet are quiet today and have been for the better part of forty-five years; that is, unless there's something to celebrate. On days like today, old memories of her trip over from Germany seem to find their way into her mind. Mostly, the memories bring smiles. Since the century turned, her long-time friend Rosa has visited

A Long Road There

several times, always bringing with her Theodor's oldest daughter, Magdalena. From their first trip east, there were tracks all the way to Central City. Magdalena managed to take her granddaughter Rosa out west to Oregon just last summer. It was beautiful country, indeed—just as Buffalo had promised. Mitch's orchards covered the hills as far as the eye could see.

Neither Magdalena nor Rosa ever did see Buffalo again, though Magdalena wrote her boss faithfully for over twenty years. He even scratched a letter back a few times. Eventually, they lost touch, but not before Magdalena congratulated him on the Montana spread he and Clint finally got around to buying. Mitch heard that the old bison had passed peacefully, looking out on the cattle from his own front porch.

Magdalena still thinks of Fritz and Will now and then, at times wondering what might have been—not wishing, just conjecturing. She even thought of Sir Biscuit Bottom and her three royal guardians the other day—still grateful.

A few years after she and Gunner had Hans, their second child, Magdalena and three friends from the quilting circle—all about her age—took the oath of allegiance to Uncle Sam. They joined Gunner, Marta, and Stan as full-fledged Yankee Doodle Dandies. Becoming an American citizen was a proud day for Grandma—a cap piece to a long journey.

With Gunner gone these past two years, Magdalena is a little lonely but not sad. She continues to quilt every Tuesday. The people sitting in the circle are mostly different than when Marta first took her, but the spirit to heal hearts is just the same.

The grandkids keep her plenty busy. Spoiling ten, and counting, is no easy job. And chasing after them keeps her young.

Magdalena and the plasterer raised quite a family. Five of their seven kids attended the university in Denver for at least two years. Their youngest daughter, Johanna, like her namesake, chose to study literature and was one of only twelve women in the class of

1909 to receive a bachelor's degree. Their middle boy, Stephen, still manages the city's opera house. Stan, the oldest, hauls freight. His namesake left him the business in '98 when he went home to see his best girl, Marta. Gunner never struck it rich looking for gold, but that didn't stop him from digging until the day he died. Now, there's only a few fellows left in town with even a touch of the fever.

Grandma is a little down this morning. That doesn't happen very often anymore, probably because she doesn't ask *why* much. She goes along as best she can, taking whatever comes. It's taken her a while to get to that.

The news in the paper this morning is especially discouraging. Her adopted country has entered the war. That means her grandsons will be fighting against the grandsons of Hans and Elsa Emma. War is such a waste, she thinks. Reading all the classics and great thinkers didn't get her to that conclusion. They helped sort things out a little, but living her life in the midst of what seemed like constant war is what made her certain she's right. So many campaigns and so much lost with so little gained all weigh heavy on her, especially today.

For a long time now, she's been able to write home without a cold shiver coming over her. Any notion that she let people down by leaving is long gone for her and all the family in Germany. It feels good to be loved unconditionally in two places.

Comforted, she reaches for the compass in her pocket like she does a time or two on most days. The pathfinder is the one Hans gave her over forty-six years ago. The inscription he had done is worn and barely readable. She knows what it says by heart, though: *To help you find your way.* As she returns the treasured keepsake to her pocket, she feels a shiver down her spine. The war is responsible for the chill coming over her.

Her German comes a little slowly at first as she begins to write her brother. They've written often over the years, sharing pretty much every up and down in their lives.

A Long Road There

6 April 1917

Dear Hans,

Today would have been Papa's ninety-first birthday. He's been gone over five years, which forces me to realize I left over forty-six years ago. I had every intention of getting back home—I knew I would. Seven kids and ten grandchildren later, I still haven't made it, though my heart has traveled back many times. I feel like I'm with you often. Your steady stream of letters over the years is a major reason I feel like this. In so many ways, your words have kept me smiling. I hope you know that.

As you probably learned this morning, America is in the war. I can't allow myself to think of that for long. The horrible possibilities that it portends for our grandchildren are too much to consider. I can only pray they don't come to pass.

You asked me in your last letter if I would change anything if I could. I don't think so. Even if I could—and I can't— I wouldn't because everything feels connected. Those decisions are made in heaven.

When things are all said and done, I guess everyone has to find their own way to happiness and contentment. I just took the long road there.

Love,
Magdalena

Laying her pen aside, she sits for a while beneath the blue sky. Soon, she notices Rosa still wrestling with Scooter. Laughing at the truth in the old adage that *the apple doesn't fall far from the tree*, she shoos her granddaughter toward her chores.

Times past on porch sitting days like, she might have sat like this grappling with confounding questions. But not anymore. She leaves those up to heaven.

———

The first fall leaves are starting to float to the ground today— an early October beauty. Magdalena's great-granddaughter is celebrating her 70th birthday, cleaning Mama's china. Yes, miraculously, most of the pieces she gave Magdalena survived all the way from Willenstat to Central City in Grandpa Mok's old college trunk. Today, some of them are sitting in Alexandria's great-great-granddaughter's china cabinet. No, she hasn't misbehaved; in fact, she's chosen to tend to the porcelain while pondering her great-grandmother's journey. Smiling to herself, she's glad Magdalena took the long road and didn't change a thing.

ABOUT THE AUTHOR

Virginia Pickett grew up in Billings, Montana and attended Montana State University. After she and her husband graduated from Gonzaga Law School in 1976, they remained in Spokane. This is her first novel.